The Body in the Attic

Books by Judi Lynn

Mill Pond Romances
COOKING UP TROUBLE
OPPOSITES DISTRACT
LOVE ON TAP
SPICING THINGS UP
FIRST KISS, ON THE HOUSE
SPECIAL DELIVERY

Jazzi Zanders Mysteries

THE BODY IN THE ATTIC

Published by Kensington Publishing Corporation

The Body in the Attic

A Jazzi Zanders Mystery

Judi Lynn

LYRICAL UNDERGROUND
Kensington Publishing Corp.
www.kensingtonbooks.com

LYRICAL UNDERGROUND BOOKS are published by

Kensington Publishing Corp.
119 West 40th Street
New York, NY 10018

All Kensington titles, imprints, and distributed lines are available at special quantity discounts for bulk purchases for sales promotion, premiums, fund-raising, educational, or institutional use.

Special book excerpts or customized printings can also be created to fit specific needs. For details, write or phone the office of the Kensington Sales Manager: Kensington Publishing Corp., 119 West 40th Street, New York, NY 10018. Attn. Sales Department. Phone: 1-800-221-2647.

Lyrical Underground and Lyrical Underground logo Reg. US Pat. & TM Off.

First Electronic Edition: November 2018
eISBN-13: 978-1-5161-0836-7
eISBN-10: 1-5161-0836-1

First Print Edition: November 2018
ISBN-13: 978-1-5161-0839-8
ISBN-10: 1-5161-0839-6

Printed in the United States of America

Acknowledgments

I have many people to thank for this book. My agent, Lauren Abramo, who went over and over the synopsis with me to make it as good as possible. This is a much better book due to her efforts. My editor, John Scognamiglio, for offering me the chance to write a mystery. And my critique partners—Mary Lou Rigdon, Ann Staadt, and my daughter, Holly Post—who went over and over my rough drafts to keep me honest.

I'd also like to thank my friend Ralph Miser, who's worked on many houses to fix them up. He generously gave me ideas for clues that might be found in an old house to help solve a murder—and he had LOTS of ideas. I hit the jackpot!

Chapter 1

It was sweltering. The sun beat down, and perspiration dripped along Jazzi's spine. Uncomfortable and impatient, she wished the auctioneer would hurry up. She wanted this house. She and her cousin, Jerod, had walked through it, top to bottom, at the initial showing and hadn't seen any major problems. They'd flipped houses together for four years now. Mostly successes.

Jerod rambled back to stand beside her. Tall and hefty, he towered over her. At five-six, she didn't consider herself short, but the top of her head came only to Jerod's chin.

"We should get this at a decent price," he told her. "To buy it 'as is,' along with all the garbage the renter left inside, scares most people. The ones I talked to came to bid on the '70 Nova found in the garage."

Good news. Cal Juniper's house had good bones and oozed charm. A cobblestone cottage style with a rolled roof and an "eyebrow" near the front door, it was two stories with a storybook feel. The roof was in good shape; the trim just needed a little paint. They'd barely made a profit on their last flip, but they'd be making only cosmetic changes to this one.

Once upon a time, Cal had almost become a part of their family. Jazzi still remembered stories about Aunt Lynda's engagement party here. People said Cal had beamed all night as if he'd won the grand prize. Lynda's vitality made people feel alive. That was before she ran off to New York and never returned. Cal never married. He died six months ago of a sudden heart attack. The house went downhill fast after that.

Jerod bumped her arm, signaling for her to pay attention. The bidding would start soon. Jazzi's hair stuck to the back of her neck, and she lifted it to cool off. She and her hair had a love-hate relationship. Thick and honey colored, she got lots of compliments on it, but on hot days, if she didn't slap it into a ponytail, she always regretted it. She'd pulled it up today, but the stupid rubber band had died. Her own fault. If she'd have looked for her hair tie like she should have, this wouldn't have happened.

Jerod glanced at her and shook his head. "What's the matter, *Jasmine*, can't take the heat?"

She tossed him a sour look. He only called her by her birth name to annoy her. "Shut it, cuz. Maybe you should clean out this one yourself."

He grinned. She'd already told him she couldn't wait to get inside the place and get down and dirty. Dirty was the key word. The renter threw everything—empty pizza boxes, drained beer cans, and greasy paper wrappers—on the floor, a fly and rodent's paradise. She didn't want to know how many maggots were happily living in there.

The auctioneer finally got to the car and bidding went crazy. The good news? After a gray-haired guy with black grease under his fingernails—most likely a mechanic—got it, the crowd thinned out. Jerod had been right. Not many people were interested in the house. Jazzi was even more surprised when everyone else dropped out at fifty-six thousand and they won the bid.

Jerod raised his hand for a high five. "We did it! I'm going to give Ansel a call and let him know."

Ansel. Their tall, blond construction contractor. Quite the distraction. Jazzi wished he were here. He worked with them on most houses. He'd meant to come with them today, but this was his girlfriend's, Emily's, first day off after three twelve-hour shifts and she'd informed him he was spending time with her. He never went against Emily's orders. At six-five, he was taller than Jerod, but thoroughly under the thumb of a five-four nurse. He had white-blond hair and sky-blue eyes—looked like a Viking, but was easygoing. Emily wasn't.

If all people with Norwegian backgrounds looked like Ansel, Jazzi would welcome Norwegian immigrants to River Bluffs with open arms and possibly groping hands. If only Emily weren't in the way.

She stayed to finalize the paperwork with the auctioneer while Jerod made his call. They'd worked with this auction house many times, always paying cash so they could start work right away.

She braced her shoulders and walked into the house. Putrid pulled pork, sour milk, and moldy tomato sauce combined into a foul stench. She couldn't stomach it and walked to her pickup truck to don a white face mask. She grabbed two flat-blade shovels and a box of trash bags, too. A broom wasn't going to cut it.

When Jerod joined her, he dragged in the huge trash container they'd brought with them. She handed him his face mask and he slapped it in place. The living room was monstrous, spanning the front of the house to the back. They spent the next four hours slogging through stinking, sweaty work. The tenant must have lived in this room, maybe even sleeping on the sofa. Its cushions permanently sagged and were covered with stains she didn't want to think about. When they finished, the room stood completely empty. The dining room was bereft of table or chairs. The kitchen had a long worktable that served as an island. It was so filthy, there was no way she was ever going to get it clean.

Jazzi looked at the avocado-green stove and shook her head. It was history. She opened the pink refrigerator and quickly slammed the door. Things might live in there she didn't want to meet. The countertops and sink were covered with dirty plates and utensils with remnants of rotting food.

At one time, Cal had professional Viking appliances in here. Jazzi sighed. "Remember how this kitchen looked when Cal was alive? Mom said Lynda loved to give parties and to entertain. This was the perfect house for it."

"I'm guessing the tenant sold anything worth anything," Jerod said. "It's a good thing he was too lazy to bother with the attic." It had some interesting antiques stored in it when they'd done the walk-through.

Jazzi held up a hand and motioned to the side door. She needed some fresh air. Jerod nodded and followed her into the backyard. A rusted, dead gas grill sat on the patio. A tire tilted against the garage. Jazzi shook her head and went to the garden hose. Using lots of soap, she scrubbed her hands and arms. Finally satisfied, she walked to her pickup to open the cooler on the backseat. Lots of ice and lots of beer. She needed something stronger than soda for this job.

Jerod twisted the cap on his bottle and walked into the shade of an old oak. "Who could live like this? You'd think the fumes would kill you."

Jazzi took a long swig of cold beer. "We should have bought a window air conditioner and plugged it in before we started."

Jerod motioned to a unit sitting at the side of the house. "According to the auction brochure, we have central air."

Yeah, right. When they'd switched it on, nothing had happened.

Jerod drained his bottle and belched. On purpose. When was the man ever going to grow up? He was twenty-nine, two years older than she was. Would thirty be the magic number? Somehow, she doubted it.

"The upstairs is pretty much empty, remember?" Jerod shook his head. "The bum sold all the antiques, probably paid for his pot."

They'd found two broken bongs in the living room.

She went to their food cooler and grabbed two deli sandwiches. She handed one to Jerod. "I'm starving, but I had to get the stink out of my nose before I could eat."

Jerod had finished his sandwich and gone for another before she was halfway through hers. "The good news is that we're making money with sweat equity. So far, we haven't found any expensive repairs."

"It's still early." She finished her sandwich and pulled her mask in place, then headed back inside the house. Three hours later, she was starving again, but neither she nor Jerod wanted to stop work until the kitchen was finished. If they stopped now, Jazzi wasn't sure if she could stomach it again.

When Jerod pulled the last black trash bag through the door, Jazzi sagged against the kitchen worktable and the thing nearly collapsed. It only looked sturdy. One of its legs was broken.

Jerod returned and gave the kitchen one last scan. "We have all the windows open. Hopefully, it will smell better when we come for demo tomorrow. Let's go check out the attic."

Jazzi groaned. "It's hot. I'm tired and hungry. It'll be an oven up there."

"So? You can't look much worse than you already do."

That's what she loved about family. They were always there for you. Whether you wanted them or not.

When she gave him a dirty look, he laughed. "I'll bring a window air conditioner tomorrow. Will that win you over?"

She could be had with bribes. They climbed the stairs to the three bedrooms and two baths on the second floor and then climbed a small, narrow set of steps to the third-floor attic. She breathed in stale air. Jazzi pulled on a string dangling from the overhead lightbulb. The room proved to be decent size with a low-pitched ceiling. No insulation, so they'd have to install some, but it provided needed storage.

Old paintings and mirrors leaned against the side walls. Wrought-iron furniture for the patio was shoved to the back. An armoire was smashed against a matching chest of drawers in the highest part of the room. Old trunks sat under rafters. A long, deep cedar chest caught Jerod's eye.

"Franny would love that." Jerod's wife refinished old furniture and ran a business out of a shed on their property. Tallish and shapeless with carrot-orange hair and a face covered with freckles, Franny would never have attracted Jerod if a friend hadn't set them up on a blind date, but once he spent an evening with her, he couldn't stop talking about her. She exuded warmth. To meet Franny was to love her. Down to earth and practical, she wouldn't put up with any of Jerod's BS, but she loved him with every fiber of her being.

The cedar chest was scratched and scarred. Its bottom half was discolored, but it was long and deep. Even the floor under it was stained. Jazzi looked at the ceiling. Had there been a leak at one time? The boards overhead looked fine.

"If you want the chest, it's yours."

Jerod smiled and started to drag it toward the door. Something jostled and rattled inside. Jerod flipped open the lid to see what, then jumped back and stared. "Holy crap!"

A skeleton was lying inside, its head cradled on a pillow, its knees pulled up. A hand and wrist bone had fallen off and formed a small heap of bones on the bottom of the trunk from when Jerod jostled them. Thick blonde hair—dry with a reddish cast—fanned to its shoulders. From old pictures, Jazzi recognized what was left of the cotton spring dress it wore and there was no mistaking the oval silver locket dangling around the neck bones.

Holy crap.

Jazzi shivered and rubbed her arms. Her mom's sister had disappeared twenty-six years ago, the year after Jazzi was born. Lynda had left for New York and never returned, never wrote, never called. Jazzi's mother insisted she wouldn't do that. According to everyone else, she would.

Mom swore if Lynda didn't want to marry Cal Juniper, she'd have called off the wedding. Others remembered Lynda disappearing to New York when she got cold feet with Maury, her first serious contender. No matter. It had taken years for her mother to give up hope of finding her. And now it looked as though Mom had been right. Lynda had never left Cal's house.

Jerod let out a long sigh. "It's who I think it is, right?"

Jazzi nodded.

He shook his head. "The Sunday meal at your place this week is going to be a blast."

A blast wasn't the exact words she'd use, but there'd be plenty of gossip, that's for sure. She cooked for her entire family every Sunday and people pitched in on the cost. They talked over each other so much, they could double as Italians, and no one could have a conversation without waving their hands. This time, maybe it would help her mom to have her family around for support. She was going to be devastated when she heard the news.

Chapter 2

Jerod called 911. While Jazzi waited for the detective to arrive, she went from room to room upstairs, checking them out. She needed to keep busy to distract herself. Her aunt was folded into a trunk, and her mom was going to relive a crappy memory. When Lynda had accepted Cal Juniper's engagement ring but told him that she needed to leave River Bluffs for a year to think things through, friends had lined up behind Cal, not Lynda. And now here Lynda was, stuffed in a trunk in Cal's attic.

Detective Richard Gaff and crime scene experts arrived before Jazzi could sort out her thoughts. Gaff looked at the trunk, frowned at the stains halfway up it, and shook his head. "How long did you say she'd been here?"

Jazzi watched the techs take one picture after another. "She disappeared twenty-six years ago, a few months after she got engaged. Why is everything stained there?"

A tech answered automatically. "A body liquefies when it decomposes— all the fluids draining and organs breaking down."

Jerod grimaced at the floorboards.

"A cleanup crew comes when we find a body or remains. They can fix anything." Gaff looked at the diamond ring caught on the knuckle of the bony finger on her right hand. "And who was she going to marry?"

"That ring came from Thomas Sorrell. She broke up with him." Jazzi pointed to the small heap of bones that had fallen off when Jerod moved the trunk. Another diamond glistened among them—a little smaller, but classier. "That's Cal's ring. She was going to marry him."

He stopped writing and frowned. "Those are both big diamonds."

Jazzi shook her head. "Both men were rich."

"You said she was engaged when she disappeared."

"To Cal Juniper, but she asked him to give her a year in New York to think things through."

"And he was all right with that?"

"He wasn't happy, but he agreed to it. My mom told me that it bothered him so much, he left River Bluffs before Lynda did. He was going to travel across Europe on business trips until Lynda was supposed to come back."

"So he wasn't in the house. For a year? That makes sense. It would stink to high heavens for a long time." Gaff scratched his head, confused. "Okay, let's start at the beginning. Can you tell me what you know about your aunt?"

Jerod and Jazzi exchanged glances.

"That could take a while," Jazzi said.

Gaff raised salt-and-pepper eyebrows. The man was built like a tank, maybe five-ten and stocky, looked to be in his early fifties. "Want to go somewhere to talk?"

"On the back patio?" Jazzi asked. "There are chairs out there."

Gaff gladly accepted a soda when Jazzi got beers for her and Jerod, and then he leaned back in the lawn chair, his pen and pad at the ready. "Go for it."

Jazzi started. "As far as I can tell, my aunt had a wild side, and she loved expensive things. The problem was, she couldn't afford them."

Gaff rubbed his chin. "The man who owned this house and property, Cal Juniper, had money. I met him a few times. He was active in the community and well liked. Lots of people attended his funeral. He didn't flaunt it, but he had deep pockets."

"Every man Lynda dated did."

"How many were there?"

Jazzi pursed her lips, trying to remember what her mom had told her. "Maury was the first—he owns the deli on State Street."

"She was engaged to him, too?"

"No, but they talked about getting married. They were high school sweethearts. When they graduated and Maury got too serious, Lynda got cold feet and ran off to New York for a year."

Mom was a junior then, and none of her friends had anything good to say about her sister. Mom swore they were just jealous. Some of them even spread ugly rumors that Lynda was pregnant, but Lynda wrote to Mom every Sunday, telling her about plays and restaurants. She never mentioned a job, so rumors spread that she was some rich man's mistress.

Gaff made his notes, then looked satisfied. "So your aunt ran off because she didn't want to marry Maury, then came home and met Thomas Sorrell."

"She got a job as a receptionist at the Chamber of Commerce and met lots of men, but I only remember the ones who asked to marry her. Mom doesn't like to talk about it." Jazzi sighed. "You're going to have to question her, aren't you? Do you mind if I tell her about the trunk first? Make it a little easier for her?"

Gaff finished his soda and handed her the empty can. "You can tell her, but I want to be there when you do, in case it jogs a memory or she realizes that something back then was important and she hadn't realized it. First, though, I have a few things to finish up here, but I won't be long."

Jerod cleared his throat. "Is the house a crime scene? Can we still work on it?"

"Might as well, but give us until tomorrow. It's not like this is breaking news. After twenty-six years, I don't think we're going to find much evidence, especially after the renter lived here and you started to work on it, but the crime scene crew will go through every room before they pack up. We'll leave the body in the chest to take it away."

Relieved, Jerod motioned to Jazzi. "We can't do anything more today. Let's go. We can stop by your folks' and tell Cyn the news after Gaff gets there."

Cal's house was on the north side of town. Jazzi's mom lived southwest of the city. Jazzi took Union Chapel Road to Hillegas to avoid heavy five o'clock traffic. She thought Mom would take the news better from her, but she dreaded how it would affect her. Mom had so many conflicted feelings about her sister, they usually avoided the subject.

Jerod followed her in his pickup. He lived ten minutes farther south from her parents. River Bluffs didn't have the massive commuting snarls of Indianapolis or Chicago, but the more it expanded, the longer the lines of cars to make lights. Mom complained about traffic all the time.

"I used to be able to drive from one end of River Bluff to the other in twenty minutes," she'd tell them. At this time of day, it took Jazzi forty minutes to reach her parents' house. Thankfully, Dad's car was in the driveway.

Her parents lived in a tri-level in a small addition off Aboite Road, convenient to stores and restaurants. The yards here tended to be large. Most were fenced for pets. Jazzi and Jerod walked to the front door and rang the bell. Nerves jangled inside her. She swallowed down worry. How would Mom take this? She tried to think of the best way to tell the news.

"It's open!" her dad called. "We're in the back."

Mom's two labradoodles raced to greet them, yipping with excitement. Jazzi bent to pet Lady, and Jerod stooped for Ebbie before they followed

Dad's voice. They found him in the family room off the kitchen, watching the evening news. Mom was heating food she'd bought at Fresh Market for supper. She didn't like to cook. Neither did Jazzi's sister, Olivia. Jazzi had learned her love of cooking from her grandma.

Mom looked up. "What brings you two here?"

They couldn't tell her until Gaff came. Jazzi tried to think of a way to lead into it. "Jerod and I bought Cal Juniper's house to restore and flip. It made me think of you."

Mom stopped fussing with the food. "You know, when Lynda moved in with Cal and invited us to his house for the first time, I was jealous. Your dad and I were renting a two-bedroom apartment that was nothing to brag about. Cal's house was so spacious, so charming. Lynda loved it, couldn't wait to live there."

Jazzi nodded. "It's a beautiful house."

Tires crunched in the driveway, and she felt relief. Her mom walked to the doorway to look out the window and frowned. "A strange man's coming to our house."

"Detective Gaff. Jerod and I wanted to be here when he talked to you."

Mom and Dad both turned to frown at her. Jerod went to let Gaff in. He led him to the family room and introduced him. Gaff looked at Jazzi. "Have you told them?"

"No, I waited for you." Her mouth went dry. Her throat pinched. She took a deep breath. "I told you that we bought Cal's house, and we started cleaning it. When we got to the attic . . ." She couldn't think of any good way to say it. "You know how you never believed Lynda ran off and forgot you? Well, she didn't. We opened a cedar chest and found her skeleton inside it."

"You what?" The color drained from Mom's face. She was still dressed in the black slacks and button-down shirt she'd worn to work today. She and Olivia never saw clients until their hair and makeup were perfect. They were sharp professionals, but Mom's blush and lipstick looked painted on right now, she was so pale.

Dad turned off the TV and went to stand next to her. He put an arm around her waist.

"Lynda never left town. Someone carefully laid her body in a wooden trunk and put a pillow under her head."

Dad asked, "How do you know it was Aunt Lynda?"

Jazzi dug her fingernails into her palms, sorry she had to tell her mom this part—the locket was such a personal touch. "The locket you gave her was around her neck, and her engagement ring was still on her finger."

Mom put out a hand to grip the kitchen island and steady herself. Jerod helped her into the family room where she sank onto a recliner. "I never believed she'd run away and never write me, but . . ." She put her hands over her face.

Dad came to sit on the arm of her chair. "Are you going to be okay?" Mom turned and glared at him. "It all started with your brother . . ."

"Not fair. He was only the first of many, Cyn."

Mom's full name was Cynthia, but everyone called her Cyn. Come to think of it, her dad's name was Douglas, but everyone called him Doogie.

Gaff poised his pen over his notepad. "Did your brother have a thing for Lynda?"

Dad pinched the bridge of his nose. "He was obsessed with her. Every time she broke up with someone, he drove to River Bluffs to take up where they left off. He always thought eventually they'd end up together."

"Lynda had that effect on men." Mom glanced at her wedding ring. "Arnold came to town for our wedding, took one look at my sister, and was hooked."

"He didn't live here then?" Jazzi asked. She hadn't heard much about Mom and Dad's early years. Lynda's disappearance had tainted it all.

Her father put his arm around Mom's shoulders. "Arnie moved to Chicago when he finished college. He started a business there, and it did really well. When I graduated, I started the hardware store here."

"Arnie was my sister's type." Mom leaned against Dad for support. "He didn't play by the rules and got his wrists slapped by the law a few times. Whenever he came to town to visit, he took Lynda to some fancy restaurant or took her shopping. My sister could never say no to a good time."

Dad nodded. "They both liked to party, but Arnie liked Lynda more than she liked him. He was a little too reckless for her, and then she met Thomas Sorrell."

Mom went to one of the built-in bookshelves and took down a photo album. She flipped to a page and pointed. "My sister was beautiful."

Jazzi, Jerod, and Gaff bent to study the picture. Jazzi bit her bottom lip. Lynda was wearing the same dress she wore in the trunk. Her aunt had Mom's cascade of blond hair, but large, gray eyes and full lips. She had a look about her—independent, headstrong.

Mom blinked and wiped at her eyes. "Thomas had money and liked to spend it. He swept Lynda off her feet. The ring he bought her was the biggest I'd ever seen."

"How old was Lynda when she got engaged?" Jazzi thought she looked to be in her early twenties in the picture.

Mom looked to Dad for the answer.

He started counting on his fingers. "She was eighteen when she was with Maury, and then she left for a year. She dated a string of guys after that until she met my brother at our wedding. She strung him along for two years before she met Thomas."

Mom's eyes narrowed. "She didn't string him along."

"She never turned down a date when he came to town to see her."

"She thought of him as a friend."

"She knew he wanted more."

Jazzi interrupted. There was a reason she never brought up Lynda. It always caused friction. "How old was she when she met Thomas?"

Dad pursed his lips. "I'm guessing she was twenty-four or twenty-five when that picture was taken."

"Did all the men have money?" Gaff asked.

Mom's expression changed, now defensive. "Those were the type of men she met at the Chamber of Commerce."

Jazzi couldn't keep track of Lynda's suitors. "Why did she leave Thomas?"

"Everything was about him, wasn't it?" Mom shrugged. "He had to leave River Bluffs to close a few deals before the wedding. He said he'd be gone a few months, but there was always something that needed his attention. Lynda finally realized his business would always come first, and she'd always come second, so she broke it off with him."

Jerod snorted. "And that big, freaking ring . . . ?"

Mom gave a tight smile. "He asked for it back. Lynda decided to keep it. She said it was his fault they broke up and she'd earned it."

Gaff nodded, finishing adding the last thing to his notes. "So, I'm guessing she lay low for a while, right? Worked and let herself regain her balance?"

Mom looked uncomfortable. "People started seeing her around town on Cal Juniper's arm."

"Your sister didn't waste any time, did she?" Jerod's blue eyes twinkled. He was getting a kick out of Lynda's scandals.

Mom scowled. "I talked to Lynda about not rushing into things, but she never listened to anyone, especially Mom and Dad. She told them they were too middle class, too conservative. Cal's family had always had money. He'd traveled a lot and built his house in the country to look like houses he'd seen in England."

Jazzi could see the European influence. It added to its charm. "What happened to Thomas? Did he just disappear?"

"He returns to River Bluffs only when he's doing business here, but we never saw him again." River Bluffs was the second largest city in Indiana. If people wanted to avoid each other, it was easy to do.

Jerod scrubbed a hand through his thick brown hair. "What happened with Cal? Did she find someone richer?"

Mom raised an eyebrow, irritated, then turned a few more pages in the album and stopped at one with a photo of a tall, lean man with soft blue eyes and a gentle smile. "She really loved Cal. I'm sure she did. I don't know why she left him. He was devastated when he came home a year later and she'd disappeared. She sent me one postcard from New York when she got settled there with *X*'s and *O*'s on it, but that's all we heard from her. A year later, Cal and I each got a postcard from Florida. It was typed, just like the letters she'd sent me. Lynda said she'd met someone new and was happy. Then we never heard from her again."

"Do you still have the postcards?" Gaff asked.

Mom flipped to the back of the album and took them out. She handed them to him. Jazzi glanced at the Tampa postmark on the Florida one. Not a bad place to settle, but she'd expected Lynda to end up in Miami on the beach in an expensive condo with some rich husband.

"That's the last I heard from her." Mom's voice quavered.

Gaff frowned. "So, everyone thought she'd left town?"

Mom shook her head, confused. "She *did* leave. Maury saw her get on the bus with her suitcases. No one saw her again."

"But how did she write postcards when she was dead in a cedar chest?" Gaff persisted.

Mom's eyes went wide. "I don't know."

Jazzi bent her attention to the photo album again. Lots of pictures of Aunt Lynda in one beautiful dress after another. Men sure loved to dote on her. And if she'd actually gone to the train station to go to New York, how did she end up in Cal Juniper's attic when the man wasn't even home?

Chapter 3

Mom closed the album and handed it to Jazzi to put away, then glanced at Detective Gaff.

He kept a tight grip on his notes. "Do you mind if I ask you a few more questions?"

Jerod reached for his cell phone. "I'll tell Franny I'm going to be late, so she and the kids can go ahead and eat supper."

"Good idea. This might take a while." When Jazzi motioned for Gaff to change places with her, he sank onto the couch opposite Mom.

While Jerod called Franny, Gaff explained about going through Cal's house. "We didn't find anything interesting. The last tenant took whatever he thought was valuable. We could see where things had hung in the basement that are gone now."

Jazzi frowned. "Why do you think he didn't bother with the attic?"

"Too much work. The steps are too narrow."

Thank heavens, or he might have sold Lynda's trunk.

While Mom and Dad answered questions about Lynda's last few months in town, Jazzi sat back and listened. Her heart hurt while Mom told how happy Grandma and Grandpa were when Cal had invited their family to his house for a fancy engagement party. Grandma, who usually pinched pennies, had bought herself a new dress with matching shoes. She'd gotten her hair done at an upscale parlor. Grandpa bought a new suit and even had it tailored. Cal had served shrimp cocktail, small crab cakes, and slices of beef tenderloin on toast points. It had been a beautiful evening with gorgeous place settings and gold-rimmed flutes of champagne.

By the time Mom finished talking, Jazzi had lived through her mom's and grandparents' disappointment and misery when Lynda told them she was putting her engagement on hold and leaving River Bluffs.

"Did Lynda say why?" Gaff asked.

Mom shook her head. "She told us she wasn't ready to get married yet, that she needed time to sort things out, but there was something she wasn't telling us. I could sense that. Mom and Lynda hadn't gotten along since Lynda left for New York the first time. They didn't even speak to each other when she left the last time."

"Were you and your sister close?" Gaff asked.

"We played together when we were little, but once Lynda started high school and guys asked her out on dates, she was done with me."

Gaff frowned. "Then why did she write you once a week when she went to New York?"

"I don't know. She'd walk past me when she was home, even if I was upset and wanted to talk to her. But I think she missed me when she left. That made me feel better."

A pizza box sat on the counter and Jerod glanced at it.

"There's a piece left if you're hungry," Dad told him.

Jerod was always hungry. He got up and stood at the kitchen island to eat. Mom's dogs begged, but when he slipped each of them a slice of pepperoni, Mom raised an eyebrow.

Her tone was crisp. "Girls!"

Lady and Ebbie grabbed their one cheat and slunk away.

Gaff looked up from his notes. "What happened when Lynda returned? Were you two close then?"

Mom looked sad. "No, she came back and got a job at the Chamber of Commerce. Found a small apartment. Met men and ignored me. I guess when I was there, in the flesh, I was boring again."

Gaff took a minute to think about that. "It sounds like she didn't meet a guy in New York."

"That's what I decided. When she was with a man, he was what she focused on." Mom crossed her arms over her chest and looked at Gaff. "Will someone be able to tell how Lynda died? It would help if I knew what happened to her."

Jazzi didn't think he'd answer her, but he gave her a sympathetic look. "Usually, I couldn't tell you, but this time is different. You've carried the baggage a long time and secret information isn't going to help us break the case. It hasn't been confirmed, but it looks like her neck was broken. It might have happened in the trunk, but it might be cause of death, too."

Mom took a deep breath. "Does that mean someone hit her from behind?"

"It could mean lots of things. It happened so long ago, we might never know for sure."

Mom thought about that. "But Lynda would only be sixty if she'd lived. Everyone she was involved with is still alive except Cal." She shivered. "Do you think one of them might have killed her?"

Gaff closed his notepad and stood. "I didn't say we wouldn't investigate. I just want you to realize the odds are against us." He smiled. "It's getting late. If I have any more questions or news, I'll get in touch with you. Thank you for your time."

They watched him leave, and Jazzi replayed her mom's words in her mind. Whoever killed Aunt Lynda was probably still alive. He might even live in River Bluffs. That creeped her out.

Jerod rose, too. "I'm going to take off. I'll grab a sandwich on the way home. Franny's probably ready to sell my kids by now. I've left her stranded long enough."

Jerod and Franny might complain about their kids, but they adored them. Gunnar was four and Lizzie was one and a half.

"Tell everyone hi for us," Jazzi called.

"Will do." With a wave, he was gone.

Once they were alone, Jazzi stood to clear the table. Her mom looked wiped out. "Are you going to be okay?"

"I'm staying home tomorrow. I'm not going to the salon. Once this hits the news, every client will want the scoop. I'm not up to it."

"I don't blame you."

Then her mom shook her head and sighed. "Who am I kidding? I might as well go in and get it over with. It's not going to go away."

"What if I call Olivia? She should know about Lynda. You two can have each other's backs." Her younger sister worked with her mom at the salon. They were partners. Since she'd moved in with her boyfriend, Thane, they didn't spend evenings together like they used to.

Mom nodded. "You tell her. I can't go through the story again. I'm talked out."

A rare occurrence. Her mom was usually a chatterbox, but this problem was too close, too personal. Jazzi called her sister and filled her in on the news.

"Crap! Is Mom all right?" Olivia asked.

"She's hanging in there. At first, she didn't want to show up at the shop tomorrow, but now she wants to go in and get it over with."

"I'll be there to help her through it." A man's voice asked something in the background. Olivia paused, then said, "Tell Mom I love her. I have to go. Thane just got home."

"And you have to drop everything? Has he got you on a leash or something?"

Her sister laughed. "No, but I want to go out tonight, and if I don't catch him before he hits the couch, I've lost him. He won't want to get back up."

Jazzi chuckled. "I know the feeling. When I get home tonight, I'm going to crash and burn."

"Thanks for the phone call," Olivia told her.

Jazzi smiled as she hung up. She and her sister were close, unlike her mom and Lynda. She and Olivia got together every Thursday night. Jazzi didn't enjoy anyone more than her smart, funny sister. Mom looked like she was wilting, and Dad looked stressed.

"I'm packing it in," Jazzi said. "Hang in there, you two. Love ya."

Dad went to sit next to mom, wrapping an arm around her shoulders and pulling her close.

Jazzi took Jefferson into town and turned into the historical West Central neighborhood she loved. She parked at the curb in front of her first-floor apartment on Berry Street. The old Victorian was painted three shades of pink with a wide wraparound porch. It had plenty of charm. Not as much as Cal's house in the country, but enough. The large front room and arched dining room was so long, she could set up tables and chairs for Sunday dinners with her family, but the kitchen was so small, it proved inconvenient. When she and Jerod got busy on Cal's house, she wanted to knock out the wall between the kitchen and dining room to have a big, open space for entertaining. It would take some work since it was a load-bearing wall, but someday, someone would thank her.

She'd decided to start looking for a fixer-upper of her own. She used to think she'd wait until she met Mr. Right, and they'd choose a house together, but she'd turned twenty-seven at the end of March and no Till Death Do Us Part was in sight, so she might as well skip that step and move on. She'd considered Cal's house, but it came with too much property. A huge yard meant lots of work. Just fixing the poor house would be work enough.

Ansel would be part of the crew soon, and then the remodeling would go faster. Jazzi smiled. She was always more inspired when their hottie contractor was on the job. Eye candy was nothing to sneeze at. But for now, she pushed all thoughts of remodeling and trunks out of her mind and went to stretch on her sofa and watch some mindless TV.

Chapter 4

Jazzi took a deep breath and prepared herself. Time to gut Cal's kitchen. She knew it would be bad, but when mice scurried from behind the refrigerator, she let out a small scream. They didn't scare her, just surprised her. She didn't even want to think about what they'd find when they finally started work on the basement.

They'd brought two window air conditioners with them and plugged them in, but her T-shirt still stuck to her like a second skin, drenched in sweat. Her hair frizzed, and smears streaked her face and arms. Yeah, she wouldn't win any beauty pageants. They'd carried everything to the dumpster in the driveway when Jazzi's cell phone buzzed.

"Bet it's Hollywood, ready to make you their newest HGTV star," Jerod teased.

Her cousin had a warped sense of humor. She glanced at the ID. "Detective Gaff," she said.

Jerod's face fell. He put down his sledge hammer and leaned against the wall to listen in on her conversation.

"Jazzi here!" she said after lowering the white mask on her face.

"I only have a few things to tell you, but I can confirm that your aunt died because she broke her neck. When we opened her locket, there was a picture of a baby. Your mother showed me the pictures of her sister, and this baby's a dead ringer for Lynda."

Jazzi bit her bottom lip. "There were a few rumors when Lynda went to New York. Some people said she was a rich man's mistress, but a few thought she was pregnant."

There was a pause. Uh-oh, there must be more. Gaff said, "The medical examiner also reported that after examining her bones, he could tell that she'd had a baby."

So, the rumors were true.

"Where did she stay in New York?" Gaff asked.

"I don't know. My mom would, or at least she thought she did, but this news is going to bother her."

"I have to ask."

"I know." She didn't have to like it, though.

"I'd like to see the letters Lynda sent her. If she has the envelopes, there might be postmarks. Have you seen them?"

"No, Lynda was a touchy subject for Mom." Jazzi decided she'd stop by her parents' house again on her way home from work. Her mom would be upset after Gaff's call.

"If I learn anything new, I'll keep in touch." He hung up.

Jazzi looked at Jerod. Finding Lynda's body was bad enough, but she'd had a baby, too? A baby no one knew about. He shook his head. "That's what girls used to do when they didn't want anyone to know they got knocked up. They'd go somewhere to have the baby and give it up."

How times had changed. Now, if a woman wanted to keep her child, she could. Did Aunt Lynda want to keep her baby? Jazzi felt a quick bit of sympathy for her. But even if the baby's father refused to marry her, so many men had pursued her, surely one of them would have raised her child. Wouldn't they?

Jazzi pulled her mask back over her nose, pushing her thoughts away. "Let's finish this up today so we don't have to face it tomorrow."

She swung the sledgehammer with more gusto than before, working off nervous energy. Mom was going to be a mess. By late afternoon, all that was left of the kitchen were two-by-sixes and the outside walls.

Jerod studied the studs between the kitchen and dining room. "Wish these weren't load bearing. We can't take them down until the new support beam gets here."

They'd ordered it, but it hadn't arrived yet. They decided to rip into the downstairs half bath. Before they left for the day, that room was gutted, too.

Jerod started to his pickup. "I'm heading straight home tonight. Franny's been in a mood lately. I promised I'd take her and the kids out for supper and then I'd watch the kids swim and play in the sand while she does whatever she wants."

He'd dug a pond at the back of his property and carted in sand for a beach. He'd built a high wooden fence around their backyard and installed a play set, so that the kids couldn't get to the water unless he or Franny accompanied them.

Jazzi gave him a quick nod of approval. "Kids are twenty-four-seven. Franny will need a break. I'm going to see how Mom's doing."

They jumped in their pickups and went their separate ways.

When Jazzi reached her parents' house, Dad gave her a warning look. "Your mom went to bed with a headache. I'm giving her some space. Hearing about the baby stirred up too many memories."

"I worried about that. Did Gaff ask to see Lynda's letters?"

Dad pointed to a stack of old envelopes on the kitchen table.

Jazzi looked at the left-hand corners. No return address. "May I?" When her dad nodded, she pulled out a small single sheet of paper. *Went to see the Statue of Liberty today. Had a wonderful time.* The letter was type written. Really? It made it feel less personal. She pulled out another. *Too cold and icy to leave the house today. Stayed inside and read a book.* A third said, *Stopped at an Italian restaurant for supper. Loved their lasagna.* Jazzi stared. Where were the intimate details, the *I miss you. What have you been doing while I'm gone?* There was nothing about Lynda's job, the people she met. Nothing that mattered.

Her dad studied her expression and nodded. "Your mom called them letters. An exaggeration, but they made her happy."

Jazzi could feel tears build up behind her eyes, but she blinked them away. Poor Mom. "They're fakes, aren't they?"

"It looks that way. Lynda was probably staying somewhere to have her baby but didn't want anyone to know."

"So she sent these to Mom, knowing she'd share the news."

Her dad rubbed a hand over his chin. "It worked. When Lynda came home again, people thought she gave up being a New Yorker to return to her family because she missed us so much. Ironic, isn't it?"

Ouch. That had to hurt. Jazzi tried to think the best of her. "Lynda must have been desperate, trying to save her reputation."

"She used your mom to make herself look good."

Jazzi didn't know what to say. Curious, she asked, "How did Lynda get along with Grandma and Grandpa?"

"There was always tension. Lynda and her mom didn't even speak at the end."

A sore subject. Jazzi decided to let it drop. "Tell Mom I stopped to check on her, will you?"

"Will do."

"How are you holding out?" Dad was a rock, but Lynda's secret had affected him, too.

"I'm okay. I'll be there for her."

Jazzi gave him a hug. "You're always there for all of us. Love ya, Dad." She left to drive home.

Chapter 5

Jazzi usually went out with Olivia on Thursday night. They ate. They drank. They caught up with each other, but this time, they'd called it off so that they could check on Mom. Not that Mom wanted them, but they hadn't known that when they'd canceled their fun. Not thrilled about going home to a jar of peanut butter and a half loaf of stale bread, Jazzi called Ansel. He was working another job right now and had to finish it before he could join them at Cal's place.

"Hey, I'm on my own tonight," she told him. "Does Emily work? Want to grab something to eat with me?"

He hesitated. "She has tonight off, but she's not happy with me. She asked me to leave for a few hours. What if I pick up wings and bring them to your place? She's kicking out George, too."

George was Ansel's pug. The dog went everywhere with him. He even brought George to work when he was with Jerod and her. Jazzi liked George. "I'll pay half. See you in a few."

She took a quick shower before Ansel got there and tossed paper plates and a roll of paper towels on the dining room table. The table was normal size now, a solid square, but it could stretch into the living room on Sundays when she put all of its leaves in.

She didn't like to eat out more than once or twice a week, but she hadn't thawed anything to cook tonight, since she thought she'd be at Henry's Bar and Grill with Olivia. They rotated between their favorite restaurants, and Henry's was at the top of both their lists. They were regulars at the Dash-In downtown, too. Jazzi had a thing for their duck burgers, and Olivia loved their specialty beers. Jazzi had a more refined palate, but Olivia had a keener fashion sense. The rest of the time, Jazzi cooked. It wasn't as much fun since she'd broken up with Chad, but she invited Ansel over whenever Emily was on shift at the hospital. He loved food as much as Chad had and wasn't picky.

She'd blown her hair dry by the time Ansel pulled to the curb in front of the house. She opened the door wide for George, and Ansel followed with a huge bag of wings.

"I got mild since Jerod's not here." He plopped them on the table. "I'm starving. Emily only wanted a salad for lunch."

Jazzi never said what she thought about Ansel's beloved Emily. The woman was a control freak with perpetual PMS. How Ansel lived with her was beyond her, but she'd learned a long time ago to keep her opinions to herself.

"Beer?" Jazzi headed to the kitchen.

"Two for me." Ansel opened a small bag with a grilled chicken sandwich he'd bought for George and broke off a piece and tossed it to him. George gulped it down.

She came back with two beers for him and two for her. Wings needed proper libations. She put a half dozen wings on her paper plate and looked at him. "What did you do this time?"

Ansel was the nicest, most thoughtful man in the world, and he constantly annoyed his live-in nurse. Maybe he'd put a pencil in the pen holder upside down.

His shoulders slumped. "When I cleaned up after lunch, I forgot to wipe down the stove top."

A cardinal sin if she'd ever heard of one. "Shame on you."

He gave her a look. "Emily likes things to be kept neat."

"You two had better never have kids. I'm surprised she tolerates George."

"I clean up after him." Ansel reached to stroke the dog's head. George whimpered, and Ansel threw him two more pieces of chicken.

Jazzi decided to change the subject. "Have you heard about the skeleton in Cal's attic?"

They talked about Detective Gaff and Aunt Lynda while they ate. Ansel didn't know much of the history of River Bluffs. He'd grown up in Wisconsin on his parents' dairy farm. His two older brothers still lived there to help run it. His sister had married and lived close by. He'd moved here to work at his uncle Len's construction company, but Len's two sons let him know that he was an interloper, a third wheel, so Ansel branched out as a contractor. When he started working with Jerod and her, it was a perfect fit.

A high discard pile accumulated beside Ansel's plate, and he took one last heap of wings. "I looked at the auction notice for Cal's house and thought about bidding on it. I like the looks of it."

That surprised her. Was he thinking of flipping houses on his own? "Why didn't you?"

"Emily didn't like it when we drove past it, said it was too far away from her favorite stores and restaurants."

She finished her beer. "Are you thinking of buying a place?" He and Emily rented a three-bedroom apartment out north right now. Emily used one bedroom as her craft room, and in theory, the third was for guests, but Jerod called it the indoor doghouse since Ansel and George were sent there when they upset her.

"I'd like to find a house, but I like old homes with character, and Emily likes new and modern. Bigger rooms and better floor plans with no renovation."

Go figure. Sometimes Jazzi thought that if Ansel liked blue skies, Emily would wish for gray, dreary days. She wondered if the little control freak ever considered that Ansel was six-five with rippling muscles. Girls would crawl across broken glass for him if he encouraged them at all.

When they finished supper, Ansel glanced at his watch and said, "Do you mind if I hang out here for another hour? Emily told me she didn't want to see me until nine."

"Make yourself at home." She handed him the remote and went to change into baggy pajamas and a light robe. She didn't need to stand on formalities. It was only Ansel.

When she padded back into the living room, his eyes lit up and he quickly looked away. What was that about? She tugged her robe closer and sank into her leather chair, just settling in when her home phone rang. She used it for business, so reached for it. "Hello, Jazzi Zanders here."

"Is this the Miss Zanders who recently purchased a house on Willow Drive?"

"Yes." Maybe they already had a buyer interested once they fixed it up.

"This is Tim Carston, Cal Juniper's brother-in-law. My sons inherited the house when Cal died and rented it until they put it up for auction recently."

"What can I do for you?" The sale was final. She wasn't sure why he was calling.

"A Detective Gaff got in touch with my sons and was curious if they'd taken any paperwork out of Cal's house when they inherited it. He was hoping they had some of Cal's personal files. Unfortunately, they didn't bother with any of Cal's belongings. They simply came to River Bluffs to sign papers, give the renter keys to the house and shed, and leave. You haven't found any papers, have you?"

"No, the house was trashed when we bought it. The renter sold anything of value. Every antique was gone."

There was a slight laugh. "Can't blame a man for trying to make a buck. My sons weren't interested in them."

Was he serious? Did he realize how beautiful Cal's furniture and artwork must have been? Jazzi's mom said that Cal bought some of his paintings in Europe. She guessed that the nephews wouldn't know an antique from a flea market find. Or else they never stepped inside the house and didn't care.

Pretty callous. Didn't Cal's family value him and the things he loved? "Your wife didn't want anything to remind her of her brother?"

"Oh, don't get me wrong. We were close to Cal until we moved to Battle Creek when the boys were six and eight. But when he took up with that low-class woman, Katherine had to draw the line. Cal had no sense of propriety."

"And Cal and Katherine never reconciled, not even after Lynda disappeared?"

He sounded offended. "How could Katherine forgive him for choosing a gold digger over her?"

A gold digger? Aunt Lynda enjoyed men with money, but she didn't stalk them. Jazzi struggled for something to say. "It's sad to see a family torn apart."

"That was Cal's choice. He came to regret it."

The more she talked to this man, the less Jazzi liked him. "If I find any papers here, I'll let Detective Gaff know."

"Good, I'll let him know I contacted you. I like to cooperate with the law."

When she hung up, she went over their conversation again. Cal's brother-in-law had seriously annoyed her.

Ansel studied her face and frowned. "Is everything okay?"

She repeated the conversation. "The man didn't have any feelings for Cal at all."

"It sounds to me like his wife is the hard-ass." He paused and reached down to scratch George behind the ears. Had his words reminded him of Emily?

Hard-ass was putting it mildly. If Jazzi never met Katherine, that would be fine with her. But Tim had made her curious. She wanted to know more about Cal and his family.

Chapter 6

On Friday, Jazzi told Jerod about Tim Carston's phone call while they finished emptying rooms. "And why did he call me in the first place? Why didn't one of his sons? They inherited the house."

"Probably didn't want to go to the bother," Jerod said. "They must have been miffed they had to drive to River Bluffs to get their money."

Upstairs, she and Jerod threw the twin bed out the window into the dumpster, along with the cheap chest of drawers. They carried down a few treasures they'd found in the attic. Jerod's Franny could restore those.

They stopped for a quick lunch and then started gutting the upstairs bath. They'd nearly finished when Detective Gaff gave a quick knock on the front door, then wandered up to find them. He looked at Jazzi. "Tim called you about Cal's papers?"

"I'm guessing the renter pitched them." She felt like a limp mop, melting from the heat. She stepped into the hallway with him and pulled down her face mask. The worst of the dust was behind them. Soon, she wouldn't need it. The heat had built and built during the day, draining her energy. Thank heavens, it was almost time to call it quits.

"A pretty gutsy thing to do. That would aggravate some family members."

A bead of sweat dripped into her eye and stung. "Not Cal's. If I understood Tim, they didn't give a darn about Cal or anything he owned."

"That's the impression I got. The guy was a little too ready to be helpful when I called him. Made me wonder."

Jerod wandered into the hallway and motioned for them to follow him. He led them to the kitchen with its window air conditioner.

Jazzi wrinkled her nose. "Tim struck me as fake, the type who'd smile to your face and stab you in the back."

Gaff undid his top two buttons. "That's how Cal's friends described Tim when I talked to them."

That intrigued her. "Who were Cal's friends?"

"Business cronies and golf buddies, people who worked with him on committees and charities. I talked to quite a few of them."

Jerod wet a paper towel and plastered it to the back of his neck. "My dad said that lots and lots of people liked Cal."

Gaff nodded. "I'd heard he had an office at home. I was hoping I could find a paper trail so I could fit timing together better—when Cal left for his business trips and when Lynda died—but it's been twenty-six years. I knew I was pushing my luck."

Jerod went to grab a beer out of the cooler. It wasn't much more comfortable on the first floor, even with the air conditioner, but it was better than the rooms upstairs and the attic. "You might have had a chance if the nephews had shown any interest in this place."

Jazzi frowned. "My mom told me once that Cal had one of the most beautiful rolltop desks she'd ever seen and hand-carved wood filing cabinets. I bet the renter got a lot of money for those."

"Either that, or somebody handed him cash, then sold them for a huge profit." Gaff turned toward the front door. "I'm on my way home. I'll let you two finish up. If you hear or find anything, let me know, will you?"

"We've got your number." Jerod raised his arm to swipe sweat off his forehead.

When Gaff left, Jazzi glanced at the stairway. "We can finish ripping out the bathroom trim on Monday, then start on the floors, but I don't want to climb those stairs again and wilt. I've had it. But since you're taking things home to Franny, when we went through the house the first time, I thought I saw some pocket doors in the basement. They must have gone between the kitchen and the dining room. I think Franny might like them."

"Pocket doors? We could put those in our house between the living room and sunroom. You can tell there used to be some there, but they're gone. Franny and I could sit in the sunroom while the kids watch TV."

"Let's hope I'm right. They were propped against a wall on the far side."

They went down the wooden steps and took a left. Jazzi walked to one of the high windows and pointed to the doors leaning beneath it.

"Solid oak. These are in great shape. Franny's going to love them."

A rusted burn barrel sat in front of them to hold them in place. Jazzi grabbed its rim to tug it out of the way. It didn't move. The darned thing was heavy. She looked inside it and her jaw dropped.

"What is it?" Jerod came to look, too.

"I think we found Cal's papers. All of them." The barrel was almost full. Whoever took the office furniture must have tossed all of their contents in here. She doubted it was the renter, probably whoever bought the antiques. He must have felt uncomfortable tossing serious documents, and there was no place to put them upstairs.

Jerod reached for his cell phone, but Jazzi shook her head. "Let me look through these first."

He raised an eyebrow.

"Gaff asked me to give them to him, and I will. Just let me have them over the weekend. I deserve to be able to tell my family what happened, and Gaff might not share everything with us. His men searched the house. They didn't find them. We did. I won't keep them."

Jerod grinned. "My sweet blond cousin, bending the rules. I'm shocked, but I can live with it."

"Thanks. I'll help you carry out the pocket doors if you help me carry out the papers."

"Done."

It took four trips, but when they locked up the house and left, they each took treasures with them. Jazzi couldn't wait to wade through Cal's papers.

Chapter 7

Jazzi was on her own tonight. Usually, when Ansel's girlfriend had to work, he dropped in for supper, but Emily took tonight off, so he was taking her out to eat. Jazzi ordered a pizza, opened a beer, and started digging through Cal's papers. She spread them out on her farmer's table and began putting them in order.

The papers at the top of the pile must have come from the last files. They were over thirty years old, from when Cal had the house built. She sorted each stack of receipts and ledgers by year and clipped them together, along with Cal's appointment calendars. When she reached the year that Lynda disappeared, the pizza came. Good timing. She nibbled on her supreme while she flipped pages in Cal's date book.

The man was organized . . . and busy. Every square on every page had something scheduled on it. *Meet Chuck for lunch—12:30—The Oyster Bar. Supper at the Country Club. Airport at 4:00, 3 days in Barcelona, meetings.* She glanced over the pages as she turned them until she reached May. *Buy ring for Lynda—Fingers crossed.* And later: *Talk to Lynda. Set date.* Everything was written in smooth, flowing cursive until she came to August. Then the handwriting changed. It shrank in size and became sharper. *Lynda wants a year off to think—a year.* Followed a few days later with: *Have Isabelle buy plane ticket for my trip to Europe—can't stay here alone* Then: *Landed in Paris—too depressed to leave room.* The date for three days later was circled in red. *Lynda leaves for New York. Sad day.* A month later: *No word from Lynda.* Then: *Got a postcard, no real message.* Months of different cities and appointments followed that. Then finally: *Year's up. Time to go home. Time to marry my Lynda.*

Jazzi switched to a glass of wine. She closed the pizza box and carried it into the kitchen. The leftovers would be breakfast tomorrow. It hurt to read the next notations. Cal went from *She's late* to *Tried to call her. No answer.* To *Is she ever coming home? Why won't she just talk to me?*

By the time the book ended, Cal had come to terms with the fact that Lynda had met someone new and wasn't even going to tell him about it. Then he got the postcard from Tampa in December and knew that his suspicions had been right.

The next year's appointments were all straightforward business meetings, but at the beginning of the year after that, Jazzi found an occasional *Meet Isabelle for supper* note. Still, she knew his entire life story. He never married anyone else.

She kept stacking each year's papers into piles and clipping them. She'd flip through every appointment book, but year after year, Cal met Isabelle, traveled, and took care of business.

Her eyes started to burn at midnight. She had only a few more years to go before Cal died. She decided to plow through them. She came abruptly awake when she picked up the book for this year and skimmed to Cal's last entries. *Saw Maury today. Made me think. Could Maury have been right about Lynda giving up a baby? Hired a private detective to find out.* A few weeks later, she read: *He tracked down the unwed mother's home where Lynda stayed. Closed now. But will search for records.* Later still: *He found him, Lynda's son. Not like the old days. No closed books. Noah Jacobs. 28. I have his phone number. Going to call.* The very next day, Cal wrote: *Noah happy I called. Wants to hear about his mother. Flying to New York to meet him. Won't tell his parents. Loves them. Doesn't want to hurt them.* There were no notations in the squares for the next five days. Then: *We instantly clicked. A wonderful young man. He'll drive to River Bluffs to visit me. Can't wait.* After that, Cal rushed to get through projects at work so that he could take a week off to spend it with Noah.

Jazzi couldn't stop reading. Cal said that Noah only told his parents he had a friend in Indiana whom he wanted to visit. Noah was bringing his tools with him to help Cal with small repairs around the house. Noah liked fixing things. Cal circled the day Noah would arrive. He wrote: *Feel like a kid at Christmas. Can't wait for Noah to get here.* In the next day's square: *No Noah. Never came. Tried to call, but no answer. Must have changed his mind. Just like his mother.* The handwriting practically drooped.

Jazzi rubbed her forehead. She wanted to reach out and hug Cal. Had Noah's parents found out? Talked him out of coming, out of having anything to do with Cal? Couldn't they at least have let Cal know? A short while

Chapter 8

Gaff wasn't thrilled with her. She'd sent him a text when she got up. Jerod, too. She knew his kids got him up early. They both came as soon they got them.

Gaff stood, ramrod stiff, bristling with temper. "I asked you to hand Cal's papers over to me."

"And I am."

"*After* you read all of Cal's notes. Did you find anything interesting?"

Jazzi glanced at Jerod. Her cousin looked amused. Gaff was obviously annoyed with her, but what could he do? She was handing him evidence his team didn't find.

She offered them both mugs of hot coffee. "I found a few things. According to his appointment book, Cal left River Bluffs before Lynda and traveled all over Europe to meet with different businessmen for a year. This year, he remembered that Maury told him that Lynda had a baby. Cal hired a private investigator, and the PI found Lynda's son, Noah Jacobs. Cal flew to New York to meet him, and they liked each other so much, Noah meant to come to River Bluffs to visit Cal. He didn't tell his parents. He didn't want to hurt their feelings."

Slightly mollified, Gaff turned that over. "Noah *meant* to come here. He didn't?"

Jazzi shook her head. "He was a no-show."

"Poor Cal." Jerod looked at all of the papers carefully arranged on her table. "He finally met someone who *wanted* to be family with him, and it fell through."

"Was his sister his only sibling?" Gaff turned a page in his notebook.

Jerod nodded. "She was younger than him. When he asked Lynda to marry him, she disowned him. He never saw her or her family again. My dad went to Catholic school with both Cal and Katherine when he was growing up . . ."

Jazzi stared. She put up a hand to interrupt. "Wait a minute. Your dad went to Catholic school and mine didn't? What happened? Did the nuns kick out Dad?"

Jerod barked a laugh. "If any brother got banned, it would have been my old man. No, Arnie and Dad both learned their catechism, but Grandpa got laid off for a few months in 1958 and ran out of money. Catholics don't teach religion for free. My dad says Doogie, being the youngest, got lucky. The nuns were drill sergeants back then. His knuckles got whacked with rulers so many times, he thought he'd get arthritis when he turned sixteen. The minute Dad graduated, he was done with church."

Jazzi could see that. Jerod's dad was as irreverent as he was.

Jerod went on. "Anyway, Cal was three years ahead of Dad. Dad went to trade school to become a mechanic, and when he graduated, he got a job working on foreign cars. Cal and his friends always had money, bought expensive models. Dad worked on most of their repairs, kept in touch with Cal and his buddies that way. They thought Cal was nuts when he hooked up with Lynda, but they'd never turn their backs on him like Katherine did."

Gaff looked up from his notes and glanced at Jazzi's leather couch. She nodded for him to take a seat. "When I called Cal's nephews, they said they hadn't seen Cal in years."

"Katherine's a snob," Jerod said. "My dad said she chased dollar signs harder than greyhounds chase rabbits."

Jazzi snorted. "And Katherine called Lynda a gold digger!"

Even happier with the notes he'd taken, Gaff turned to Jerod. "Does your dad know Tim?"

"No, Tim's not from River Bluffs. Katherine met him in college. Married him because she thought he was going to make big bucks. Instead, he ran three businesses into the ground, almost went bankrupt, but Katherine still acts like royalty. Thought Lynda was beneath her."

"Beneath her?" Jazzi stared. "How?"

"She never went to college and attended public school. Katherine called her a 'commoner.' Guess how we'd rate?"

Did people still care that much about status? Katherine obviously did. Jazzi grinned. "Do you care?"

"Do you have to ask? But Katherine would take one look at your nails and snub you."

"Forget Katherine."

Gaff took a minute to collect his thoughts. "When I talked to Cal's friends, they said he never got serious about another woman after Lynda."

"Sad, huh? When I read his notes, he had dinner with Isabelle a lot, but only thought of her as a friend. Lynda was like a wrecking ball, wasn't she? She knocked men off their feet and left them off balance when she moved to the next guy." But who was she to talk? She'd moved in with Chad and couldn't make it work. She thought they were on the same page, but once they lived together, he pressured her to stay home to cook and clean and have his children. Not her style.

Gaff leaned back against the soft leather, resting his arm on the back of the sofa. "His friends said Cal was devastated when Lynda decided to go to New York."

Chad hadn't been overjoyed when Jazzi moved out and found an apartment either.

Jerod started to the kitchen. "I need something to cool me off. Got any iced tea?"

"Top shelf of the refrigerator."

"Sugar?"

"Yup, it's sweet enough for you."

"Want some, Gaff?" he called.

"Wouldn't mind."

Jazzi waited till he handed Gaff his glass. "You know, Uncle Arnold took forever to meet someone new after Lynda dumped him. Then when she disappeared, it really threw him. He always wondered why she didn't contact anyone or return home."

Jerod nodded. "I bet your dad didn't have any great love for Lynda. She didn't make his life any easier."

"It caused some friction between Mom and Dad, that's for sure." Jazzi thought of Mom's reaction when she told her about Lynda's skeleton in the trunk. She'd turned to Dad to blame his brother.

Jerod sighed. "I don't think she had many close friends here."

Jazzi hadn't really heard much about her. People in her family avoided the subject. "I wonder what Grandma thought. She never mentions Lynda. And she comes to family meals every Sunday. Not much is sacred in our family. We gossip about everything, but not Lynda."

Jerod gave her a look. "It's a little tricky talking to your grandma now. I never know if she's living in the present or the past."

Gaff leaned forward, interested. "Could I talk to her?"

"You can try." Jazzi wasn't sure how to describe her grandmother. She adored the old woman, but her mind was a slippery slope these days. "Most of the time now, Grams thinks I'm her dead sister. My whole family comes to my place every Sunday. Grams, too. You're invited if you want to meet them all."

"Can't this time," Gaff said. "It's my grandson's birthday."

"How old?" Jazzi asked.

"He's turning seven."

"A fun age." Jerod looked at Jazzi. "My buddy's kid is seven. They get better the older they get."

"Until they become teenagers." Gaff shook his head. "That's when parents call us because their kids are giving them grief."

Jazzi wouldn't know, and she was fine with that. She looked at Gaff. "If you decide to visit Grams, let me know and I'll go with you. Sometimes she's on track, and sometimes she isn't."

"I'll keep that in mind." He glanced at his watch. "Have to go. If you're having company tomorrow, you have to be busy, too. We have more homicides than we need right now." He handed Jazzi his empty glass.

River Bluffs had grown enough to be like most big cities. Someone shot someone else almost every weekend. Most were gang or drug related.

Jerod finished his tea and stood. "Franny's going to wonder what's keeping me."

Ansel had texted that Emily worked tonight and wanted a quiet apartment to sleep. He'd be over earlier than usual. No biggie. She'd preroasted four chicken leg quarters last weekend, so all she had to do was throw them on the grill with some barbecue sauce. No, make that sauce on *three* chicken quarters. George didn't like anything with a tomato base. And yes, they fed him human food and he loved it. He especially liked it when they set empty beer cans on the cement patio and he could take his front paws and tip the can to get the last sips of brew. Yup, George would be a happy dog tonight.

They never worked on weekends. Jerod spent every Saturday and Sunday with Franny and his kids. Jazzi spent Saturday cleaning and cooking during the day. She relaxed on Saturday night. Sometimes Ansel came over. Sometimes she went out. This time, she and Ansel were supposed to meet a group of friends for Mexican food on Wells Street. She'd looked forward to stuffing herself with a spicy beef chimichanga and a couple of margaritas, and they'd all be home by eleven. They were older now, and she and Ansel were the only ones in their group without kids. Their friends' weekend dynamics had changed. They drove kids to soccer games or swim meets.

And when their kids went to camp and shared germs, unfortunately, they stayed home to care for them. They'd had to cancel their plans.

As Jazzi changed into running shorts to clean, she sighed. How long could you wait to start a family? Had she made a mistake breaking up with Chad? Heck, no, but sometimes, she missed having someone to talk to. Was she in a rush to meet Significant Number Two? Not really. A girl had to kiss a lot of toads before she met a serious contender. But the big 3-0 was getting closer. Soon, it would be breathing down her neck.

Before she started her usual weekend routine, Jazzi braced her shoulders and called her mom. Her cell phone buzzed three times before she picked up. "Hey, kid! How's it going?"

"Pretty good. I was thinking of coming over to see you and Dad when you get out of the salon today."

"Can't happen. I took the day off and your dad and I are on our way to Shipshewana. There's a big craft fair today, and your dad loves Amish pies. If you haven't started dessert yet, we can bring a few to the Sunday meal."

Mom had told her about visiting all the shops in Shipshewana. Her parents oohed over anything Amish made, but it had completely slipped her mind. "That would be great. I love pie."

"Good. I don't get to pitch in very often. Anything else?"

"Nope, thanks. You're saving me some work." There was no way she was telling her mom about Noah over the phone when Mom and Dad had a day to play. The news would have to wait.

Chapter 9

It took only an hour to clean the apartment—the good thing about small spaces. Then she started to make a grocery list of things she needed for tomorrow's meal. She'd decided on bruschetta, melon slices wrapped in prosciutto, and a seafood pasta. Jerod had a thing for deviled eggs. Did she have enough eggs to make some? When she went to the kitchen to see, she glanced out the window to the small backyard.

Doggone it. Her upstairs neighbor, Reuben, had passed out on the picnic table. He wasn't there earlier, so he must have just gotten home.

Reuben didn't overindulge often, but when he did, he didn't handle it well. She went out and shook his shoulder to wake him. "Hey, Reuben! You're going to get a serious sunburn if you sleep it off here."

He stirred and mumbled. He wore expensive slacks and a silk shirt. The party he'd attended must have been swanky. With his mocha skin, blue eyes, and slight build, he was a beautiful man. He *looked* like an interior designer who worked with wealthy clients. He didn't look like he belonged passed out on a picnic table.

She gave him another shake. He cracked an eye and immediately shut it. "Isabelle?"

"Nope, just me—Jazzi."

He yawned. "Isabelle couldn't make it last night. I missed her, and I might have drunk too much."

"Looks like it. You're going to have one heck of a headache. Come on. Let's get you inside." She pushed him into a sitting position. "You can lean on me."

He stumbled to his feet and they stood shoulder to shoulder. She had to admit, she was surprised to hear him ask for a woman friend. If she'd have placed a bet, she thought he was gay. Not that it mattered.

They made their way to his second-floor apartment and she helped him to his blue velvet-covered sofa. She went to the kitchen and brought him two aspirins and a glass of water, careful to place it on a coaster on his coffee table.

"You okay?"

He nodded. "Thank you, dear." He was fifty-six, close to her parents' age, and insisted on calling her "dear." He liked to cluck over her and keep track of what she was doing. Sometimes, when she and Jerod finished a house, he'd give her ideas on how to design it. She was sure he could afford a bigger apartment, but he swore he loved his upstairs unit. And she had to admit, he'd made it stunning.

She patted his shoulder. "Do you want me to call anyone, get you anything?"

He reached for his cell phone. "I'll call Isabelle. She'll come for me."

Isabelle? Cal's friend? "You've never mentioned her before."

"We only met a while ago after Cal Juniper died. They were an item, and she was lonely without him. We started going to dinner and the theater together. We've grown quite close."

"Jerod and I just bought his house, and we're getting it ready to flip."

He chuckled. "It's a small world, isn't it? I'll have to tell Isabelle. She loved his home. She'll be happy someone's taking care of it again."

Jazzi decided not to mention Aunt Lynda's body in the cedar chest. Why ruin Isabelle's fond memories? Or did Isabelle already know about the trunk? A suspicion niggled in her mind. How much did Isabelle love Cal and his house? Enough to get rid of Lynda? She pushed the thought away.

"Feel better," she told Reuben and left.

Once back in her own kitchen, she read through the recipes she was going to use and finished her grocery list. The trip to the store didn't take long, so she stopped at Olivia's apartment on her way home. Olivia could still be at the salon, but she might have taken the day off, too, since Mom did.

She was in luck. Olivia smiled a greeting and motioned Jazzi into a large great room. The carpet was worn, but sliding doors offered lots of light. Large, colorful, modern paintings hung on the walls. She and her sister attended River Bluffs' art fairs every summer to find artists they liked and could afford.

Olivia sank onto the burnt orange sectional and picked up a bottle of teal polish. She raised her foot to finish painting her toenails. "Thane's fishing with a friend today. I'm doing girly things."

It must be home spa day. Her sister's hair was wrapped in a towel.

"Deep root treatment," Olivia said.

A green mask covered her face.

"Deep pore cleansing. You should try it."

"Someday." Jazzi sat across from her. "I can't stay long. I just wondered how Mom's doing."

"She's having a hard time. Knowing someone stuck Lynda in a trunk is bad enough, but knowing her sister purposely tricked her really hurts. You'd never do that to me, right?"

"You wouldn't judge me. I wouldn't have to."

"Mom and Grandma wouldn't judge Lynda either."

"Grandpa would."

"They wouldn't tell him." Olivia started on her other foot. "Detective Gaff gave Mom Lynda's locket and she tossed it in a drawer and won't look at it."

"How's Dad?"

"He's on the fence. Mom blames his brother, Arnie, for indulging Lynda too much. She says it changed her. That's not the way Dad sees it. He says whenever Arnie lost interest, she did the sly, push-pull flirting thing only really pretty girls can pull off. You know, that combination I-want-you, stay-away-from-me type thing. I guess poor Arnie didn't know if he was coming or going."

"Dad didn't like her."

"He calls her high maintenance. Keeps saying he's glad he met Mom, not her. Lynda was a knockout, and when she was *on*, Dad says she was something. Arnie thought they'd eventually end up together, until she met Cal. It threw him when she just up and disappeared and left Cal, too. He liked him. Everyone did."

"It took Arnie a long time to get over Lynda, didn't it?"

"He was thirty-five when he finally married his Lucy, and even Mom wishes after all he'd been through, he'd have been able to grow old with her." Olivia finished painting her toenails and screwed the lid on the polish. She held a hand next to her foot. The nails matched. Satisfied, she said, "At least they had twenty-five good years together before cancer got her."

"And he has his two kids," Jazzi added. Whenever she saw Arnie at family holidays, he doted on his son and daughter. "Um, I was thinking about Lynda and New York. Do you think Grandma and Grandpa knew she was pregnant and she was going there to have a baby and put it up for adoption?"

"Dad thinks Grandma suspected, but Lynda swore she wasn't."

"Didn't they pay to send Lynda to New York? Did they have to pay for her to stay there?"

"Lynda told everyone she got a job in New York, and all she had to pay for was her trip there. Mom said her parents footed the bill for that, and then she wrote to tell them she'd found a cheap apartment and was doing fine. Looking back, the cheap apartment was most likely a home for unwed mothers and giving up her baby for adoption paid for her stay there. Mom said she came home broke, said that it was too expensive living in New York to save any money, and that's why she came back to River Bluffs."

"I can see why people would believe that."

"All I know is when Mom got all excited when Lynda wrote that she'd spent the day in Coney Island, she said Grandma raised an eyebrow and snapped, 'You know better than to believe everything your sister tells you, don't you, Cyn?'"

"What did Mom say?"

"She just laughed and said, 'Why would she make up something like that?' And I guess Grandma just shook her head and looked away."

"But Grandma didn't *really* know?" Jazzi asked.

"No, but she told Mom once that she couldn't trust Lynda's version of any story, that she always waited to hear the other side before she made up her mind."

Jazzi bit her bottom lip. "I found out that Cal hired a detective to find Lynda's baby. Just before he died, he went to New York to meet him."

"For real?" Olivia started to jump to her feet, then thought better of it. Her polish wasn't dry yet.

"I called Mom to tell her, but I forgot about her taking the day off. I couldn't ruin her fun."

"You'll have to tell her tomorrow. I'll be there to help you."

Jazzi stayed to visit a few more minutes before she had to leave. "Ansel's coming over for supper tonight."

Olivia snorted. "What's new?"

Jazzi laughed. On the drive back to her apartment, though, she thought about Lynda. She'd hurt a few people, yet someone had carefully folded her inside the trunk and put a pillow under her head.

Chapter 10

On Sunday, Dad called to tell Jazzi that he'd talked to Arnold last night, and his brother was coming to the family meal.

"His kids, too?" Jazzi glanced at the table stretched between her living room and dining room. It would be crowded with three more people. Her lease was up at the end of August. Maybe it was time to find someplace bigger to live.

"No, it was too short of a notice for them to make the trip, but Arnie wants to hear about Lynda. He's moved on. She's in his past, but he always thought something happened to her, or she'd have contacted us. He thought maybe she caught something and died in a foreign country."

Jerod was right. Lynda was going to be the topic of conversation for the entire meal. Most Sunday meals were filled with teasing and laughter, catching up with each other, but families were there for each other through good times and bad. They'd weather Lynda's past and death together. For the moment, though, she pushed her aunt out of her mind while she cut cantaloupe slices and wrapped them in prosciutto. Then she made the toppings for the bruschetta—diced fresh tomatoes with basil for some and a white bean puree for others. She was sautéing the shrimp and scallops when Jerod and Franny came.

Jazzi added white wine and chicken broth to the pan, then turned and frowned at them. "No kids?"

Franny put a relish tray on the table—her usual contribution to the meal. Franny and stoves were never simpatico. "My parents wanted to take them to the zoo. I figured that might be a good thing if we're going to sit around talking about a skeleton today."

"Yeah, I can see that." Jazzi tossed halved cherry tomatoes and baby spinach into the pan.

Jerod went to grab a beer when Ansel gave a quick knock on the door and held it open for George. "I had to bring him today," he told Franny. "Emily locked him in the bathroom when I was getting ready to leave."

Jazzi bent to pet the pug behind his ears. She wouldn't be surprised if Ansel insisted they eat at outdoor cafés from now on, so that George could come, too.

Franny gave Ansel a sympathetic look. "I always worry about the kids when I leave them, but it's good to separate from each other once in a while. It builds strength. You don't want George to be too dependent on you, do you?"

Ansel looked shocked. "George likes alone time once in a while, but he's never been locked in the bathroom before."

Emily probably did it to bother Ansel. Jazzi gave George one last pat and started to put glasses on the table. Ansel reached for a deviled egg when there was another quick knock at the door and Dad and Mom came in with Arnie. Dad carried three pies, stacked on top of each other, into the kitchen.

"Hey, good to see you!" Jerod went to pump Arnie's hand. Their uncle had enjoyed giving Jerod a hard time while he was growing up. At Christmas, he always gave him a fake present before he gave him a real one. One year, when Arnie had heard that Jerod had been grounded for a week, he wrapped a piece of coal in an elaborate box. Jerod loved it.

Arnie looked at Jerod's waistline and shook his head. "You're not getting any thinner, kid."

With a snort, Jerod reached for a deviled egg before Ansel took another one. "How's retirement, old man? I heard you were just another Q-tip, soaking up the rays in Florida, now."

If Arnie was a Q-tip with his thatch of pure white hair, he was a good-looking one, fit and healthy. Lynda would have had a good life with him.

"Come down and visit me sometime." Arnie slapped Jerod on the shoulder. "I'll take you out on my boat and we'll do some deep-sea fishing. My house has a pool, and I belong to a golf club. I'll show you a good time."

Jerod looked at Franny, and she nodded. "Works for me."

Just then, Grandma knocked and joined the party, followed by Jerod's mom and dad. Jazzi took a second to study Grams and was relieved. She looked sharp today, like she was with them, mentally acute. She didn't have the lost look she sometimes got.

Jazzi's mom looked surprised. "I thought you weren't coming."

"And miss Arnie? I called Eli and he came to pick me up." Jerod's parents had grown as fond of Grams as Mom was, claiming her as part of their family now, too.

The front room was getting crowded when Olivia joined them.

"Sorry, Thane had to work today. I got a little bit of a late start." Her sister looked around the room and braced herself. Jazzi understood. Everyone looked wired.

Underlying tension buzzed in the air, so Jazzi said, "Let's eat. Everything's ready."

To make life easier, she'd divided the seafood pasta into two huge bowls, one for each end of the table. People jostled into their seats and passed platters. Jazzi put bottles of wine and beer on the table, and everyone grabbed for what they wanted.

Arnie didn't waste time. "Doogie called and told me about Lynda's body in a trunk."

The conversation took off from there, rehashing all of the details for him.

Mom's voice cracked when she blurted, "She'd had a baby. Did you know that?"

"Whose?" Arnie obviously hadn't known. His shoulders tensed.

Dad put his hand over Mom's before he answered his brother. "It was before she met you, Arnie. When she went to New York, it must have been to have the child and give it up for adoption."

Arnie visibly gathered himself. "So whoever got her pregnant wouldn't claim the baby and make it legitimate? He left Lynda on her own?"

"It looks that way." Dad patted Mom's hand again. "There was a picture of the baby in the locket Lynda wore."

Arnie shook his head. "No wonder she didn't trust men. Some loser got her pregnant, then walked away. She must have been desperate, afraid."

Heads turned toward Grandma. "She never said a word to us, only asked for money to go to New York."

"Why did she say she wanted to go?" Jazzi asked.

"She said she had a good job waiting for her there, that she was tired of living in a stick-in-the-mud town, that she wanted something bigger than River Bluffs."

"And it was all a lie." Mom's hands curled into fists. "She wrote to me every week, told me all the fun she was having. All lies."

Arnie's expression looked so sad, Jazzi wanted to hug him. "But what else could she do, Cyn? She was too proud to admit she'd slept with someone who kicked her to the curb. Her reputation would be ruined."

Mom barked a harsh laugh. "Would you have cared about her reputation when you met her? Would you have ignored her as a tainted woman?"

"No, it wouldn't have mattered to me. But if she told people, some of them would put pressure on her to keep the child. What would that have done to her life?"

Mom's expression pinched in anger. "If she'd have been honest with me, I'd have never told anyone. Lynda knew that."

"Her dad and I would have helped her raise it if she wanted to keep it," Grandma said. "Or we'd have supported her giving it up, but my Raymond wouldn't condone an abortion." She glanced at Doogie, Eli, and Arnie. "Not like you Catholics, but he was against it."

Arnie leaned his elbows on the table, even more determined to make his point. "See? She couldn't get rid of the baby, so she gave it away."

Jazzi wasn't sure what to think.

Mom pushed her plate away, her food uneaten. "I'd love to know who knocked her up. I'd like to give him a piece of my mind."

Arnie wasn't eating either. "I'd like to know where the baby is, who raised it, and where the kid lives today."

Ansel spoke for the first time. "Maybe the kid's better off not knowing that his mother gave him up. Maybe he's had a happy life, and people should leave him alone."

Franny agreed. "What good would it do him to know that his mother's dead and his dad didn't want him? It's selfish to burden him with that."

Arnie leaned back in his chair and sighed. "You're right. I'm thinking about what I want, not what's best for the kid."

Jazzi pushed to her feet. The pasta was gone, the food platters empty. "Hand your plates down and I'll put them in the kitchen." Should she tell them now? She decided to go for it. "Cal found the boy. He hired a detective. Noah had a good life with loving parents and was happy to meet Cal."

Mom sat up straight in her chair. "Cal found Lynda's son?"

"He flew to New York to see him."

Jerod's dad, Eli, took the leap and said what Jazzi had been thinking. "What if Lynda didn't want the boy? She never struck me as the nurturing type."

Dad squirmed in his chair. He'd obviously thought the same thing.

Mom stared. "But every mother—"

"Isn't like you," Olivia said. "Some women make crappy mothers. Your sister might have been one of them."

No one spoke. Finally, Mom admitted. "My sister wasn't perfect."

That was an understatement, but Jazzi and everyone else let it ride.

Mom repeated, "I'd still like to know who got her pregnant. And how did she end up in a trunk? I wonder if the same person was responsible for both those things."

That seemed highly likely. As Jazzi carried the dishes to the kitchen, she called, "Let's have dessert. Mom brought pies."

"Wait a minute," Arnie said, silencing them. "You said Cal found Lynda's son. Can we meet him? Would he ever come to River Bluffs to get to know us?"

Jazzi regretted the next news. "He was going to come here to meet Cal but changed his mind."

Arnie's shoulders sagged. "I can't say I blame him. It must have been a shock when Cal called him."

"Especially when it wasn't even a relative who looked for him," Eli chimed in.

Arnie's face drained of color. "You don't think Cal killed Lynda, then hired a detective to find her son?"

Jerod shook his head. "Cal wasn't even in River Bluffs when Lynda disappeared."

Arnie relaxed. "You're right. He'd left for Europe, hadn't he?"

Jazzi put the pies on the table and purposely steered the conversation to other topics. The air conditioner was struggling to keep the rooms comfortable with so many people jammed into them. The men kept running their fingers around their shirt collars. Jazzi felt sticky. Usually, they'd go outside and sit in the backyard, but the temperature was uncomfortable, and flies buzzed around glasses and bottles.

People stuck it out another half hour, then started to leave. Grandma came to hug Jazzi good-bye. "You cooked a wonderful meal, Sarah. Thanks for having us."

Jazzi smiled. Grandma's eyes had that fuzzy look again, like she'd moved miles or years away. When she called Jazzi "Sarah," she'd reverted to her younger days and was spending time with her dead sister. Today must have been too much for her. "Love ya, Grams."

Ansel stayed until the last person left. "Let me help you with cleanup."

While they rinsed dishes and loaded them into the dishwasher, Jazzi asked, "Does Emily work tonight?"

"No, I'm taking her to a restaurant for supper. She's sleeping now, so I try to stay out of the apartment and give her some quiet." He took an uneaten shrimp off a plate and tossed it to George.

George snarfed it down.

THE BODY IN THE ATTIC

They finished with the dishes and then went to fold chairs and put the table's leaves in the linen closet. Everything was back to normal, but Jazzi put her hands on her hips and looked around her apartment. "It's time I find someplace bigger. It's getting more and more crowded when we get together."

"What about Cal's place?" Ansel pushed the table back into the center of the dining room. "I haven't seen too many houses with as much room and charm."

Jazzi wrinkled her nose. "But I'd always remember finding Aunt Lynda in the attic."

"So? That was a good thing. You can finally give your family a little closure."

"There's too much property."

Ansel shook his head. "I'd love that. George would have a place to run."

Jazzi looked at the pug and laughed. He was stretched out on the kitchen floor under the air conditioner. "Yeah, I'll believe that when I see it."

Ansel grinned fondly at his dog. "Look, you helped Jerod fix up his place to sell, and then he decided to keep it and you didn't mind. You two got Cal's house at a great price. You should think about it."

"I do love the house."

"See?" He helped her finish swiping down the kitchen, and then they went to plop on the sofa and watch Sunday sports. George jumped between them to put his head on Jazzi's lap. Their Sunday ritual. They'd coast until Ansel had to pick up Emily.

Chapter 11

On Monday, the real fun began when Jazzi and Jerod started scraping layers of tile off the bathroom floors. There were three of them. They'd be lucky if they finished at a decent time today. Jerod rammed his crowbar too close to the master bath's wall and it left a hole. He was cussing when Detective Gaff came.

"I have bad news."

Jazzi and Jerod laid down their tools and followed him to the kitchen. They sat in their usual circle in the lawn chairs there.

"When I called New York to ask about Noah Jacobs, the cop at the station looked up his name and told me he'd been reported as a missing person."

Jazzi held her breath. *A missing person?* "But Noah lives in New York, doesn't he?"

"He has a wife and a kid there, plays in a band, but he left to visit a friend in Indiana seven months ago, and no one's seen him since."

Seven months. "That would be about the time he came to visit Cal."

Gaff nodded. "The case went cold after a while, but when we started digging again, we found his car in Ohio, close to Cleveland."

Jazzi blinked, trying to picture Noah's drive to River Bluffs. He'd left New York and must have stopped in Cleveland. That seemed a little out of his way, but not that much. Maybe he meant to spend a few nights there before he stopped in town. It wasn't unreasonable.

"Was there anything in it?" Jerod asked. "Luggage?"

"We found two suitcases and a guitar in the trunk. I called his parents and they confirmed he'd taken his guitar with him. Took it everywhere, I guess. He was a musician in a band and was doing fairly well. He was married with a little boy. His wife's a Web designer, so can work from home. He did odd jobs on the side when gigs got slow."

Not anymore. It didn't sound good. It sounded as though Noah Jacobs had disappeared just as thoroughly as his birth mother had. "How old is he?" Jazzi asked.

"Twenty-eight. His parents said he was well liked. All that he told them was that a friend of his moved to Indiana, and he was going to stay with him a week to help him fix up his house."

"Except he never made it."

Gaff shook his head. "It doesn't look like he did."

"Poor him. Poor Cal." Cal had been waiting for *another* person who disappeared on him. She sighed. "His body isn't lying in a morgue somewhere, unclaimed, is it? What if someone mugged him and took his ID? Can you trace things like that?"

"We'd have found him. I talked to Isabelle and she said that Cal could hardly wait for Noah to get here. It was a horrible blow when he never showed up. She even hinted that might be part of the reason Cal had his fatal heart attack."

"Have you checked hospitals? Clinics?" Jazzi couldn't stand the idea that Noah had just disappeared. Just like Lynda.

"What do you think?" Gaff gave her a look. "Tell me about your Sunday meal. How did that go?"

They filled him in and he made notes.

"Did anyone have any theories about Noah and Cal?"

Jazzi bit her bottom lip. "At first, Arnie suspected Cal, but we decided against that."

Gaff looked surprised, but then shrugged. "Noah's parents are sending a picture for us to post for missing persons. That might help."

The baby in the locket had looked like Lynda. Jazzi wondered what the grown man would look like.

Gaff tried again. "And no one in your family had any idea who the father of Lynda's baby might be?"

"No one even knew she'd had a baby, and you said there was no father's name on the birth certificate." When Lynda wanted to keep a secret, she did.

Scowling, Gaff shut his notepad. "Well, I'd better get going. This is an old case, but it intrigues me. I have plenty of new ones, though." He paused at the door. "I'll tell your mom this time. She knows me now. It might be better if this came from me."

They watched Gaff leave, then went back to work. At the end of the day, the bathroom floor was cleaned down to the base and the wall between the kitchen and dining room was gone and a new beam had taken its place. The open space was big enough to host dinners for twenty people, if you wanted to. Jazzi eyed it with greed. It would be a perfect place to have her Sunday dinners.

Jerod raised an eyebrow at her. "You gave up more profits when you helped me fix up my place and buy it. If you want this, it's yours for half what we paid for it."

She could feel herself blush. Her cousin knew her too well. "We hardly made any money on our last job."

"But we made a bundle on the one before that. This is a perfect house for you. Think about it."

"Thanks." She did like this property. If worse came to worse, she'd buy a big tractor to mow the yard.

"Ansel likes it too," Jerod said.

"Emily said no. That's why he didn't bid on it."

Jerod made a disgusted noise. "Emily never cares about what would make Ansel happy."

"He's happy with her. I guess that's enough."

Jerod snorted. "Ansel has poor taste in women."

When they left for the day, they'd patched the wooden floor where they'd taken down the wall, and the first floor of Cal's house had two huge spaces—the living room on one side and the kitchen/dining room on the other, perfect for entertaining.

Ansel was going to start working with them tomorrow, so the upstairs would go even faster. He'd finished his other job and had taken today off to spend time with Emily. She'd wanted to visit her parents near Chicago, so he was driving her there.

"She's going to spend the rest of the week there," Ansel had told her when he called. "Then I'll drive up on Saturday to bring her back. She doesn't like to drive in heavy traffic."

Emily didn't like lots of things, but that was between her and Ansel. It meant that Jazzi was on her own tonight, though. She decided to make herself nachos and rent a movie. She was browning hamburger and slicing jalapenos when someone knocked on the door. When she went to answer it, Maury Lebovitch shifted from one foot to the other on her front porch.

She knew Maury by sight, nothing more. He was friends with her dad's brothers. They'd gone to Catholic school together, so she heard about him once in a while. There was only one reason he'd come to visit her: Lynda.

She forced a smile on her face, then opened the door. "Hi, how can I help you?"

Maury walked in and took a seat on the sofa and fidgeted. "I heard about Lynda. Is your mom doing okay?"

"Just give me a minute." She went to the kitchen to turn off the stove, then returned and sat across from him. "She's struggling. She never thought Lynda would leave River Bluffs and not talk to her again. It hurts. She always thought she'd get a phone call someday, you know? Now, at last, she knows why. Then we found out Lynda was pregnant when she went to New York, and she gave up a baby. That bothered Mom even more."

Maury stared. "Are you sure—that Lynda had a baby, I mean?"

"The doctor who examined her bones could tell she'd given birth."

He sat silent a minute, taking that in. "And she gave the baby away?"

"Yes. Then she came back to River Bluffs."

"But she sent letters to your mom every week. She was working, having fun."

"All lies. Detective Gaff called and the unwed mothers weren't allowed to leave the premises while they lived there. The home was beautiful with beautiful grounds, but they didn't want the girls to meet new people, maybe meet new men."

"So Lynda was stuck there, all alone." He rubbed his forehead. "What about the father?"

"She didn't list his name on the birth certificate."

Maury let out a long breath.

Jazzi realized the news would be upsetting for him. He'd wanted to marry Lynda right out of high school. "I'm sorry. This must be hard for you."

"It had to be worse for Lynda. We had so much fun together, but we were so young. Stupid young. We thought we were in love, but we didn't even know what that meant. Then we graduated, and I went straight into full-time work at my dad's deli. Lynda got a job as a bank teller. She met people, saw what the world had to offer, and she wanted more than getting married and settling down. I didn't understand at the time. I do now. The last thing she'd want was to have a baby and be tied down. But, boy, to face the pregnancy all by herself . . . that had to be rough."

Jazzi wouldn't want to do it. "She had a boy. Cal found him. He invited him to River Bluffs, but he never made it here."

"What do you mean he never made it?"

"Police found his car abandoned close to Cleveland."

Maury surged to his feet. "When?"

"They think it happened seven months ago, a little before Cal died. He was listed as a missing person then, and the New York cops followed up, trying to find him." Jazzi stood, too. "No one knows what happened to him. Detective Gaff's investigating. You could talk to him."

"I will. It can't be a coincidence. What could have happened to him?" Maury paced back and forth across the room. "Lynda didn't look any different when she came back from New York, not one bit. Did the kid have a good life?"

"It sounds like it. He's a musician in New York with a band, and he works part-time doing odd jobs when he needs extra money. His parents are desperate. They've been looking for him."

"God!" Maury ran his hands through his gray, kinky hair. It was cut short, close to his head, probably to control it. "How did Cal find him? Back in those days, adoption files were closed. No one could see them." When Jazzi gave him a thoughtful look, he said, "My Gina had two miscarriages when we got married. The doctor said she'd never be able to have a child. We were thinking about adoption when she got pregnant and had our first son. The agency assured us that our files would always be closed if anyone tried to look at them."

"Times change. Cal hired a detective."

Maury stopped pacing. He stared. "Times *do* change, don't they? Are you going to have a funeral for Lynda?"

"Mom talked about a private graveside service. That's all."

Maury nodded. "I understand. If they find her son, will you let me know? Lynda was my first love. If the kid needs anything . . ." He trailed off. "I can't believe she gave him up for adoption."

Jazzi didn't know what else to say.

Maury gave one last sigh. "Thanks for talking to me. I appreciate it. Tell your mom I was thinking of her."

"I will."

When he left, she started back to the kitchen, but he'd ruined her mood. Nachos and watching a movie alone didn't sound as good. She glanced out the back window and saw Reuben's car parked at the back of the property. She gave him a quick call.

"Hey, I was wondering if you'd like to grab something to eat with me, my treat?"

He hesitated. "Are you okay?"

"Yeah, just a little restless."

"We'll go dutch, and you can drive, so I can have a martini. How about the Gas House?"

"I'll put on some good slacks."

He chuckled. "I'm on my way downstairs."

He looked elegant, as usual. It only took ten minutes to reach the restaurant, and Reuben decided he'd like to eat on the outdoor patio, overlooking the river. Jazzi got her usual fare—the prime rib—and Reuben ordered the crab cakes. While they gossiped about their days, Reuben dug in his wallet and handed her a business card. "Isabelle asked me to give you that. She'd love to see Cal's house one more time, if you wouldn't mind."

Jazzi put the card in her purse. "I'm halfway thinking about buying his place. My apartment's too small when I invite my family for Sunday meals. I'm ready to have something bigger."

Reuben leaned forward, excited. "When would you move? Because I'm growing quite fond of Isabelle, and she's hinted that she'd move in with me if I had more space. When she hinted that to Cal, he didn't take her up on it, but I'd like to, and our landlord has let me know he'd like to get out of the leasing business. I was thinking about making an offer on our old Victorian and restoring it into a single home again."

"You'd make it beautiful." She had no doubt that Reuben would restore it to its former glory. "My lease is up the middle of August. Is that too soon?"

"That's perfect!" Reuben finished his crab cake and took the last sip of his martini. "If you'd like any advice on Cal's house, I'd be glad to help out."

"Maybe I'll invite you and Isabelle to look it over once Jerod and I finish sanding and staining the floors. We've gutted everything else."

"It's a date. We'll bring champagne to celebrate your new home."

She grinned. "We have to stay in touch after I move. I've gotten used to you, you know."

"Likewise, my dear. I don't want to drift apart."

She intended to follow through on that. After they both finished their meals and returned to the Victorian, she waved good-bye as he headed to his upstairs apartment. She settled onto her sofa and turned on the TV to relax. Two hours later, she was more than ready to call it a night.

Chapter 12

The next day was so hot and humid that the window air conditioner woke Jazzi as it droned to keep the apartment cool. She kicked off her sheets and lay still, letting the cool air fan over her before she pushed to her feet. July in Indiana could wilt a steel beam. She pulled on jeans for work anyway. Had to protect her legs, but she tugged on a sleeveless T-shirt and scraped her hair into a high ponytail. She was going to sweat a lot today.

On her way to Cal's house, Jazzi stopped to buy stain at her dad's hardware store. Time to finish the floors. Dad was at their southwest building, but she ran into Chuck Huestis. He'd bought one of the grand old homes that she and Jerod had restored in Forest Park. When she raised an eyebrow, he grinned. "No worries. You guys fixed every little thing in that house, but my wife wants a soaker hose for her roses. We love what you did to the place."

She smiled. "Good, we try to catch everything."

"You did. Believe me." He nodded toward the cans of stain in her hands. "I hear you're working on Cal Juniper's house. We both belonged to the Country Club. I miss him. I hated it when his nephews rented out his place. They didn't give a crap about Cal. But they didn't mind inheriting all the dividends from his stocks and bonds."

That surprised Jazzi. "Cal left all his money to them?"

Chuck shrugged. "His sister was his only living relative. He wouldn't leave his fortune to her. She quit speaking to him when he got engaged to Lynda. Never forgave him. Have you met Katherine?" When Jazzi shook her head, he said, "You're lucky. She tilts her nose in the air so high, I'm surprised she can function. Cal was never like that. He was one easygoing guy, but his sister made him so mad, he told me his will left everything to

Lynda. Thing is, no one could find her, so his money went to his nephews. He couldn't name their dad in his will. Tim blew through every penny he'd ever made."

Jazzi hadn't really thought about Cal's will, but she and Jerod had bought the house from his nephews. They must not have cared how much it was worth, so she'd guess they got so much money from Cal that it didn't matter to them. It made her sad. "Cal's friend Isabelle loved his house."

Chuck nodded. "I think Cal included her in his will. She'd earned it, and she was his best friend."

He hadn't asked about Lynda, so she wondered if he'd heard the news. "You know that we found Lynda's body in a trunk in Cal's attic, don't you?"

Chuck looked shocked. "No. In Cal's attic? Cal would never harm her. He worshipped her. Like I said, he left everything to her in his will."

"He tracked down Lynda's son, too, but Noah disappeared on his way to River Bluffs."

Chuck took a deep breath. "Lynda had a son?"

Jazzi filled him in on the latest news.

"And the boy was coming here to meet him?" Chuck's lips turned down. "I hadn't seen Cal for a while. I'm behind on his news. Bet he was glad the kid said yes. He invited his nephews to stay with him every once in a while, but they always made an excuse not to come."

"They live only three hours away, don't they?"

"If that. You should get together with Isabelle sometime and talk to her about Cal. He confided in her. He told her everything. She knows things none of the rest of us do."

"I'll do that." She decided she'd like to know more about Katherine's sons. When she got home tonight, she'd look them up and start asking around about them, and sometime, she'd call Isabelle.

She and Chuck walked to the cashier together, paid for their items, then left.

Jerod and Ansel were already working on drywall when she reached Cal's house. Jazzi dragged in the tall floor sander she'd brought, then went back for the stain. She told both men about her visit with Chuck Huestis.

Jerod stopped to inspect the drywall on the outside wall. The kitchen was starting to look like a room. "I like Chuck. If he says Cal's nephews are rotters, they are."

"How's Emily?" she asked Ansel.

His lips pinched. "She isn't happy at her job. She could make more money as a traveling nurse."

Jerod stopped and stared. "Traveling where?"

"We didn't renew the lease on our apartment. I got happy about that and started to look for houses, but that's not what she wants either. She's talking about California. She got a license to work there."

"And you?" Jerod asked. "Do you like California?"

"I don't know. This was sort of sudden."

He turned back to the drywall. He clearly didn't want to talk about it. Jazzi didn't want to pressure him. Instead, she pitched in to help him and Jerod. It was a big job. It took them all day to finish installing it. They were all drenched in sweat when they put up the last sheet.

"Franny's not going to let me in the house tonight." Jerod used his shirt hem to wipe his forehead. "She'll make me stand in the backyard and hose me off."

"How's she doing lately?"

Jerod had said Franny was touchier than usual, that she snapped at him and the kids more. She'd seemed all right at the Sunday meal. She hadn't talked and laughed as much as usual, but no one did. They all answered questions for Arnie.

"I've nicknamed her Moody Mama. This heat isn't bringing out the best in her. She's tired a lot, too."

Jazzi wiped her face and neck with a damp paper towel. She tried not to stare at Ansel. He'd taken off his shirt while they worked, and muscles glistened everywhere. "I think everyone's a little moodier than usual. This heat just saps your energy."

"Not yours." Jerod patted her head. "You're motivated to fix this house."

She *was* excited to see how it turned out. She went to the sink to wet another paper towel to cool off her neck and listened to the water gurgle as it slid down the pipes. "We're going to have to check the plumbing. Things are sluggish. There are enough trees on the property, we might have to snake out roots."

"I kind of figured on that. I checked on when the septic tank was cleaned last, and it should still be good." Jerod started putting away his tools. "I'm going home and I'm going to jump in the pond with the kids. Want to come?"

"Thanks anyway, I want to stop and check on Grandma tonight. She went a little fuzzy before she left my place on Sunday. Hopefully, she's clear again today."

"I'll come," Ansel told Jerod. "Want me to stop and buy Coney dogs on the way to your place?"

"I love you, friend. Franny doesn't like to cook to start with, but in hot weather, forget it."

"I'll meet you there." Ansel tugged his shirt back over his head and he and Jerod started to their trucks.

Out of curiosity, Jazzi went to flush the toilet on the ground floor and shook her head when the water took forever to go down. Yup, tomorrow they'd have to check the pipes in the house. Thankfully, Ansel and Jerod were as good at plumbing as they were with hammers.

Chapter 13

Jazzi drove home and grabbed the slow cooker to take to Grandma's. She'd started brats and sauerkraut before she left for work this morning—one of Grandma's favorites. She wasn't sure if Grandma would remember she was coming or not, but she pulled into her drive at six sharp. No time to take a shower, but she'd done a quick rinse-off at the sink, so she didn't look too bad.

Grams was sitting on the front porch, fanning herself with a magazine. She lived in a little town south of River Bluffs and raised chickens. Today, they were loose and scratching in the side yard. She'd planted a garden, as usual, but the tomato plants looked a little droopy from the heat. Grams always brought fresh produce and eggs to Sunday meals—when she remembered.

"Sarah!" Grams stood to wave Jazzi into the house.

Jazzi grabbed the bag of hoagie buns she'd brought, along with the slow cooker. Grams held the door so she could carry them inside.

"It's a hot one today," Grams told her. "I made us a pitcher of lemonade."

Good, she'd remembered Jazzi was coming. She just had the wrong decade. She was a young woman again, getting together with her sister.

When Jazzi made her way to the kitchen, Samantha came up from the basement with a load of folded laundry. A widow, Samantha had moved in with Grams for free room and board and kept an eye on her. So far, it had worked out well for both women.

"How's it gone lately?" Jazzi asked.

"We've been fine, moving a little slower than usual since it's so hot, but nothing to complain about."

Grandma poured them each a glass of lemonade. "I told Samantha the good news about Lynda having a baby. Isn't it wonderful?"

"Babies are miracles." Jazzi searched in the cupboards for paper plates. Grandma was worse today than usual.

"Jerod's going to be so happy it's a boy." Grandma put silverware at each place setting.

Poor Jerod. He was the first of their generation to get married and have kids, so he must have stuck in Grandma's head as Noah's father.

Grandma shook a finger at Jazzi. "Franny's pregnant, you know. I saw the mask, always do. I can tell what a woman will have. She'll have another boy."

Jazzi stared. Where had that come from? Grams gave her a severe look. "If you want to make babies, you'd better get to it. Hens get old, and their eggs stop coming. Same will happen to you."

Oh, Lord! Time to change the subject. "I brought you bratwurst and sauerkraut."

Grams smiled, and her eyes cleared. "We need mustard. Samantha, Jazzi brought us supper."

The conversation turned to Grandma's crop of green beans, how young the new minister was at Grams's church, and how the neighbor's dog got loose and came to scare her chickens. When they finished their meal, Grams studied Jazzi and asked, "How's your mom holding up?"

Jazzi didn't want to talk about Lynda. She was afraid she'd lose Grandma again to the past, so she tried to keep her answer light. "She's doing fine."

"That girl always put her sister on a pedestal, always stood up for her. Lynda wouldn't do the same for her. I tried to tell Cyn that."

"She's learned that the hard way. It's bothered her."

"Why wouldn't it?" Grandma sighed and leaned back in her chair. "You always were the best cook in our family, Sarah. I don't suppose you'd want to leave me the leftovers, would you?"

Sheesh. She was Sarah again, but Jazzi smiled. "I'd be happy to leave them. I even brought plastic containers for you to store them in."

Grams chuckled. "You always did spoil me. Mom said it was a wonder I turned out decent at all."

"I like spoiling you. It makes me happy." Jazzi helped Samantha transfer the food into the disposable containers, and then she kissed Grandma on the cheek. "I'd better get going. I have a big day tomorrow."

"You work too hard. Always have. A body needs a rest sometimes, or you're going to wear yourself out before your time." Another truth. Sarah had died before she was seventy. "And find yourself a nice man. Life's better with a partner." But Sarah never had. Is that why Grams lumped her and Sarah together? Because she worked too hard, too, and still wasn't married?

Come to think of it, though, Jazzi didn't want to end up like Sarah. She'd owned a dry-cleaning shop and didn't retire until she was sixty-eight. A year later, she died. Jazzi bent again to kiss Grandma's cheek. "Love ya."

"The next time you come, I'll teach you how to make strudel. You asked me about that."

She had. Grandma's head was one giant jumble. "We'll try some day when it's not so hot."

"I have eggs for you to take home."

Samantha had put three dozen cartons of eggs in a tote bag.

"Thanks. I'll come again soon." On the drive home, Jazzi was grateful once again that Samantha lived with Grandma. She wouldn't be safe on her own anymore.

Later that night, she called her mom. "I went to see Grandma."

"How was she?"

"Sometimes I was Sarah. Sometimes I was me."

Her mom sighed. "At least she's not getting worse."

"That's a blessing." Jazzi paused a second. "Did you ever meet Cal's nephews? I ran into Chuck Huestis at the hardware store today, and he didn't have anything good to say about them."

"The apples don't fall far from the tree. Their mother's ego could suck all the air out of a room, and their dad can make money disappear. If those boys had spent more time with Cal, they might have had a chance, but they chose not to."

"Did they come to River Bluffs when Cal died?"

"They were here for his funeral. Stayed in his house until the lawyer read his will, and then they grabbed his money and ran."

"That's pretty much how Chuck described them."

Mom sighed. "It's too bad. Cal deserved better."

That's how Jazzi was beginning to feel. First, Cal fell for Lynda, and that didn't end well. Then his sister shunned him. And finally, he found Lynda's son, but Noah never reached River Bluffs. The man might have had lots of money and friends, but he had his fair share of grief, too.

"I'll let you go, Mom. Are you hanging in there?"

"I'm starting to focus on how thoughtless my sister was, and it's making me feel better."

Not what Jazzi had expected, but if it worked, why not? "Anger can be a good thing."

"Yes, it can. It's going to get me through this."

When Jazzi turned out the lights and went to bed, she thought about Mom's words. Mom had every right to be mad at her sister. It was a little late, but better late than never.

Chapter 14

Jazzi sanded the living room floor on Wednesday while the men ran snakes down every drain in the house. She'd started in the living room, so she'd be out of their way while they cussed in the bathrooms and kitchen. The water still didn't drain right.

"Looks like we're going to have to rent a backhoe and check for broken pipes," Jerod said.

Her cousin loved it when he had to rent heavy equipment. If she weren't careful, he'd be ripping out the privet hedge that bordered the entire backyard.

"I like the bushes that line the property," Jazzi warned him. "They stay. Don't get crazy."

"They have stuff growing in them. You're going to have to dig out saplings. Why not just start over?"

"Because it takes years for a privet hedge to get that thick. Hands off."

He threw his arms in the air in mock defeat. "Whatever you say, *Jasmine*."

The man was a menace. He and Ansel jumped in his pickup to go rent what they needed. As always, where Ansel went, so went George. Jazzi started on the red oak floor in the kitchen while they were gone. If she was lucky, she'd get most of it done before Jerod and Ansel returned. As she worked, she wondered if George would like California. He could probably go outdoors every day. Would a pug miss snow? She doubted it. George wasn't a fan of cold weather. He wore a sweater as soon as the temperatures dropped below thirty.

Would Ansel miss River Bluffs? She couldn't imagine him staying if Emily left. Would she miss Ansel? She couldn't dwell on it.

When the men got back, they headed to the basement to check where the main pipe and drain were situated. George took one look at the wooden stairs and began to whine. Ansel had to carry him down with them. Jazzi was curious where things were located, so she went down, too.

The foundation had cement-block walls and a cement floor. Windows were spaced high on each side, a little above ground level. Enough light came in to see, but Jerod switched on overhead fluorescent bulbs anyway. They made the area more cheerful.

"You got lucky. This is a solid basement," Ansel said. "There are a few cracks in the cement floor, but they're shallow. Easy to fix. Nice high ceiling, too. You could finish part of this if you wanted to."

Jazzi went to look at the furnace. It was eight years old. "Cal must not have replaced the central air when he replaced the heating system."

"That happens," Jerod said. "Maybe it was newer, and he thought it would last a long time."

Ansel stopped to look at the hot water heater. "New enough. You shouldn't have to replace much for a while."

"Good, then all we have to worry about is drainage." Jerod headed for the basement door. "I found the drainpipe. I know where to start the backhoe."

A few minutes later, the rumble of an engine came from outside. Ansel frowned and bent to look at a wooden toolbox pushed between the furnace and water heater. He pulled it out to inspect it. It had a high handle that peaked in the center with wooden flaps tented as lids on each side. He opened one flap and gave a low whistle. "Look at these tools. They're antiques. You can't even find some of these now."

The box itself was beautiful. Carvings of hammers, chisels, and other tools covered every inch of it in an intricate design. A soft brown stain glowed with a satin finish. He frowned at initials carved in the handle. "NJ. Was that Cal Juniper's father or grandfather's initials?"

"No, his dad's name was Casper—like the friendly ghost." Kids these days wouldn't even know who Casper was. A chill slithered down Jazzi's spine. NJ. "Noah Jacobs." She shook her head. "He worked odd jobs and was going to help Cal fix up a few things in the house. But he never made it here."

The initials were a small detail, and probably not important, but it bugged her. She called her dad at the hardware store. Maybe she had the wrong names for Cal's family. "Do you happen to remember Cal's dad and grandpa's names?"

"His dad was Casper—Casper Juniper. I always thought his parents got a little too cute with that. His grandpa was Ora—talk about a character. Why?"

"We found an antique toolbox in the basement with the initials NJ."

Her dad laughed. "You're barking up the wrong tree. Cal's family didn't know a wrench from a screwdriver. They were all businessmen, always hired everything done."

"Thanks, Dad." When she hung up, she braced her shoulders and called Detective Gaff. "This is probably nothing, but we went to Cal's basement today and found a toolbox . . ."

She didn't get to finish. "An antique one with Noah's initials carved in the handle?"

How did Gaff know? "Yup, that's what we have."

"As soon as I finish here, I'm on my way over. Noah's parents said he took it with him to help Cal around his house. That means the kid made it to River Bluffs and stopped at Cal's place."

"But Cal didn't see him. How could they miss each other?" If Jazzi remembered the timeline right, Cal died a month after Noah traveled to see him.

"Something's off," Gaff said. "I talked to Cal's friend Isabelle. Cal flew out to meet Noah in New York. The two men hit it off. That's why Noah was driving here to spend time with Cal, only he never showed up. Cal waited and waited but finally flew to the West Coast for a business trip."

"And had a heart attack and died there."

"Right." Papers shuffled on the other end of the line. Gaff must be sifting through a file. "Look, got to go, but Noah must have made it to that house. I found the picture his parents sent me. I'll bring it with me. See you soon."

Jazzi blew out a long breath when she pushed her phone back into her pocket. "The toolbox belongs to Noah Jacobs."

Ansel frowned. "Then where is he? Why didn't he meet Cal?"

"And how did his car end up close to Cleveland, Ohio?" Did Noah and Cal have a falling out? Did Noah leave River Bluffs not long after he got here?

The rumble of the backhoe outside stopped abruptly. Jerod bellowed, "Ansel! Jazzi! Get out here. Quick!"

What now? Ansel scooped up George, and they sprinted for the stairs. Outside, Jerod pointed to the hole he was digging. He'd made a sweep out the back gate to dig behind the thick hedge. He'd stopped near the septic tank. About two feet down, black curls surrounded a decomposing face.

Jazzi looked away. She pulled out her cell phone and called Detective Gaff. "You might want to bring your crime scene unit. I think we found Noah Jacobs."

Chapter 15

The kitchen floor was only half done, heavy plastic taped over its doors to seal them. Everything was covered with dust, so they set up lawn chairs in the living room to wait for Gaff. Jazzi had sanded the floors in there and cleaned them.

Jazzi looked around the room at the curved fireplace mantel, gorgeous trim, and latticed windows. The house was so lovely, filled with so much charm, it felt surreal to find two dead bodies here. She shook her head.

"It's not the house," Jerod told her. Her cousin could read her as well as Ansel did. "This house and Cal welcomed people. When you think of these rooms, think of Cal. They're like him—warm and gracious. This house deserves laughter and happiness again."

How could her cousin be such a tease most of the time, and so perceptive when it mattered? No wonder Franny kept him.

"Thanks, that helps." Could she live here without picturing Lynda in the trunk in the attic and Noah buried in the backyard?

Ansel's blue eyes glittered. "Are you thinking of buying it? If you do, we'll add special touches when we renovate it."

She patted his arm. "You're so sweet. I was talking about buying it, but two dead bodies sort of spook me."

Ansel lowered his hand to stroke George's head. "George likes it here. He's sensitive to vibes. This house makes him feel secure."

Jerod nodded in agreement. "It's not the house, Jazzi. It can't help who walks in and out its doors."

Jazzi wasn't sure how much faith to put in their advice, but they were trying to reassure her, and that was nice.

Tires crunched and Gaff gave a brief knock before joining them. His dress shirt looked like it had lost the war today—damp and wrinkled. "Are you guys doing okay?"

Jerod ran a hand through his brown hair. "We'd rather quit finding bodies while we work, if that's what you mean."

Gaff grinned. "Better you than me."

At Ansel's scowl, he laughed. "Really, you guys have been great to work with. Are you sure you don't want to sign up as cops?"

"Very funny." Jerod stood and motioned for Gaff to follow him. "He's out here, and we found the toolbox in the basement."

A team of experts had gathered around the hole.

"When I saw the hair, I turned off the backhoe," Jerod said.

Ansel, Jazzi, and George had followed them. Jazzi stared at the dark curls. She'd seen them somewhere before but couldn't pull the memory to the surface. A tech jumped into the hole to start sifting through the dirt to examine the body. Jazzi didn't want to watch.

"We'll have to look over the basement," Gaff called to her as she headed to the house. "It would be best if you didn't go down there."

Had Noah been killed near the furnace? She closed her eyes, trying not to envision that. She took a deep breath and decided to concentrate on what she knew best—fixing old houses.

She went to work on the rest of the kitchen floor. She could swim in sweat when she finished sanding and cleaning it. Jerod and Ansel stained the oak floors in the living room while she worked in the kitchen. By the time Gaff knocked and stepped inside the house, the three of them were finishing up for the day. They taped up cardboard to block the entrance to the living room. The stain had to dry before anyone walked on it.

"If there was any evidence in the living room, we've ruined it," Jerod told Gaff, "so there's no reason for your team to go in there."

They'd wait to stain the kitchen until they left the house tomorrow to give it time to dry.

Gaff glanced inside the room and smiled. "Looks good. No problem. We still want to look over the basement, but the rest of the house is okay. I took a picture of the toolbox with my cell phone and sent it to Noah's parents. I'll call them when I get back to the station."

Ansel grimaced. "We touched it. Sorry. We couldn't see the initials where it sat."

"I'm just glad you found it." A tech poked his head into the room and held up a gadget while another tech motioned for Gaff to join them in the basement.

"You three might as well come."

Jazzi squirmed. Did she want to? Ansel put a hand under her arm to guide her down the steps. Once they were all there, another tech flipped off the overhead lights. When the handheld instrument scanned the floor near the furnace, discolored drops and stains showed up on the cement floor.

Gaff nodded. "This is where Noah died. Someone tried to clean up the blood, but you can't trick Alex's toy." He nodded at the tech and his light meter.

Ansel, Jerod, and Jazzi looked at each other. As far as they knew, Noah should have arrived in town while Cal was still alive, but when Gaff found Noah's car in Cleveland, they'd assumed Noah never reached here and Cal never got to see him. That had been their working theory until Jerod dug up a body near the septic tank and Ansel spotted Noah's toolbox. Now Gaff found blood splatters on the basement floor. Jazzi rubbed her arms. "So Noah *did* arrive here. Could Cal have killed him? And Lynda, too? Maybe he *looked* like a nice man but had problems."

"Anything's possible," Gaff said, "but if Cal killed them, he was one good actor. His ledgers sure looked convincing to me, and everyone I talked to told me that he never got over Lynda and that he'd been distressed before he left for his business trip to California."

Jerod scratched his head. "Why would he spend years searching for Lynda's son and then kill him when he got here?"

Jazzi shrugged. None of it made sense to her. And why would Cal write fake feelings in his appointment books? She remembered her promise to Maury, though. "I told Maury Lebovitch that I'd call him if I heard anything about Lynda's son. Can I do that?"

"Not until we ID the body for sure and talk to his family. I'll let you know when it's okay."

"Can I tell my parents about another dead body?"

Gaff motioned to a van parked across the street from Cal's house. "The news already sniffed us out. Just don't mention a name."

No longer needed, Jazzi, Ansel, and Jerod went upstairs to rinse off before they left the house. She walked to the window that overlooked the backyard, but the privet hedge was so thick, it hid most of whatever was happening behind it. A lilac bush grew nearby. Its roots had probably sought out the fresh, organic material of Noah's body and grown into the drainage pipe. An easy fix—once Gaff removed the body.

Jazzi pursed her lips, thinking. Where had she seen Noah's dark curls before? And then she remembered. In her mother's photo albums. She'd go there tonight and ask to borrow a few of them.

Satisfied, she walked to her pickup with Jerod and Ansel. Emily didn't work tonight, so Ansel was taking her out for supper. Jazzi would have the night to herself. She decided to grab a pizza, take a long bath, and try to make her cuticles and fingernails look decent again, and then go through old pictures. But first, she'd stop to see her parents. She couldn't tell them the new news, but she could borrow Mom's albums.

Chapter 16

When Jazzi pulled into her parents' drive, she was surprised to see her sister's car. Olivia and Mom worked together and saw each other all day at the shop. They usually separated in the evenings to go home to their significant others. When she knocked on the door, her mom called, "It's open!"

Giggling, her sister and Mom sat next to each other on stools at the kitchen bar. They were digging into a huge plate of nachos and drinking wine. They both looked a little happier than usual.

Her mom grinned. "Thane's taking some kind of training tonight, learning something new about heating and air conditioning. Your dad's bowling with his buddies. We won't see him for a while." She snickered. "You know how much that man loves bowling and playing cards, so we decided to enjoy ourselves."

Jazzi smiled. When the cats were away, these mice would play. "Looks like you're having a good time."

"We are. How's it going for you?" Olivia handed Jazzi a paper plate when she went to stand across from them.

Should she ruin their fun? The news van had parked across the street. The story would be on the late-night news. She'd rather tell them now. "I hate to be a spoilsport, but we found another dead body in a shallow grave at Cal's house." Stalling, Jazzi reached for a nacho and watched the cheese stretch super long before it broke. "I can't tell you a name until the body's identified. It was buried in the backyard near the septic tank."

"Another one?" Mom looked curious, not horrified. She must be feeling pretty mellow.

"Old or new?" Olivia asked.

"Newer. He hadn't been there long."

Her sister raised an eyebrow, gave her an assessing look. She was putting two and two together, could probably guess whom they'd found. She glanced at Mom and took another sip of wine. In a flippant tone, she said, "Maybe Cal was a serial killer. I've read they can come across as the nicest guys in the world."

Their mom sputtered. "Cal?"

"I'm not buying that." Jazzi licked her fingers. The nachos were delicious, but there weren't that many left, and Olivia still looked hungry. She'd wait and eat later. "Serial killers don't mourn for the people they bury. They just move to the next one."

"This time you found a guy?" Olivia drizzled salsa on top of a big chunk of chips that were held together with melted cheese. Was she trying to lead Mom to whom it might be? Give Mom a heads-up?

When people first met Olivia, they always underestimated her, but she was smart and clever. Her dark blond hair was pulled up in some kind of a spiky bun today, making her look edgy. She'd rimmed her eyes with blue liner. All three women in their family were different shades of blond, but Olivia had Dad's brown eyes. The blue looked good with them. Mom was thin, Olivia willowy, and Jazzi curvy. Alike, but different.

"Could you tell how old the victim was?" Mom picked at her food, as usual. She'd always been a light eater, probably why she stayed so slender and possibly why the wine was hitting her harder.

Jazzi couldn't give away too much. "He looked younger, but it was hard to tell for sure. Once Jerod saw his curly hair, he stopped digging and called Detective Gaff."

"I'm surprised Cal had someone that young visiting him." Mom frowned. "He had to be close to retirement age when he died."

Jazzi couldn't say much more, not until Gaff okayed it. "I stopped to see you to ask if I could borrow some of your photo albums and look through them. You and Dad talk about old friends, but I don't know most of them. All of the stuff that's been happening at the house has made me curious."

Mom wiped her hands on a napkin and shook her head. "Won't do you much good to look at them alone. I was never good at marking who was in which picture, but I'd be happy to go through a few of them with you. I'm curious, too."

"Good, we have plenty of time!" Olivia finished the last of the nachos and went to rinse her hands at the kitchen sink. "Let's look at some old pictures."

Mom sat in the middle on the sofa, a daughter on either side, and they began to go through the first album. The first page was all pictures of Mom with her sister.

Mom pointed. "Lynda had come back from New York, and I was about to graduate from high school."

"Lynda's clothes always look expensive." So did Olivia's tonight. She wore a long, silky tunic over straight-legged pants.

"She bought those in New York." Mom's tone had a bitter tinge. "Probably used the money from selling her baby."

Jazzi winced. "Is it going to bother you to look at these?"

"No." Her mom's words were clipped. "I've come to terms with my sister. I'm glad she gave the baby away. She was too young, not ready to settle down. But all we ever showed her was love and respect. I wish she'd have trusted us more." She turned the page.

There were pictures of Mom in her cap and gown. On the next page, there were photos of her mom standing in front of a cosmetology school.

Mom smiled. "Your dad was in his third year of college when I started hairdressing. That's when we started dating. Lots of good times."

"What did Lynda do then? Did she have a job?"

"She was the receptionist for the Chamber of Commerce, met lots of important business men there." She rolled her eyes. "Okay, I'm still a little angry at her for writing me a fake letter once a week, and then when she came home and started dating, she dropped me out of her life . . . again."

Jazzi could see how that would rankle. The next page showed her mom and dad when they were young, at different spots around town. In one of the pictures, they were at a New Year's Eve party with streamers and balloons overhead. A laughing man with dark, curly hair had his arm over Dad's shoulders.

Jazzi pointed. "Who is that? He looks familiar."

Smiling, her mom pressed a finger to the picture. "It's Maury before he went gray and cut his hair short to try to tame it a little."

"Maury Lebovitch?" The Maury who was Lynda's high school sweetheart? The Maury who was upset when Lynda broke up with him and took off for New York? Noah had his father's hair. Jazzi stared at the picture. Did Maury know Lynda was pregnant when she ran away from him? Did he hate her for giving up their son?

Olivia looked at her. "Are you all right?"

Jazzi couldn't say anything. Yet. "Mom and Dad have sure aged better than Maury has. It's sort of sad how gray he is now."

Mom sighed. "Maury went through a rough patch for a while. It takes its toll. He was really upset when Lynda left him, and then he met Gina. Talk about being in love! They were so happy, and then Gina had two stillbirths before she finally had two healthy babies. Maury told everyone he was being punished, but that was silly. Maury's a great guy."

Stillbirths? Maury had told her Gina had miscarriages. Those were sad enough, but to carry a baby for nine months who died at birth? Could Maury's story get any more depressing? No wonder Maury was so interested in Cal finding Lynda's son. Noah had Maury's wild, unruly hair. Noah was his. And now Noah was dead. She needed some excuse to get out of here. She couldn't stand much more. She pressed a hand to her stomach.

"I'm sorry, guys, but I did heavy work all day, and I only ate a nibble of your nachos. I'm starving. I've got to go get something to eat."

Olivia turned to study her. She wasn't buying it.

Mom closed the photo album and slid it onto the coffee table. "I'm glad you asked to look at these. It brought back lots of good memories of your dad and me. If you want to see more, come back again."

Olivia knew something was bothering Jazzi, but she put on a smile. "Nice seeing you, sis! Let's keep up the momentum and go someplace fun tomorrow night."

It wouldn't matter. Jazzi would have answers tomorrow, and she'd share them with her sister. That would be enough to ruin any good times. Maybe they should find a restaurant that served gruel for supper.

With a wave, Jazzi left them. She really was starving, so on her way home, she stopped to buy a box of chicken tenders and fries. Not healthy, but she didn't care at the moment. Then she called Detective Gaff.

Once she explained about Maury's visit to her and the pictures in Mom's album, Gaff sighed. "Noah's dad identified the picture of his toolbox. He's flying in tomorrow to ID the body. Once that's done, would you come with me to talk to Maury? It doesn't make sense to me that he'd kill his son, and I have a feeling he'd be more honest with you than me. Sometimes, cops tie people's tongues."

"Sure, I like Maury." But she wasn't looking forward to the visit. It was going to be just plain depressing.

Chapter 17

Jazzi, Jerod, and Ansel finished the downstairs floors Thursday morning and she took back the rented sander. Yellow police tape still circled the hole in their backyard, so Jerod couldn't jump on the backhoe and get rid of roots. Jazzi expected Gaff to call, but when he didn't, she decided Noah's father had caught an earlier flight and Gaff was doing detective things. She might hear from him tomorrow, but there were no guarantees. Part of her was relieved; part of her wanted to get the whole thing over with. She hated knowing secrets she couldn't tell. She was always afraid she'd accidentally open her mouth and out they'd come.

When they broke for lunch and sat in the kitchen to eat sandwiches, Ansel was quieter than usual. There'd been no friendly chatter while they worked. George had to put a paw on his thigh to get his attention before Ansel tore off small pieces of ham for him.

"Does Emily work tonight?" Jazzi asked.

"Yes."

"Do you want to come out with Olivia and me for supper?" She'd never invited him before, but he seemed so moody, she thought he might like company.

"No."

Okay, then. He didn't want to talk about it. She let it drop. She glanced at Jerod, and he rolled his eyes. Luckily, none of his usual oddball humor popped out of his mouth.

After lunch, the three of them went upstairs to work on the bathrooms. They'd chosen to install porcelain floor tiles that looked like wood in the smaller bath and an old-fashioned black-and-white floor tile in the master bath. Cal had a claw-foot bathtub in perfect shape that Jazzi had saved in the garage. After a long, hard day—when her muscles felt tired—a good, hot soak made everything better. She'd chosen polished subway tiles for the shower enclosure. She'd bought a long antique chest of drawers that Franny refinished to hold two sinks.

"This is going to turn out nice," Ansel said.

She knew he'd like it. They'd worked together long enough that she knew his tastes, similar to hers. "Thanks. I haven't picked a sink for the small bathroom yet. Any ideas?"

He pulled out his smartphone and showed her a picture he liked. Hmm, the man had gotten serious about finding a place of his own. Too bad for him. If he loved that sink, Emily would veto it.

"How much?" she asked.

He looked it up, and it was reasonable. "I'll order it," she told him.

"It's just a suggestion. This isn't my house." He sounded put out. He really had meant to bid on it until Emily nixed it.

"You'll visit a lot." When his expression turned moody, she bit her bottom lip. *Maybe* he'd visit—if Emily didn't move to California.

He scowled and turned back to his work. It took them the rest of the day to lay the floor tiles.

"Thank God the central air gets installed tomorrow," Jerod said, peeling his T-shirt a few inches from his chest and stomach. "A window unit doesn't cut it."

Ansel was the first to leave, scooping up George and stalking to his truck. Jerod blew out a breath of relief. "I hope he's in a better mood tomorrow."

"He doesn't want to move."

"Then he should give Emily an ultimatum. If she stays, they're a couple. If she goes, she goes alone."

"Do you think he'd let her?"

Jerod frowned, considering his answer. "This time, he might. He's given up a lot of things to be with her, but he likes River Bluffs. He likes his job, his friends. She might be asking too much."

"He's always done whatever she wants."

"And that's just made her worse." Jerod wasn't a fan.

Neither was she. "I'm just saying, he'll cave this time, too."

The only thing that might make him unhappy enough to take a stand was if Emily told him he had to get rid of George. Someday, she might. Jazzi shook her head. "We might have to start looking for a new contractor soon."

Jerod's frown turned thunderous.

It was a good time to get out of there. "I'm off. It's Thursday, my night with Olivia." Jazzi was glad she was going out with her sister tonight. Olivia always made her laugh.

Jerod locked the door and headed to his truck. "Lucky me, I got to work with a moody Ansel today, and I get to go home to a moody wife tonight."

"Franny's still out of sorts?"

"I can't do anything right. Neither can the kids. We all try to stay out of her way."

"Is something going on? Bothering her?"

"Beats me. I try not to be in the same room with her."

"Jerod . . ."

"I know, but honestly, I've tried to talk to her. It doesn't go well. I love her, though. We'll ride this out."

Jazzi thought about that on her drive home. Maybe that's what love was. Sticking in there and riding out the bad times together, because you care.

When she got home, she had to hustle to be ready in time. Her sister never left the house without doing her hair and makeup. Jazzi swore she wore a new outfit every other week. She felt like a slacker if she didn't at least look decent. Tonight, she let her hair fall in thick waves past her shoulders. She even put on eyeliner.

When Olivia pulled to the curb and Jazzi hopped into the car next to her, Olivia nodded approval. "Good, you went to a little bother. Sometimes on Sundays, you skimp."

Jazzi grimaced. "If the kitchen gets hot while I'm cooking, my makeup just melts."

"Then don't cook. Make us a big salad."

Yeah, like that would go over well. "Where are we off to tonight?"

"I'm in the mood for something special. I was thinking about Paula's Seafood on Main Street."

"I'm flush enough. Let's do it."

When the hostess started to lead them to a table, Reuben stood up on the other side of the room and called, "Hey, why don't you join us? Our friends had to cancel. We have plenty of space."

Jazzi looked at Olivia. It was their girls' night out, but her sister grinned. "I love meeting new people!"

Jazzi didn't share that sentiment, but she liked spending time with Reuben. He was with a female friend tonight. She looked intimidating—thin, sophisticated, and poised.

Once they were seated, Reuben made the introductions. "Jazzi, this is my friend Isabelle. She knew Cal Juniper. Isabelle, this is my downstairs neighbor and friend, Jazzi, and her sister . . ."

"Olivia," Jazzi supplied. "Nice to meet you." She'd meant to call Isabelle and had never gotten around to it.

"You're the person who bought Cal's house and is fixing it up, aren't you?" Isabelle glanced at Reuben. "Thanks for calling her over."

Reuben grinned. "Isabelle's more private than I am. She doesn't like to meet new people."

Jazzi could relate. "I understand. It always takes me a while to get comfortable with someone I don't know."

"You're funny about that," Olivia agreed. "But every stranger is just a potential friend you haven't met yet."

Jazzi didn't make new friends easily. It took a while before she let a person in. "Is that some kind of new age slogan?"

Olivia laughed. "Nope, just my perspective."

Isabelle took a sip of her wine, then shook her head. "I don't want many friends. I'd rather have a select few. A friend is an emotional commitment. I have only so much energy."

Reuben picked up his menu to study it. "I'm glad you made room for me."

"So am I." Isabelle sent him a look that could curl toes.

The waitress came to take their orders. Jazzi chose the breaded fried scallops—her favorite—and hard to find. They weren't on the menu, so she was excited they were one of tonight's specials. After the others ordered and the waitress left, she turned to Isabelle again. "Reuben said that you were a close friend to Cal."

"He was my best friend for years. Hard on my ego, though. I always hoped someday he'd want more, but he never really got over Lynda."

It must suck to compete with a dead woman. "You heard about the trunk?"

She nodded. "Reuben told me. I wish he'd have opened it a long time ago. Then he'd have known she was gone, and maybe he would have moved on."

Reuben put his hand over hers. "In that case, I'm glad he didn't."

She gave a soft laugh. Everything about Isabelle felt contained, restrained. Jazzi took a swallow of beer. "And you know Cal found Lynda's son?"

"He hired a detective. He wanted to find someone to connect with other than his sister and her family."

"Can't blame him for that." Olivia's willowy figure belied her appetite. The girl could put food away. She reached for a slice of bread when the waitress placed the bread basket on the table. A minute later, the waitress brought their salads, and there was a slight pause in the conversation while they took a few bites.

Isabelle pushed her plate away with half of her salad untouched.

"She's like that," Reuben said. "Never finishes her meal."

"Mom does that, too." Olivia buttered another slice of bread. Jazzi had to admit it was delicious, but she made herself abstain.

After a sip of wine, Isabelle sighed. "Cal flew to New York to meet Noah. It was a wonderful experience for him. He said Noah looked exactly like Lynda except for his hair. It was dark and curly, completely unruly."

Olivia frowned and turned to Jazzi. "That's why the pictures upset you yesterday."

"I can't talk about it. Not until Detective Gaff gives me permission."

Reuben's expression lit up. "A secret! How wonderful!" And *that's* why Jazzi hated secrets. They could bite you in the ass.

Isabelle shook her head. "I don't like secrets. They're a burden."

Lord, she and Isabelle had a lot in common. Except that Isabelle oozed high fashion, dressed all in black with her dark hair scraped back into a tight bun. And she had poise out her yin-yang. And . . . Jazzi stopped counting.

Isabelle lowered her eyebrows, turning serious. "We won't pressure you, but when you're allowed to share the news, I'd like to be informed."

Jazzi nodded.

Isabelle sat silent while the waitress brought their entrees, then said, "I felt so sorry for Cal. He could hardly wait for Noah to visit him. He'd taken the day off work so that he could greet him, but then he got an emergency call in the early afternoon. He left a note on the door and the key in the lock, but when he got home, no one was there. He waited and waited and tried to call, but no one ever came or answered."

"He got an emergency call?" Jazzi leaned forward in her chair. "Did he say what the emergency was?"

Isabelle's eyes went wide. "I'd forgotten. It was so odd. When he got to the office, no one knew anything about it. We tried to track it down, but it remained a mystery."

Jazzi's shoulders slumped and she took a deep breath. "It was a setup."

Isabelle's fingers went to her throat. She bit her bottom lip. "Don't tell us anymore. I didn't mean to pry information from you."

"No, you've helped me. Everything makes so much more sense now. Do you happen to know if anyone else, anyone at all, knew about Noah coming?"

She gave a wan smile. "Noah didn't tell anyone. He was determined not to hurt the parents who raised him, but I think Cal told the world about it. At first, it bothered me that he was so happy to find Lynda's child, but then he told me about his sister and her family and I understood. And then there was Thomas Sorrell. He wanted to meet Noah, too."

"Thomas? Why?"

"He still blames Cal for 'taking' Lynda. He's part owner of a business in River Bluffs. That's why he came here in the first place. Lynda's lucky she left him. He strikes me as a vindictive, controlling person."

"Vindictive enough to kill Lynda and stuff her in a trunk?"

Isabelle pursed her lips, considering her answer. "Yes, I believe he is. He tried really hard to drive one of Cal's companies out of business. Cal had enough clout and money to buy the shares he needed to fend off Thomas, but it was a personal attack, not based on sound finances."

Jazzi had never given much consideration to Thomas. After they broke up, he never came to town that she knew of, except to ask for his ring back. She'd crossed him off her list.

Olivia frowned. "Why did Thomas want to meet Noah?"

"It irritated him that Cal had found him. Noah belonged to Lynda, so Thomas thought he had just as much of a claim to him as Cal did. Which, of course, might be true, except that Cal wanted to meet him for all the right reasons, and Thomas wanted to win him away from Cal just to punish Cal."

Olivia's eyes went wide. "But that was twenty-six years ago, at least."

"Exactly. Once Cal made an enemy of Thomas, he had an enemy for life. I got the feeling that Thomas never forgives and forgets."

Reuben drained his martini glass and picked up the olive to nibble on. "It sounds as though Thomas could benefit from counseling."

Isabelle gave a low laugh. "He definitely has issues of some kind."

More issues than Jazzi had realized. "Did Thomas know that Cal flew to New York to meet Noah?"

"He might have. Cal couldn't keep it to himself. Everyone was happy for him."

Jazzi sighed. "Thank you. Unfortunately, you might get a visit from Detective Gaff soon. He'll answer your questions, but then he'll want to ask you some of his own."

Isabelle spoke slowly and carefully. "I'm going to get sad news, aren't I?"

"I'm afraid so."

Isabelle straightened her shoulders and gave Reuben a brittle smile. "In that case, I think you should be ready to visit me at a moment's notice in the next days. I'll need you. But we've made new friends tonight, and we're at a wonderful restaurant. We need to enjoy ourselves. Entertain us with your wit, dear friend."

Jazzi felt relieved. Isabelle wanted to change the subject and, hopefully, the mood.

"When you call, I'll come," Reuben told her, then visibly shifted into host mode. "Now, on to serious things. When do you mean to depart your apartment, downstairs neighbor?"

Jazzi stared at him, caught off guard, then laughed. "I'm guessing the landlord's willing to sell you the house."

"Overpriced, but I'm happy to pay it. Isabelle would love to see your apartment if you wouldn't mind giving us a tour."

She reached into her purse and took out her extra key. "Just leave it on the kitchen table."

"What do you think the house would look like painted lavender?"

Her jaw dropped, and Reuben clapped his hands together, delighted. "You're so traditional. I love it!"

Olivia got excited, though. "There's a Victorian on Spy Run that's purple. It has two different shades for its trim."

"Do you like it?" Reuben asked.

"It's eye-catching." Olivia finished her almond-crusted walleye and wild rice. She leaned back in her chair with a satisfied sigh.

Jazzi glanced at Isabelle's huge bowl of mussels, half-eaten. She finished her last scallop as Reuben ate his last bite of Dijon-roasted salmon.

"Where are you ladies off to after this?" he asked.

Olivia glanced at her watch. "I'll probably have one last drink at Jazzi's place and then head home. I start early in the salon tomorrow."

Isabelle studied her. "You look like a hairdresser. You have flair."

"Thank you, so do you. Where do you get your hair done?"

Isabelle hesitated slightly, then said, "I travel to Chicago every five weeks to a salon and spa."

Reuben smiled. "And I go with her for the weekend. A great city! Lots of inspiration for a designer."

They were both too classy for Jazzi. She had to admire their style, though.

Reuben motioned for the bills, and they said their good-byes. When Olivia pulled to the curb in front of Jazzi's apartment, she gave her an apologetic look.

"Do you mind if I beg off early tonight?"

"Not a bit. I'm beat."

Impulsively, Olivia stretched across the seat and hugged her. "Hang in there, sis. Sorry about Noah, and I hope Maury takes the news well. He couldn't have done it. He's too . . . Maury."

Jazzi nodded. "Don't say anything to anyone."

"I don't want to. What a downer. I'll leave that to you."

"Thanks." Jazzi wasn't looking forward to it. She climbed out of her sister's car and trudged to her apartment. She didn't even turn on the TV. She just fell into bed and slept.

Chapter 18

Jazzi didn't want to get out of bed, but she reminded herself that it was Friday. Nothing terrible could happen on a Friday, could it? Then she remembered that Gaff would probably show up at Cal's house today, and she needed to tell him about Thomas Sorrell. He might even bring Noah's father with him. Her mood plummeted. Maybe she should never leave the apartment, hide under the bed, and pretend she wasn't home.

Her dad's words spoke in her mind. "Problems don't go away just because you ignore them."

Sad, but true. They weren't *her* problems. She didn't inherit them just because she bought the house. But she couldn't really avoid them either. So she slung her legs out of bed and padded to the bathroom to get ready for the day. No use worrying about hair and makeup. She'd sweat so much, it didn't matter. The new central air was getting installed today, but when you did hard physical labor, air conditioning only helped. It wasn't a cure-all.

She pulled on her worn work jeans and a sleeveless tee. When she glanced at her arms in the mirror, she did a double take. Her biceps could intimidate desk jockeys. She flexed her muscles. *Look out, world. I'm a strong woman!* Then she thought of Ansel and laughed at herself. No competition.

On her drive across town, she glanced at the orchard she passed every day. Apples clung to the trees, not ripe yet but plentiful. Jazzi had a thing for apple dumplings. That made her think of the upcoming Sunday meal. What in the world would she make this time? Somehow, in hot weather, her menu muse deserted her.

She thought of the electric smoker on her back patio. Last April, she'd had the flu and spent a day on the couch watching QVC, and doggone if she hadn't ended up buying the stupid thing. She didn't regret it. She loved it.

She'd make ribs and potato salad, she decided. The meat would cook outside, and the kitchen would stay cool. Making a decision made her feel like she'd accomplished something. The day might not be fun, but at least she'd taken a step forward.

When she reached Cal's house, she was the first one there. She was upstairs, installing beadboard in the master bath when Jerod and then Ansel arrived. Jerod narrowed his eyes to study her work.

"Yeah, I like it. It gives it an old-fashioned look."

Ansel gently lowered George to the floor. The pug immediately stretched out on the cool tiles. George was tired. It took a lot of work to be constantly pampered.

The doorbell rang, and Jerod poked his head into the hallway and smiled. "The air-conditioning men are here."

She was surprised the three of them didn't break out into a happy dance. There was no break in the heat predicted for days on end. They'd hired the company Olivia's Thane worked for. Thane took heating and cooling as seriously as they took flipping.

Jerod raced down the stairs to let them in. When Thane entered the foyer, they cheered for him. He blushed all the way to his hairline. Ansel might be on the quiet side, but Thane was downright shy. He was as tall as Jerod with a heavier build, but Olivia was the aggressive one in their relationship. Olivia's outgoing personality was good for Thane, who tended to brood. And Thane's steadiness balanced out Olivia's spontaneity. Gaff had given them permission to work in the basement, so Jerod led them to the furnace, then returned to help with the baths.

Jerod chuckled as they worked in the bath. "I can't believe your sister fell for a guy whose favorite hobbies are camping and birdwatching."

It had surprised Jazzi, too. Thane wasn't exactly a showstopper. He had auburn hair and gray eyes, a crooked nose, a long chin, but he gave off an aura of being solid and dependable. And he was. "They say opposites attract. They complement each other."

"I guess." Jerod reached for his hammer. The master bathroom was big enough that the three of them could work together. After they installed the beadboard, they carted in the cabinet for the double sinks. Last, they installed the toilet and glass shower doors. When the room was finished, Jazzi was one happy girl.

"What do you want in the small bath?" Ansel asked.

She hadn't gotten that far. "What would you do with it?"

"White wainscoting on the bottom half and dark blue paint on the top half. A big mirror with a white frame." He'd obviously thought about it.

"Sounds good to me. Let's do it." She felt sorry for Ansel. He wanted to make a house his own so much, and Emily wasn't going to let him. They had plenty of beadboard for the wainscoting and installed that. "We'll have to wait to paint," she said. "Why don't you pick out the blue and white tonight?"

He gave her a look. "It's your house. Are you babying me?"

"Maybe."

At first, he looked miffed, but then he relaxed. "The look will go with your house, and I'll have my perfect bathroom."

"Why don't you plan out the two guest bedrooms, too? You and I like the same styles."

Ansel's blue eyes lit with excitement. "Really? Emily never let me pick things out without her."

Jazzi decided not to comment on that. "You have great taste. Make them pretty. I'm painting the master bedroom a rose color."

"What? You never expect to invite a guy over?" Jerod fluffed his short hair. "Rose is a little froufrou, isn't it?"

Ansel scowled. "I like rose."

"Oh, brother, you would," Jerod complained. "Jazzi's babying you. She never babies *me*."

"Franny does. You're spoiled enough." Jazzi knew better than to humor him. If she encouraged him, Jerod would use fake martyrdom status every chance he got.

Jerod laughed. "She used to, before bitch mode, but let's break for lunch before we start on the next project. It's past noon."

On their way down to the kitchen, Jazzi asked Ansel, "I've been debating between butcher block countertops or stainless steel. What do you think?"

"Stainless steel." He didn't hesitate. "It will go with the white tin ceiling tiles you want."

Not real ones. She couldn't afford those, but they made great replicas now. "You don't think it will look too modern?"

He put George down. George didn't like stairs, so Ansel always carried him. "It's according to what you use for a backsplash and cupboards."

Ansel was right. If she stuck with everything else traditional, stainless steel would work. "I went with a robin's-egg blue Shaker-style cupboard. I'll order the stainless steel. It will match the knobs and hardware."

"Backsplash?" Jerod asked.

Jazzi looked to Ansel when she said, "Subway tiles?"

Ansel grinned his approval. How could Emily resist pleasing a man with a smile like that?

When they reached the kitchen, the air-conditioning men had left for lunch, too. Thane would be chowing down at a nearby bar. The three of them were grabbing sandwiches out of the cooler when there was a quick knock on the door and Gaff led a tall, thin man with gray hair into the house.

The guy looked like he hadn't had any sleep for weeks, and his eyes were puffy. She hoped seeing where Noah died and was buried would give him some closure, but he was going to be more miserable at the moment. She looked at her sandwich, her appetite gone. She rewrapped it and put it back.

Gaff pressed his lips together. "Sorry. I ruined your lunch."

Even Jerod tossed his half-eaten sandwich into the trash. Who could eat in front of a grieving father?

Noah's dad looked so *nice*. And so *sad*. She was depressed. Gaff had told her that Noah's dad was a music teacher and his mom played in the symphony orchestra. Music was an everyday part of Noah's life growing up.

Noah's dad looked at them, apologetic. "We should have called before we came."

"No big deal." Jazzi stood to greet him. "You came to see the basement?"

Gaff nodded. "He ID'd the body. It's Noah. He'd like to take the toolbox home with him. Noah's grandfather gave it to him."

"My father," the man said. "He was a handyman and taught Noah his skills."

Jazzi bit her tongue before she could blurt out, "Lucky Noah." He must have been dearly loved, but he'd died much too young. Instead, she flicked her head toward the basement door. "I'll lead you to the furnace. That's where we found the box."

She stopped walking with them for the last few feet, and Gaff took charge. He motioned to the toolbox, set between the furnace and water heater. "This is where they found it. We think Noah was killed while he inspected the furnace. Right here." He pointed to tape marked in an *X* on the floor.

Tears rolled down Noah's dad's face. "I wish Noah had told us about Cal, about meeting him and coming here. We could have come with him. Maybe then . . ." He had to stop to regain his composure. "Maybe we'd still have him. But he was always so thoughtful."

Grief was hard to hear and see. Jazzi clenched her hands, wishing she had something comforting to say. But what can comfort a grieving parent?

His dad went on. "When he was young, we told him he was adopted, and he told us over and over again that we were his real parents. We were the ones who loved and raised him. But we'd have understood that he wanted to know more about his birth mother and father. We'd have been all right with that. If only . . ." He swallowed and looked away.

Jazzi heard footsteps enter the kitchen and looked at Gaff. "The air-conditioning crew's back from lunch. Someone might come down here."

Gaff nodded. "Let's go outside and look at where we found his body."

Ansel was talking to Thane when they climbed the stairs and went outside. Bless their Viking friend! He'd stalled the crew so that Noah's dad could have some privacy. She sent him a grateful glance, and he nodded.

Thane strained to see Gaff and Noah's father. He'd obviously heard all of the latest news from Olivia. His expression saddened. No one could look at the dad and not feel his pain.

Jerod was waiting by the police tape in the backyard. When they joined him, he said, "I was using the backhoe to check our drainage system when I saw Noah's black curls two feet down. I called Gaff."

The dad looked like he might collapse. Gaff stepped closer in case he needed to grab him. "Someone just threw his body in a hole. No tarp to cover him. No blanket. Nothing. No respect for his body at all."

That bothered him, Jazzi could tell. Would Noah's flesh have lasted longer if he'd been wrapped in a tarp? Maybe. She wasn't sure. She didn't know what to say, so went with the standard lame words most people used. "I'm so sorry for your loss."

The dad turned to her and pumped her hand. "I'm so grateful you and your friends bought this house to fix it up, or we still wouldn't know what happened to Noah. You've spared us lots of agony."

She doubted that. They finally knew what happened to Noah, and that would ease some of their pain, but there'd be plenty left to last a while. Experts said the first year was the worst, but she'd watched people, and the second year wasn't much better. Knowing did help, though. She thought of her mom and Cal, always wondering if Lynda was still alive and why she never got in touch with them. Closure was a good thing.

She felt uncomfortable, uncertain if Noah's dad would like some time alone. She took a step back, and Gaff said, "I'd like to take Noah's dad to visit Maury Lebovitch. You said you'd come with us."

Oh no, Gaff *and* Noah's father? She hadn't counted on that. She'd promised to tell Maury if they found Lynda's son, though, and she'd rather he heard it from her than Gaff. This was going to suck. How could it go well?

Her expression must have shown how much she was *not* looking forward to it, because Noah's dad said, "I know we're asking a lot, but we'd really appreciate it."

How did you walk away from that? She nodded and turned to Gaff. "You should call Maury and have him meet us in his office. He deserves some privacy when he hears the news."

Gaff didn't argue. He reached for his cell and made the call as the three of them walked to his car.

She glanced at Jerod. He gave her a thumbs-up. "Don't worry. Do what you need to do and we'll work on the smaller bedrooms upstairs."

He really was a pretty neat cousin. Ansel stepped out of the house and handed Gaff Noah's toolbox. Gaff carried it to his car. Jazzi and Noah's dad followed him. It was a short drive to Maury's deli. The place was packed. For good reason. River Bluffs didn't have another true deli. There was a chain deli on the south side of town, but it couldn't compete with corned beef or pastrami made from old family recipes.

Maury was working behind the counter with his two sons, but when he saw them come in, he nodded to a door on the left near the rear of the restaurant. He finished a sandwich for a customer, then came to join them.

The office was cramped, and that was putting it kindly. Maybe it had been a pantry at one time. It had room for a desk, a file cabinet, three chairs, and not much else. That worked for Jazzi. She planted herself by the wall near the door. Noah's dad looked at Maury's tight, gray curls and looked away for a minute.

Gaff and Noah's father took chairs across from Maury's. When everyone settled, Gaff made introductions. "Maury Lebovitch, this is Noah's father, Alan Jacobs. Alan, this is Maury." He turned his attention to Maury. "Jazzi asked me to tell you about Noah Jacobs. He was Lynda's son. She gave birth to him and gave him up for adoption when she went to New York for a year."

Maury leaned forward, excited, staring at Noah's father. "Did you adopt him?"

Alan nodded. "My wife and I did. We couldn't have children of our own. We were older, in our early forties, when we got lucky enough to adopt Noah." He fumbled in his coat pocket and brought out pictures. He shoved them to Maury, and then Gaff passed them to Jazzi.

An infant Noah had the same wild, unruly curls Maury had once had, but he looked like Lynda. There was another photo of Noah with "five-years-old" scribbled on the back. If there was a cuter kid in the world, Jazzi hadn't seen him. Next came a high school graduation picture of Noah in his cap and gown. The last photo showed Noah playing a guitar with his band. Maury sucked in a quick breath. "I'm Catholic. Lynda never told me that she was pregnant when she left for New York. She just broke up with me. She said we were done, she wasn't ready to get married yet, and then she left town. It wasn't until years later, when she was angry with me for telling Arnie that he was better off without her, that she told me she'd had my child. She did it to hurt me, which was pretty low, considering she'd hurt me to start with. I tried to find the boy, but I finally gave up and hoped the best for my son."

"Does your wife know?" Gaff asked.

"No, I never worked up the courage to tell her. Lynda and I were a thing before I met Gina. I couldn't bring myself to tell her about Lynda having a baby after my wife's second stillbirth. I just couldn't. And to be honest, part of me suspected Lynda just said it to hurt me. I didn't completely believe her."

"But you checked?" Gaff asked.

"I called agencies in New York. They wouldn't tell me anything."

Jazzi raised an eyebrow at Gaff. Maury sure didn't sound like a man who'd kill Noah. He'd probably run to him and embrace him. He was going to take this news hard.

Maury looked at Noah's father. "Does Noah have a good life?"

Alan flinched, but reached across Maury's desk and shook his hand. "You have no idea how much you blessed us. We'd given up hope of ever having a baby, and then we got Noah. He was such a funny, wonderful child. A delight."

Maury scrubbed his fingers through his tight curls. "Does he want to see me? Or does he hate me for not finding him, for not being there?"

Gaff turned to Jazzi and motioned for her to join the conversation. She'd told Maury about Cal hiring a detective to find Noah, how Cal flew to New York to visit him, and how Noah had driven to River Bluffs to see Cal. "Noah disappeared, remember?"

Before she could say more, Maury leaped to his feet. "Alan's here. So did Noah come, too? When can I meet him?"

Gaff pressed his lips in a tight line and nodded to Jazzi. "Tell him. He deserves to know."

Maury sank back onto his chair, alarmed. He frowned at Jazzi. She took a deep breath. "We found Noah's body buried in Cal's backyard."

"What? No! Impossible." Maury shook his head, denying the news. "Who'd hurt him in River Bluffs?"

Alan lowered his head. He folded his hands together, as though in prayer, in his lap.

Maury stared. "What sense does this make? Who'd want him dead?"

Gaff grimaced. "We don't know, but Jazzi insisted we tell you."

Maury's face went blank. He looked at Jazzi. "Who'd do this? I wanted to meet him. What would that matter?"

"Someone must have felt threatened by him," she said. "Why else would someone kill him? No one even knew him here."

"Threatened? How?" Maury turned to Gaff.

Gaff hesitated a moment, then said, "Do you have a will?"

Jazzi frowned. Where was Gaff going with this?

"Sure, I do. I left everything to my wife. If she dies, too, then my sons inherit . . ." Maury stopped abruptly and shook his head. "Even if my property and holdings were divided into thirds, my sons would be fine."

Alan spoke. "Noah didn't need anyone else's money. We have more than enough."

"But no one knew that, did they?" Gaff turned to Maury again. "Did your sons know Noah was coming to River Bluffs?"

"How could they? I didn't even know." Maury's hands started shaking and he couldn't stop them. He finally sat on them.

Noah's dad drew in a long breath. "I'm so sorry for all of us. This should have been a grand celebration instead of an investigation. Our families could have joined together. We'd have liked that."

"Us, too." Maury finally put his elbows on his desk and lowered his head into his hands. "This is too much."

An understatement. There was a lot of pain in this room. Jazzi was glad when Gaff drove her back to Cal's house.

Chapter 19

When Jazzi got out of Gaff's unmarked car, she leaned close to his window and said, "I have something to tell you if you can call me later this evening."

"I'm driving Alan to the airport at four. What if I stop by here later?"

"I'll wait." She watched Gaff's car pull away and then turned to go back into the house.

Jerod and Ansel were waiting for her. Ansel studied her. "Are you okay?"

"That was the pits."

Jerod patted her shoulder. "Do you want to stop work early today? It's Friday. We can have an early weekend."

Jazzi grimaced. "Gaff's coming back here after he drops Noah's dad at the airport. I want to tell him about Thomas Sorrell."

"Sorrell?" Jerod looked confused. "No one's seen him for years. He still comes to River Bluffs for business once in a while, but he doesn't want anything to do with us."

Jazzi told them what Isabelle told her.

Jerod let out a low whistle. "The guy sounds like a candidate for a violent stalker."

The air-conditioning men had left. Jazzi had hoped to see Thane, but she'd missed him. She comforted herself by remembering that she'd see him on Sunday. The house was still warm and sticky. It would take a while to cool it off. "Is the central air working?"

Jerod waved her farther into the house. "Enjoy the luxury of seventy-two degrees."

It hadn't reached that yet, but Jazzi exhaled a breath of relief. The front rooms didn't feel like a sweat house. "Nice. What have you guys been up to while I was gone?"

Ansel beamed. "I drove to Lima Road and bought paint for the bedrooms and bathroom. Want to see it?"

"Sure do."

Ansel picked up George, and she and Jerod followed him upstairs. He had a drop cloth on the wooden floor, along with blue painter's tape, rollers, and paintbrushes. He lifted the lids on three cans.

"This is the blue for the bathroom." It was darker than she'd expected, but she liked it. He pointed to a caramel color. "This is for one bedroom. The dusty amethyst's for the other one."

She liked them all. "You done good."

He grinned at her deliberate bad grammar. "If you'd like something else, I can take them back."

"They're perfect choices. I can hardly wait to see how they look."

"Want to paint a room now?" Ansel was excited. He clearly wanted to see how his colors looked on the walls. "Emily works tonight. I don't have to be home at any certain time."

She thought about it. "Why not?" She didn't have any exciting plans for the night.

"Count me out," Jerod said. "I have a wife and two kids to hang out with."

Jazzi loved how crazy Jerod was about his family. "Why don't you take off early, and we'll paint?"

"Sounds like a plan." He tapped the top of her head. "Hang in there, cuz. Don't let Gaff rattle you tonight. And cook me something wonderful on Sunday. Why don't you move your dining room table over here for the family meal? You'd have a lot more room."

"The cupboards and appliances haven't come yet."

"You'd better get on that then. In the meantime, you could buy a mini fridge and use the cooler. The sinks work."

"I've ordered everything," Jazzi told him. "Stainless steel and a farmer's sink. They're coming on Wednesday. We need to install the tin ceiling and paint the walls so we're ready."

"Piece of cake." He was enjoying himself, taunting her. But he had a point about having the family meals here. "If you decide to have everyone here, Ansel and I will each bring our coolers for the drinks. They're big ones. We use them when we go fishing."

"Will you be here on Sunday, Ansel?" Jazzi had lost track of Emily's work hours.

"No, Emily has the day off, but you can use my cooler anyway. Emily doesn't like picnics. I won't need it." He looked disappointed, and she realized that he'd like to be here for the first meal in the house.

She shook her head. "I can't get everything moved and done in time. But for the meal after that? I'll be ready."

"Thank the heavens!" Jerod did a small two-step happy dance. "I'll finally be able to stretch my legs at a Sunday meal. It's so crowded in your apartment, we're all jammed together."

"You never complained about that before."

"Down, *Jasmine*. Your cooking makes it worth it, but it will be nice to eat *and* stretch. We're moving up in the world." He dodged her smack and hurried down the steps to the door. He called up, "Have fun, you two!"

Ansel picked up a paintbrush. "Which room first?"

The man was ready to go. Jazzi chose the caramel bedroom, and they got started. They had three walls done when Gaff knocked and yelled up to them.

"Give us a minute. We're coming down!"

"You go," Ansel said. "I'll finish painting."

Lord, the man was determined.

Jazzi went down to see Gaff alone.

Chapter 20

Gaff walked into the kitchen and took a deep breath. "It feels good in here."

They hadn't turned off the window air conditioner, and it had actually made the room comfortable since it didn't have to cool the entire downstairs. "The central air's hooked up. Life's going to be better."

He smiled, sank onto a lawn chair, and looked around. "The place is starting to come together."

"The bathrooms are done upstairs and Ansel and I are painting the bedrooms. The floors are good. The biggest project is going to be this kitchen."

"The heart of the home." He tilted his head, thinking. "Since the kids have grown up, my wife and I carry in food or go out more than we used to."

Jazzi laughed. "You probably have more money."

"There's that, for sure. Kids are expensive." He glanced at the cooler, and Jazzi took the hint.

"Want something cold to drink?"

"Wouldn't mind. I can sip while you tell me about Thomas Sorrell."

She handed him a soda and sat across from him. She shared everything Isabelle had told her, and Gaff raised his eyebrows. "This Sorrell wanted to meet Noah, and Isabelle thinks it was just to annoy Cal?"

Jazzi put her elbows on her knees, leaning forward. "You know, I've been thinking, and Cal's nephews inherited his house and money, but what happened to Cal's businesses? Will's a plumber. Wade's an electrician. They don't know squat about finances. Who runs Cal's companies now? He even had some overseas, didn't he?"

Gaff nodded. "I talked to his lawyers. He left them all to Isabelle."

"Isabelle?"

Gaff looked at her, surprised. "She was his assistant, even invested in a lot of his projects, and owned shares in most of his companies. She'll run the businesses as well as he did. You didn't know?"

"Why would I?"

Gaff gave her a sheepish look. "Sorry, that was my fault. You've shared everything with me, and I didn't return the favor."

"I'm surprised Isabelle didn't tell me."

"She probably thought you knew."

Jazzi considered that and decided Gaff was right. Isabelle assumed Jazzi knew she and Cal were more than friends. They were business partners, too. "Did Cal and Isabelle work together when Cal met Lynda?"

Gaff's lip quirked up on one side. "Yes, they did, but Isabelle swears they were just partners back then. They didn't grow close until after Lynda disappeared and Cal struggled with his grief."

"Still, Lynda would be a threat to Isabelle. Lynda was smart and ambitious. I could see her wanting to get involved in Cal's work."

"Isabelle wasn't in River Bluffs the day Lynda disappeared. Four hours after Cal left for Europe, she was in New York, covering a conference for him."

Jazzi grinned. "You checked."

"I'm a detective."

A knot of worry unraveled in Jazzi's chest. She was glad Isabelle couldn't have killed Lynda. She liked Isabelle.

Gaff waited a minute so that Jazzi could sort her thoughts, then said, "Guess who *was* in town when Lynda died."

Jazzi's eyes went wide. "Thomas Sorrell?"

"On business."

"What made you look into that?"

"I went through every person you named who was involved with Lynda. I like knowing who's where at the time of a murder."

Jazzi bit her bottom lip, frowning. "Isabelle made it sound as if Thomas was in River Bluffs when Noah arrived, too."

"I'll check into that."

"Where does he live? Is it easy for him to pop in and out of our city?"

"His home base is Cleveland, Ohio. Within driving distance. And he travels a lot."

"Does he come here often?"

Gaff drained the last drops from his soda can and got up to throw it away. "Only once or twice a year. That's why I haven't paid much attention to him. He's got my attention now." He glanced at his watch. "It's Friday. I still have paperwork to do. I'll let you know what I find out."

"Thanks." She walked him to the door, then went upstairs to check on Ansel. He'd almost finished the last wall. The paint still needed to dry, but Jazzi could tell that she was going to love the color. "It's gorgeous."

He gave it the last strokes it needed, then stepped back to admire his work. "It's even better than I pictured it. If I ever get a house, do you mind if I use this color, too?"

"It was your idea. Go for it."

A quick look of frustration passed over his face. "Emily probably won't like it."

That was for sure. The more Ansel wanted it, the less likely he'd ever get it. The week was catching up with Jazzi. "I'm beginning to drag. Let's clean up our gear and then order in some food."

"It's only five thirty. We could finish the second room."

"We could, but we're not going to. I'm starving. I vote for food."

"Crap. I forgot. You didn't eat lunch. Gaff came with Noah's dad. You've had a terrible day, and I pushed you to help me paint. I've been selfish."

She shook her head. "You're never selfish. I'm glad we painted the room. I could have said no. But now, I'm hungry."

He laughed, and the rumble resonated through his chest. It was a wonderful sound. "What do you want?"

You. But she couldn't say that. She was going to have to be careful until he and Emily left. "I know fried chicken isn't healthy, but I'd love a bucket of it with coleslaw and mashed potatoes and gravy."

"We Norwegians never trust someone who doesn't love fried chicken."

Yeah, right. She'd guess they never saw the stuff. "Then fried chicken it is! I'll grab some. Do you want to meet at my apartment and watch a movie together?"

"If I get to pick."

She stared at him. "You picked the last movie. You're getting a little full of yourself."

"That's true, but there's one I really want to see."

Uh-oh. "It's not gloomy like some of the Swedish mysteries you like so much, is it?"

He grinned. "It's older. I bought the CD. *The Thirteenth Warrior* with Antonio Banderas and Vikings."

"Vikings?" *Like him? Tall, blond, and beautiful?*

"You'll love it. The bad guys dress like bears and rip off heads."

Okay, he had her. The movie sounded like it was right up her alley. She loved English movies like *Pride and Prejudice* and *Sherlock*, and she loved offbeat thrillers like *Sleepy Hollow* with Johnny Depp and every single Harry Potter. "You win this time, but you owe me. Remember that."

"You won't let me forget. I'll see you at your place."

They went their separate ways, and she stopped for food, but when she got to her apartment, his pickup wasn't there. He pulled up behind her a minute later and opened his truck door with a smile. "I stopped at George's bakery and bought your favorite cake—the torte filled with kiwi and strawberries with whipped cream."

When he heard his name, George's ears perked up and he panted happily. *The torte? From George's? That was only a zillion calories a bite?* "I love you!"

She reached for her food bags, and he reached for the cake, but not before she caught the grimace that flickered over his handsome features. *Why had she blurted that out?* In the dining room, sitting across from him, she hurried to say, "I shouldn't have said that. I love you like a brother, and I'll miss you when you move to California, but I understand about Emily's job. She'll make a lot more money as a traveling nurse and have a lot more learning experiences."

He looked even more miserable. "Yes, she will, but I'll have to start over. I'm not sure I want to."

Jazzi stared. "But Emily—"

"Can't always get what she wants. I'm willing to concede on small points, but this is major. I get a vote, too."

Would Emily cave? Would she stay in River Bluffs and choose Ansel over California? Jazzi doubted Emily had ever compromised before.

Ansel tore off a piece of white chicken meat to give to George. "Let's forget about Emily right now."

They dropped the subject and chose to enjoy their meal and their time together. Jazzi loved *The Thirteenth Warrior* as much as Ansel did, and they finished the night in better moods than they'd started it.

At eleven, Jazzi waved Ansel off and plopped onto her couch to watch a half hour of mindless TV before going to bed. Tomorrow, she'd clean the apartment and go to the grocery store like she always did. But after Sunday's meal, it was time to start packing things up. When the kitchen was finished at Cal's house, she wanted to move all of her cookware and dinnerware there. Her dining room table, too. That way, Ansel could be there for the first meal in her new home.

Chapter 21

Gaff called her before noon. Three lemon meringue pies were already cooling on the countertops. Potato salad and a watermelon salsa waited in the refrigerator. She was ahead of schedule. A good thing.

"Guess who's in town this weekend?" Gaff asked.

Jazzi looked at her reflection in the kitchen window. Her hair tended to frizz when she cooked. Humidity was not her friend. "Thomas Sorrell?"

"I'd like it if you'd come with me when I talk to him. You know the family history better than I do."

"Why not?" She didn't have to look good to talk to Sorrell. "When should I be ready?"

"I'll pick you up in half an hour."

"Good." They'd finish up and she'd be home in time to buy the ribs for tomorrow.

She pulled her hair up in a ponytail, tossed on a pair of khaki capris and a cotton T-shirt. She could wear those at the grocery store. When Gaff pulled to the curb, she went out to climb in his car. "Where to?" she asked.

"An addition out north." Gaff threw her a look. "He's staying at a friend's house. Whenever he comes to town, he stays with her."

Jazzi frowned. "He's married, isn't he?"

"Yes, to his fourth wife."

"And he still has money?"

"He always insists on a prenup. He must not mind losing three million a pop. Maybe to him having a young woman on his arm is worth it, but they get paid only if they stick it out for two years."

"What a guy."

"It goes both ways. The girls know what they're getting into."

Jazzi let out a long breath. The money wouldn't be worth it to her. "It sounds like Lynda made the right choice when she left Thomas."

"At least he didn't ask her for a prenup. It must have been true love."

"They were still young. He wasn't happy when she wouldn't give him back his ring."

The traffic on State Street wasn't as bad as usual on Saturday. Jazzi strained to glance down Forest Park Boulevard when they passed it. Big stately homes lined both sides of the street. Gaff crossed over Anthony and kept heading north. When he crossed Coliseum Boulevard, the older two-story homes and bungalows gave way to ranches and additions. He turned left on Maplecrest and then turned left into an addition Jazzi had never been in before. It was a lot like her mom and dad's neighborhood southwest—some split-levels and ranches mixed with a few more modern two-story homes, large yards, and everything well-kept.

Gaff parked in the drive of a charcoal-gray split-level that had boxwood bushes sculptured like sphinxes on each side of the yellow front door and a fountain near the corner. Jazzi followed Gaff and stood behind him when he knocked. No one came. He stepped back and stared at the bronze pyramid plaque near the door frame—a doorbell. He rang. They waited. No one came again.

"Maybe they're in the backyard." They were walking to the rear of the house when the front door opened and a woman called, "Hello? Is someone there?"

They retraced their footsteps. Gaff flashed his badge and said, "I'm Detective Gaff. I called to see Thomas Sorrell."

"Oh, please come in." She stepped back to let them enter the front room. Her dark hair, pulled up in a knot, was mussed. So was her eyeliner. She wore a floaty-style skirt that barely covered her butt and a low-cut, sleeveless top. Jazzi guessed she must be in her early thirties. "I'm Beth. Thomas will be here in a minute."

They settled themselves into chairs and she said, "Can I get you something to drink? A cocktail? Beer?"

"I'll take a glass of water." Gaff took out his pen and notepad.

Jazzi shook her head. "I'm fine."

When Beth went to the kitchen, Jazzi studied her surroundings. The white carpet was so thick, feet sank into it. The walls were painted the same charcoal gray as the exterior of the house. The modern sofa was a shock of bright yellow; the chairs blazed bright red. A bronze sculpture protruded from the side wall, and modern paintings hung on the long wall between the front room and the kitchen.

Beth came back with Gaff's water. When she looked up and saw a tall, silver-haired man walk down the hallway toward them, her smile dazzled. "Here's Thomas!"

Thomas's hair was still damp. He wore casual slacks and a crisp white shirt that set off his deep tan. With a brisk nod, he sat on the sofa across from Gaff and raised an eyebrow. Beth sat at the other end of the sofa, out of his way.

Gaff looked at his notes. "I've come regarding the death of Lynda Remington. I'd like to ask you some questions about her." He nodded toward Jazzi. "This is Jazzi Zanders, her niece. She agreed to accompany me."

His long, narrow lips turned down. "You're related to Lynda?"

Didn't Gaff just say that? "She was my aunt."

"Too bad, you're quite lovely, but I've sworn off anyone from the Remington family."

Was that a backhanded compliment? The man was older than her father. Did he really think she'd be interested in him?

Thomas turned to Gaff. "Let's get this over with. What do you want to ask me?"

"I'm assuming you know that Lynda's body was found in a trunk in Cal's attic."

"I read about it in the paper. Somebody disliked her more than I did."

"You were in River Bluffs the day she died. How much did you dislike her?"

Thomas's eyebrows rose in surprise. "You've obviously heard about our argument the day before she was due to leave. Cal was too weak for her. She'd have grown bored with him. I was a better fit. Besides, I'd invested a great deal of money in her."

"But not very much time, according to the sources I've talked to." Gaff waited for his reaction.

Thomas shrugged. "My time is valuable. I can't squander it."

What an ego! Jazzi glanced at Beth, but nothing Thomas said seemed to faze her.

He expanded on his statement. "Every time I came to River Bluffs, I spent an entire day with Lynda. I made sure she enjoyed herself."

Big deal. Thomas must think his quality time was life shattering.

Gaff went to the next question on his list. "You left River Bluffs the day after Lynda disappeared. That's a little suspicious."

"Is it? Why? I came here to confront Lynda. She wouldn't listen to reason. I waited for her to call the next day, but she left town instead. There was no reason for me to stay."

"That's one explanation. Another view is that you knew Cal had left for Europe. You went to his house to see Lynda. You argued, and you lost your temper and killed her."

"I might lose my temper, but I never act on impulse. That scenario would never happen."

Gaff moved to the next question. "I've been told that you wanted to see the son Lynda gave up in New York. Why?"

Thomas half-smiled, amused. "To irritate Cal, of course. He didn't have any more claim to Lynda's son than I did. That's why I've kept a business here, too. Cal took something that was mine, and I intended to keep reminding him of that." He steepled his fingers and sat in thought for a moment. "I'm selling my interests here now that Cal's died. They don't entertain me anymore."

Beth's shoulders stiffened and she frowned. "But what about me?"

He glanced at her. "What about you? I bought you this house. I've paid for your jewelry. You're a beautiful woman, but there are beautiful women everywhere."

Jazzi had to look away. The pain that crossed Beth's face was too hard to watch.

Gaff moved to his next question. "I'm also assuming you know that Lynda's son was murdered in Cal's house and buried in his backyard."

Thomas's expression turned thunderous. "How did I miss that? I saw on the news that a body was removed from the house, but there were no details. I assumed it was related to Lynda's murder twenty-six years ago. I haven't seen one article about Noah. The son was supposed to meet Cal before Cal died, but he never came."

"The news couldn't print it until Noah's father came to identify his body. You can read about it tomorrow morning." Gaff looked up from his notepad. "Were you in town when Noah was supposed to arrive?"

Beth answered. "Yes, he was. He made a special trip."

Thomas's expression made Jazzi shiver. She rubbed her arms. Then she glanced at Beth. Gone was the doting mistress. If the floor opened and swallowed Thomas in flames, Jazzi wouldn't be surprised.

"I drove here, hoping to see him. I knew that would bother Cal, but I shouldn't have wasted my time. When Noah never came, the kid devastated Cal more than I ever could. Actually, though, I enjoyed watching that, so it was worth it."

What a hateful man! If Lynda had married him, Jazzi would be related to the jerk. A horrible thought.

Gaff gave Thomas a long, serious look. "You had motive to kill both of them to hurt Cal and because you were so angry with Lynda. And you had opportunity. You were in River Bluffs for each death."

Thomas laughed. "Prove it. I'd have to stand in line behind people who weren't fans of Lynda. As for Noah, I don't even know when he finally showed up at Cal's. You're fishing, and you don't have enough bait. I don't kill people. Where's the fun? I'd rather watch them dangle and suffer."

Gaff closed his notebook and tucked it into his pocket. "Thank you for your time. If I need anything else, I'll call you."

"Any time, detective. I'm always happy to cooperate." Thomas stood and held out his hand. It was time for them to go.

Beth stomped down the hallway and slammed a door.

Thomas smiled. "An eventful day."

Jazzi and Gaff didn't talk as they got into the car and left the addition. Then Gaff gave a low whistle. "You don't meet many like him."

"Thank goodness!" Jazzi felt like she needed a shower just for sharing the same air as Thomas.

When she got home, there was a message from Ansel on her machine. "Emily has to work again tonight, so she needs her sleep. George and I had to clear out of the apartment, so we went to Cal's house to paint the second bedroom. We started around nine. If you want to check it out, I won't put you to work."

She checked the time. A little before three. Crap, she'd just missed his call. She dialed his cell and was relieved when he picked up. "Are you still at Cal's?"

"Yup, you want to come see the room? I like it."

"I'm on my way." It took her half an hour, so she'd filtered out most of Thomas Sorrell's comments before she got there. She tried to push them away. She didn't want to dwell on them. When she walked inside the house, she ran up the stairs to find Ansel.

George came to greet her, his curly tail wagging. Jazzi stepped into the second bedroom and put a hand to her throat. The soft, dusty amethyst was soothing and relaxing. "I love it."

Ansel smiled. "So do I." He was just finishing up.

"Did it take more than one coat?" He'd been at it a long time.

"No, come and see." He led her down the hall to the master bedroom and opened the door.

She gasped. "It's beautiful!" The rose walls complemented the wooden floors and oak trim. She almost choked on emotion and blinked away tears. It was so sweet of Ansel to paint this for her. And it was everything she'd hoped it would be.

"It's my favorite room," Ansel said. "You should buy new furniture and put your queen-size bed in one of the guest rooms."

"What's wrong with my bed?" She'd bought it when she moved into her apartment. It was still fairly new.

"Not special enough."

"And what do you picture in here?"

"A sleigh bed."

She rolled her eyes. "You must have a thing for them. Can you even fit in one? You're so tall, you'd have to scrunch up."

"Not if I buy a king."

She could picture Ansel in a long bed, shaped somewhat like a Viking boat. Not that she should. She swallowed her lust. *Down, girl.* "Those are expensive. What if the next guy I meet is under six feet?"

Ansel winced. His expression turned fierce. "What if he's not?"

He had a point. She sighed. "Why get cheap on the furniture when the room's so pretty?"

He grinned. "Your cannonball bed would look perfect in the caramel room."

"I can see it in there." She went to one of the long, narrow windows and looked outside. The view from the master bedroom looked over the street and the wheat fields that stretched for miles. A great view.

"Do you like it?" Ansel asked.

She nodded. "It's more than I pictured. I love this house."

"The armoire and chest of drawers in the attic would fit in here. The room's big enough to handle them."

He was right. She wondered if this was where they'd been originally.

Ansel went on. "When Jerod and I are together on Monday, we can carry them down here. All you need is the bed." The man was sure attached to this house. She hoped he'd be as happy with whatever apartment he and Emily found in California.

"Want to go look at furniture?" she asked him. "Then we can grab something to eat, and I need to buy ribs for tomorrow's meal."

"I love your ribs."

She patted his arm. "I'll make an extra slab. You can heat them up later."

He grinned. "What if we leave George here and come back for supper after you find the bed?"

"Works for me."

After an hour, they agreed on which sleigh bed they wanted. They even agreed on the comforter to put on it. It was odd how much they had in common. They grabbed Chinese take-out on the way back to Cal's. Ansel could plow through a dozen crab Rangoon like he was eating a handful of peanuts. Jazzi ordered pork lo mein, and he ordered Mongolian beef with extra rice. They stopped to buy an Arby's Jr. for George. The pug wasn't partial to soy sauce.

As usual, time passed quickly when they were together and Jazzi was surprised when she looked at her watch. "Holy crap! It's almost nine. I have to stop at the store and buy a few things for tomorrow. Thanks for losing your free day to paint for me."

"I like making you happy," he said simply. And she realized she felt the same way about him.

"Emily doesn't work tomorrow night?" she asked.

"No, she's planning on coming home tomorrow morning and staying awake for most of the day. She likes brunch, so we'll go somewhere for that. We'll have the day together, and then when she falls asleep at about five thirty or six, she'll sleep straight through until lunchtime on Monday."

"Not a bad plan." Jazzi wasn't sure she could be sleep deprived that long, but nurses must get used to it. She turned to Ansel again. "Thanks for everything."

He nodded, grabbed George, and followed her out of the house. They waved as they drove in separate directions. On the drive home, Jazzi realized that the second floor of Cal's house was mostly done. The only thing that needed a little more polish was the hallway.

She stopped and grabbed a half-dozen slabs of baby back ribs and an extra slab for Ansel, then took the time to season them with a rub before calling it a night. Tomorrow, she'd throw them in the smoker early in the morning. And she'd save a slab for Ansel.

When she finally put things away and settled on the sofa in her apartment, she noticed the message machine was blinking on her phone. She punched it, expecting to hear someone ask if they'd renovate a house for them, but a woman's voice snapped, "If you know what's good for you, you'll quit playing detective. Keep your nose out of other people's business."

The voice was muffled. Jazzi didn't recognize it, but that was the point. She looked at the caller ID. *Private number.* At first, the message made her nervous, but then she remembered the look on Beth's face when she and Gaff left her house. Did she blame them for upsetting Sorrell enough to leave River Bluffs? He would eventually have dumped her anyway.

Who else would call to warn her off? And what was the point? Gaff was the detective, not her. Jazzi shrugged. It had to be Beth. Once the girl calmed down, she'd come to her senses. Right?

Jazzi put the call out of her mind, crawled into bed, and dreamed about phantom phone calls off and on through the night. Okay, when she woke the next morning, she had to admit the call had spooked her a little, but she was meeting people she normally would never deal with and Gaff was putting them on the spot. They weren't going to like her, and some of them were going to lash out. Hopefully, that's all they'd do.

Chapter 22

Jerod walked through the door at two, sniffed, and smiled. "Pork heaven. I'm a happy man."

Franny laughed at him. "If there's meat and potatoes, you're doomed."

Gunner and Lizzie went straight to the cookie jar. Jazzi always filled it for them. In the winter, she baked the cookies. In the summer, she visited the bakery or store. Gunner, at four, lowered the jar for his year-and-a-half-old sister to choose. She dug to find the Oreos and he grabbed the Chips Ahoy.

"Only two each," Franny told them. "We're going to eat soon."

Jerod looked at the table. "No deviled eggs?"

Jazzi knew her cousin. There were *always* eggs. "I haven't put them out yet. You do the honors. I'm going to get the ribs off the grill."

"Want the potato salad, too?" Franny called as Jazzi went out the door.

"Yeah, thanks! There's watermelon salsa if you want some. The chips are on the counter."

When Jazzi carried in six racks of ribs, Jerod and Franny had the rest of the food on the table and people were looking for spots to sit. It was the usual crowd—Mom and Dad, Dad's brother, Eli, and his wife, Grandma, and Olivia and Thane.

Thane saw the ribs and grinned. "My favorites."

It must be a guy thing. Jazzi liked ribs, but she liked other things every bit as much. Potato salad ranked high on her list.

People yakked and gossiped about what they'd been doing lately, avoiding the Lynda-Noah issue, and the meal was filled with a lot of laughter. The only hiccup was when Grandma looked at Franny and said, "It's going to be a boy, Lynda. Choose a good name for him."

Franny grinned and said, "Will do."

And everyone returned to other topics.

When it came time for dessert, everyone had a big piece of lemon meringue pie. Thane finally looked at Jazzi and said, "I heard you had to deal with Thomas Sorrell."

She wrinkled her nose in disgust. "What a nasty human being."

Thane nodded. "He hired our company to install huge roof air-conditioning units for his factory, and he tried every trick he could think of to argue down the price and say that we didn't install them properly. He even came up on the roof to harass us while we worked."

"Did he win?" Eli asked. "Because he tried the same crap with me. He brought his car into the garage with a scratch down its passenger side and then tried to say that we'd scratched it while we did the repairs. It's a good thing we had it documented before we started work on it."

"We've dealt with his type before, so he didn't get anywhere, but I have to say, he was one of the worst." Thane looked to Olivia to agree with him. Olivia always backed him up.

Eli chuckled. "He rubbed me the wrong way, too."

Thane looked at Jazzi. "Did it go okay for you?"

"Gaff just wanted to interview him about Lynda. He got enough information, but Thomas was so arrogant, I could hardly stand being around him."

"Yeah, the world revolves around him," Eli said.

Grandma finished her pie and smiled. "It's a good thing he wasn't the father of Lynda's baby."

They all turned to stare at her. Jazzi asked, "Did you know Lynda was pregnant when she left for New York?"

"She had the mask. I can always see the mask." Grandma shrugged. "She shouldn't have run the second time. Ansel would have been a good father."

The second time?

Grandma gave Jazzi a pointed look. "He'd be a good father to your children, too."

Jazzi blushed. Ansel as the father of her babies? A nice fantasy. "I'm not ready for kids yet."

"Then just enjoy trying to make them," Grandma told her. "That boy's good looking."

She felt her blush deepen. Enough. Jazzi looked around the table. "Does anyone need anything else?"

Jerod chuckled and popped another can of beer. Mom reached for a second glass of wine. Olivia and Jazzi joined her. Gunner told everyone how he'd gone to Franke Park summer camp and got to see frogs. "We got to hop like them, then walk like crabs and camels, too. Lots of different kinds of animals." He led them into the backyard to show them his newfound skills.

People started leaving after that. It had been a nice get-together. When everyone was gone, Jazzi finished rinsing dirty plates and loading the dishwasher. When she took out the table's leaves this time, she propped them against the wall. She'd wrap them and take them to Cal's house this week. Then she poured herself another glass of wine and plopped onto the couch. She hadn't been a couch potato for too long, and she had a lot of shows that she'd missed and recorded. Today was catch up for all of them.

Chapter 23

By the time the ceiling tiles were delivered on Monday, the three of them had painted the large kitchen and entertaining area a soft cream color to match the living room. The guys decided to drag the armoire and chest of drawers out of the attic while the paint dried. Jazzi went up with them to carry down one of the mirrors that might work in the caramel-colored bedroom.

Jerod clunked his shin on the armoire on his way down the narrow attic stairs. A curse word followed. He tilted the tall piece a little too much and the door cracked open enough to pinch his finger. The curses escalated.

Jazzi agreed they were a hazard. "They're a pain, or the renter would have sold everything in the attic. He was too lazy to bother with them."

On the third curse, Jazzi frowned at him. "Are you okay? You cussed through most of our painting, too." It's not that it was unusual for her cousin to cuss, but he tended to be in a good humor most of the time. Something was bugging him.

When they reached the bottom of the steps, and it was easier to carry their load, Jerod blurted, "Franny's pregnant again."

Lizzie was a year and a half old; Gunner was four. "Did you want a third baby? This would be a good spacing between kids. They'll be close enough together to be friends."

"Nah, we meant to stop at two rug rats. But Franny takes her pill before bed, and she fell asleep without taking a few. I swear, though, every time I hang my pants on the bedpost, that woman conceives."

Jazzi gave him a look. "Knowing you two, I doubt that's all you do."

Jerod laughed. "Yeah, we're both a bit on the horny side. Can't deny that. Ah, what the heck? We make the best kids around. Why not go for a third one?"

"You don't want to stop at three." Ansel shook his head. "My sister's between my two older brothers and me. Always whining about something. Middle-child syndrome."

Jazzi wasn't buying it. "Either that or she was sick of so much testosterone." Ansel laughed. "There was a lot of pushing and punching, too much smack talking."

"You?" Jazzi couldn't imagine Ansel talking smack. He usually played down how good he was at anything.

"You have to establish your place in the pecking order," Ansel explained. "My sister thought she should have a tiara and be treated like a princess since she was the only girl."

"Doesn't matter. Every kid blames their parents for anything that goes wrong." Jerod wedged the armoire into the bedroom, being careful not to chip the door frame. "The oldest complains that they expected too much from him. The youngest says he was babied. The middle didn't get enough attention. Parents can't win."

"I was the youngest, and I wasn't babied," Ansel argued.

Jerod snorted. "Ask your older brothers what they think about that."

They placed the armoire on the wall Ansel had chosen. He stepped back to survey it and nodded. "It looks good there."

"What about you?" Jerod asked him. "Do you ever want kids?"

"Emily doesn't. Not ever, but I'd like to be a dad someday." Ansel bent to scratch George behind the ears. "I think I'd make a good one."

"Not if you spoil a kid like you do that dog."

Jazzi had never seen anyone dote on a pooch like Ansel did George. Mom sure never paid as much attention to her and Olivia. A good thing. If Mom had jumped to meet their every want or need, they'd be as spoiled as the pug. "I can't imagine how hard it must have been for Lynda to give up her baby and pretend nothing ever happened. I bet she thought about him all the time."

Jerod stared. "That's not the way I see it. I think Lynda's like Emily. She didn't want kids. Not every woman does. Maury's admitted he was the dad. He wanted to marry Lynda and he'd have raised their son. It was Lynda who didn't want him."

"She didn't want to have to marry Maury. And she'd have had to if she kept the baby."

"Maybe. Maybe not. Maybe Maury would have raised Noah by himself. I can tell you this, though, if I found out that I had a baby that I never knew about, I'd be furious."

Ansel nodded agreement. "Lynda shafted Maury. And I'd guess she didn't think twice about Noah after she left New York."

"Do you know what's worse?" Jerod started back up the attic stairs to get the chest of drawers. "If she wanted to keep her secret so that she'd look good when she came back to River Bluffs, that's one thing. But to throw what she did in Maury's face years later was a low blow. She knew he couldn't do anything about it by then. She just wanted to twist the knife and make him suffer."

"I don't get why she told him. Maury was always nice to her." She followed Jerod up. Before the men moved the chest, she'd take out the drawers and carry them down separately.

"What did you tell us?" Ansel trailed behind her. "Maury warned Arnie and Cal off her. Lynda didn't like anyone interfering in her business."

"If you ask me," Jerod said, "Lynda and Thomas Sorrell were perfect for each other."

Jazzi pulled out a top drawer. "That's a little harsh."

Jerod took out the second drawer to put aside. "Think about it. Sorrell would have met his match. Lynda would nail him if he tried to push her around."

Not a very flattering view of Aunt Lynda, but Jazzi had to admit her mom's sister wasn't the martyr type.

When they took out the last drawer, the men carried the heavy chest down the steps and Jazzi went up and down, carrying the drawers. When Ansel placed it where he wanted it, they returned the drawers into their proper slots. Then all three of them stood back to decide what they thought.

Jerod smiled to give his verdict. "Looks good in here."

Ansel grinned, pleased. "The sleigh bed's coming on Thursday. Then we'll know for sure."

But Jazzi could already tell the furniture was going to be perfect for this room.

Ansel carried George downstairs and they circled the cooler. They'd take their lunch break before getting busy on the tin ceiling. It was easy to install, but the area was big enough, it would take the rest of today and most of tomorrow to finish it. Jazzi wanted it in place when the cupboards and appliances arrived on Wednesday. They had to cut the plywood countertops, too, for the stainless steel to wrap around. They'd measured and then measured again to make sure they'd fit.

Jazzi had gone to a little extra bother with their lunches today. She'd brought three bread bowls and scooped them out and made a hoagie-style filling with shredded lettuce and pickled banana peppers to put inside them. She even sprang for Michelob instead of their usual beer.

"Wow, cuz! What made you get all fancy on us?"

Ansel took a chunk of bread to scoop up the meat mix. "How do we get you to do this again?"

"The mood moved me last night," she told them, "but that doesn't happen very often. It'll be back to deli meat sandwiches tomorrow." She'd had a nice, relaxing night last night and had most of the ingredients in her refrigerator. Serendipity blessed them. What could she say?

Jerod reached for more filling. "I've learned to appreciate what I get. My Franny is fun and wonderful and a great mom, but it's safer when I cook the meals."

"I like to cook, too," Ansel said.

Jazzi almost choked on her swallow of beer. "Since when? I've never seen you cook."

"I help you, don't I? Emily doesn't like it when I make a mess in the kitchen."

Jerod looked skeptical. "Even if you're cooking for her? You do all of the cleanup, don't you?"

"She'd rather I ran and brought food home."

Jerod sighed. "I forgot that people without kids can afford to eat out all the time."

"I'd get tired of that." Jazzi finished her lunch and went to throw her paper plate in the trash. "Fast food and restaurant food get old after a while."

"I think so, too," Ansel and Jerod said in unison.

George enjoyed his last nibbles of lunch when Ansel took his last bite. Jazzi decided that what Ansel liked, George liked. When the guys finished eating, they tossed their paper plates and the three of them started work on the ceiling tiles.

They measured and applied the glue for the kitchen area. Pressing the fake tin tiles in place went faster than they expected. Once, Ansel had to climb off his ladder when he caught George finishing the last dregs of the beer he'd left on the floor beside his chair, but Jazzi welcomed the break. Holding her arms above her head for so long got tiresome. She'd feel it tomorrow, and there were more tiles to go.

"That was too much for you," Ansel scolded the dog. "I had enough for a last drink before I left for the day."

The can was empty, and George lowered his head on his paws and closed his eyes, unrepentant.

By five o'clock, they'd finished the ceiling all the way to the island that would help divide the kitchen from the dining area.

"Is Emily home tonight?" Jazzi asked as they cleaned and locked up.

"She has tonight and tomorrow night off. I'm taking her out to eat. Keep your fingers crossed we can call a truce."

"That bad, huh?"

"Emily's relentless when she wants something."

Jazzi had suspected as much. She decided to stop at the Tower Bar on her way home. She was hungry for chicken wings and meant to order their citrus-chipotle grilled version, some of her favorites. The restaurant was a little east of Hillegas Road, not far out of her way home.

When she walked in, Maury was sitting at a table with a group of friends. They'd finished eating and were getting ready to leave, but Maury waved her over and motioned for another beer.

"Hey, how are you doing?" he asked.

"Fine, we're making headway on Cal's house. It's turning out really nice."

Maury's beer came and the waitress took Jazzi's order—wings, fries, and half an order of Greek salad. The Tower's fries and salads were delicious, too. More people came in, and tables started to fill. The noise level amped up. The bar did a great business.

Maury let her take a sip of her wine and relax a little before he asked, "Have you and Gaff made any progress?"

"Not much. We went to see Thomas Sorrell over the weekend."

Maury blinked. "You're a brave woman, but then, Thomas didn't intimidate Lynda either. He never figured that out. He always thought if he wanted something, he'd get it. He could never bully her." He snickered. "He didn't have much luck in River Bluffs, period. Cal and Isabelle side-stepped him, too. Isabelle makes her own decisions. She's quiet, but purposeful."

Purposeful. Jazzi liked that word to describe her.

The waitress came with Jazzi's salad, and the dressing tasted delicious. "Thomas told us he was going to sell his businesses in River Bluffs, that they weren't fun since Cal died."

Maury grimaced. "He loved baiting Cal. Thomas isn't the type to say the best man won. It never occurs to him that he's not the best man."

"Did you do business with him?" Jazzi asked.

"No, I stayed as far away from him as possible. I warned Arnie to do the same thing."

"You two were close growing up, weren't you?"

"Yeah, we hung out together at school. I never got to know your dad very well, since he went to public school and was younger than us."

Jazzi still found it odd that her dad's two older brothers went to Catholic school and he didn't. "Did Arnie listen to you?"

"No, he always thought Lynda would burn through men, and then eventually, she'd see that he was always there for her."

She'd bet Sorrell didn't appreciate that. "Did Arnie have a run-in with Thomas?"

Maury chuckled. "Oh, yeah, but Sorrell didn't count on how free and loose Arnie played. When Sorrell ticked him off, somehow Arnie found out everywhere Sorrell took Lynda and had huge bouquets of flowers delivered to her there. It drove Thomas nuts until he finally called Arnie and made peace. It's the only time I think that ever happened."

Jazzi had to smile. Her uncle was what Dad called a loose cannon. He'd always been fun to be around at family gatherings. He loved to do the unexpected. She could see how Sorrell wouldn't have any idea what to do with him.

Maury grew serious. "I suppose Noah's family had his body sent to New York for a funeral."

Jazzi nodded.

Maury sighed and looked down, avoiding her gaze. When he looked back up, anger blazed in his eyes. "I called Gaff after I met Noah's dad. What a neat guy! I'm so grateful Noah ended up with a father that nice. Gaff said someone bashed in the back of Noah's head. That only happened seven months ago. I want Gaff to find the killer."

"He's trying."

Maury finished his beer. "Well, I'd better get going. I'm ruining your meal. Sorry. If you hear anything, though, will you let me know?"

"Will do." She watched him leave the bar and motioned to the waitress. "I'll take another wine." That was a weenie move, drinking to restore her mood, but tonight, she didn't care.

Chapter 24

On Wednesday, Jazzi woke so excited, she flew through her morning routine to speed to Cal's house. The kitchen cabinets and appliances would come today. She, Jerod, and Ansel had finished the ceiling tiles yesterday, put up beams to rim the room's ceiling, and cut out the plywood base for the stainless-steel counters. The beams gave the room a little more of a European look. Once the cupboards and appliances were in place, the three of them could work on the backsplash, install a hood, and start moving in all of her kitchen utensils and goods.

On Sunday, she could start entertaining here!

Ansel's pickup was already parked in Cal's drive when she got there. When she entered the house, he was in the kitchen, laying cardboard over the floor to protect it when the men entered at the side door. "I have more in the back of my pickup," he told her.

She went to bring in more big sheets to help him.

He made sure to leave enough space from the chalk marks they'd drawn for the layout for each cupboard. She accidentally stepped on the chalk line and smudged it a bit, and he scowled at her. Somebody was a little testy today.

"You okay?" she asked.

"Emily and I had an argument last night."

A rare event. Ansel usually agreed with anything she told him.

"Are you two good?"

"I don't want to move. Neither does George." Hearing his name, the dog's tail wagged, but he didn't manage to sit up or open his eyes.

Jazzi couldn't help but feel the dog's vote was prejudiced, but she felt sorry for Ansel. "When does Emily have to make a decision?"

"Our lease is up August fifteenth. We have to renew it or move, but Emily found a hospital in Berkley she's interested in. If she doesn't snatch up the position, someone else will."

Jazzi remained quiet a second. "So, Emily wants to say yes now."

Ansel nodded.

"What happens if you don't move with her?"

"We're through. She won't even talk about staying in River Bluffs."

"I'm sorry, Ansel. It sounds like a lose-lose situation."

"That's how I feel. If I go, I'll feel bullied into it. If I stay, Emily goes without me."

He sounded so frustrated, Jazzi asked, "Is there someplace else you two could agree on? What if she found a hospital in Wisconsin, close to your family? Would you like that?"

"She says she's tired of winters."

"What about the East Coast? You have friends in Florida, don't you?"

"She doesn't like anything out East, says there's too much humidity."

That narrowed things down quite a bit. "Good luck, whatever you two decide."

He grunted. Thankfully, just then, Jerod walked in. He clapped his hands and rubbed his palms together. "The trucks are here. Let's make ourselves a kitchen."

Jazzi held the door while men carried in kitchen cupboards and appliances. Later in the afternoon, another crew would deliver the stainless-steel counter. Jazzi had considered buying the tops ready-made instead of making the plywood base, but Jerod and Ansel were sure they could make them work, and they were lots cheaper this way.

When the men left, the three of them started putting cupboards in place. They stopped for a quick lunch and worked solid until after three in the afternoon. Then Jerod made the call and the countertops came. Jazzi held her breath, but the guys were right. The plywood and stainless steel were a perfect fit. By five, the kitchen was put together. They still had finishing details to complete, but Jazzi couldn't stop looking at the room.

Robin's-egg-blue Shaker cupboards spanned the entire back wall except for the windows over the sink. More cupboards and a matching pantry lined the outside wall with the kitchen door and the side-by-side refrigerator freezer. The inside wall held the six-burner stove centered between more cupboards. An island stretched in the middle of the room. Jazzi had more work space than she'd ever imagined.

"Lord, it's beautiful."

Jerod laughed at her. "Did you ever doubt it?"

"I always worry everything will come together. I love this."

Her cousin nodded. "Makes me want to change the countertops at my place. I was all about saving money back then. Went with Formica."

"We'd help you," Ansel said.

"Thanks, man." Jerod slapped him on the back.

Ansel studied the large space for dining. "You have enough room for a sitting area on the far end."

Jazzi didn't own enough furniture to fill this house. She sighed with relief, glad she'd gotten a loan that was large enough to include that.

Jerod gave a knowing grin. "You're still coming in under budget, cuz. This place is going to be worth top dollar when we're done, and you got it on a shoestring budget."

"Not exactly shoestring." She shrugged. "But way under price."

When they'd worked on Jerod's house and finished it, he'd gotten a bargain, too. A huge, four-bedroom farmhouse, it felt spacious when he'd moved in. With a third kid on the way, it was filling up fast.

Ansel walked to the back wall and held up a subway tile. "This is going to look great." He glanced at the long, stainless-steel hood for the stove. "You have a nice balance of old and new."

Jerod glanced at his watch. "We got a lot done today. I might show up an hour later than usual tomorrow."

Jazzi smiled. "Why not? You and Franny can have a little extra cuddle time."

"With a one-and-a-half-year old? You've got to be kidding."

Ansel went to get George. "Emily's home. She's hungry for Italian tonight."

"I'm stopping to see Mom." On Sunday, everyone kept the meal as carefree as possible, but Jazzi suspected Mom was still struggling. She took one backward glance at the room, then grabbed her purse and followed them out, locking up as she left.

On the drive to her mom's house, she tried to shift gears from being happy about her house to thinking about Lynda and Noah. She wasn't sure if Detective Gaff had kept Mom up to date or not. It felt like plenty had happened lately, but Gaff still didn't have answers for Mom, and that's what she wanted.

Chapter 25

Jazzi found Mom and Dad sitting on the back patio, watching Ebby and Lady run to the back fence to bark at a marauding rabbit. A tall maple in the center of the yard provided shade, and Dad kept the grass at a respectable length, but other than that, there was no landscaping. Mom would never be accused of being Little Miss Homemaker. When Olivia had moved out of the house and empty-nest syndrome moved in, Mom had bought the two dogs. Now, Mom looked up, saw Jazzi, and waved for her to join them at the umbrella table.

"What's up, kiddo?" Dad asked. He wore gym shorts, a T-shirt, and flip-flops. His brown hair was beginning to thin, but he didn't comb it over or try to hide the bald spot growing at the top of his head. A small paunch stretched the shorts' elastic waist, but that didn't deter him from enjoying the rum and Coke in his hand.

The patio was on the west side of the house, so the sun didn't blast down on them. The temperature hovered in the high seventies, but in the shade, sitting and sipping, her parents felt comfortable. Jazzi sat across from them. "I came to tell you that the kitchen's done at Cal's place, and I'm going to have our next Sunday meal there."

Mom's face lit up. "I love that house. I'm so glad you've bought it and are taking good care of it."

Jazzi released an inward sigh of relief. That's how she felt about the house, too. She'd worried that Mom would be bombarded by bad memories when she thought of it, but there was something about Cal and his home that created warm, fuzzy feelings.

"When do you move in?" Dad asked.

"Soon. Jerod and Ansel will help me move my furniture. Reuben bought the old Victorian in West Central, and he's going to make it into a single-family home again."

Mom looked even more excited. "Good! *Two* homes will be loved and restored."

Jazzi leaned back in her chair and stretched her legs. "I want to make something special for our Sunday meal, something to celebrate our first get-together there."

"Like party food?" Mom loved party food. Jazzi usually didn't have the patience to make small bites, but if it would make Mom happy, why not?

Mom didn't stop there. "We need something wonderful for dessert, too."

Jeez, she was pushing it. "Cakes? Pies?"

"Cupcakes and tiny tortes. Irresistible."

Jazzi hadn't been thinking about going all out, but she'd obviously thought wrong. "I guess I could do that."

Mom immediately looked contrite. "I didn't mean to push you. Everything you make is good. It's your party."

It was a party now. Doggone. "I'll think of something."

Dad chuckled. "Are we going to drink champagne?"

"Is that safe? I remember your telling me about Grandma and champagne." Jazzi immediately regretted the comment. The last time Granny drank the bubbly that she knew of was at Lynda and Cal's engagement party. Grandma loved the stuff so much, she ended up twirling in circles to background music until she collapsed on Grandpa's lap.

Mom threw back her head and laughed. "Boy, that was a sight! I'll never forget it. Mom looked so happy. We'll bring a few bottles."

Jazzi felt pleased. Maybe Cal's house could provide lots of happy memories for her family.

Tired of chasing the rabbit, Ebbie and Lady came to flop down next to Mom's chair. She leaned to pat each of them, and then her expression grew serious. "Have you heard anything more about Noah?"

Jazzi brought Mom up to speed. "Sorrell was in town when both Lynda and Noah died."

Mom shook her head. "Thomas is a coward and a bully. He loves to push other people around, enjoys it when he hurts them, but when he gets any serious resistance, he's a wimp. The man can give it, but he can't take it."

"Did he love Lynda?"

"He thought he did. I wouldn't call it love. He wanted to own her, but that's not love."

"You don't think he'd lose his temper and kill someone."

Mom frowned, thinking about that. "I suppose anyone can be pushed too far, but when Thomas felt threatened, he usually gave some kind of scathing comment, tucked his tail, and ran home."

Dad nodded. "Most bullies are like that. They pick on people they think can't fight back."

A car pulled into the driveway with waiter on the way printed on its side. Dad went to pay the delivery man. "Want to stay for supper?"

Jazzi knew her parents ordered only enough for the two of them. If she stayed, someone wouldn't get enough to eat. She smiled and stood. "No, I only stopped to tell you to come to Cal's house for Sunday meal. If you spread the word, that would be great."

"We'll bring champagne," Mom promised

Jazzi didn't tarry. She went out the front gate to reach her pickup. On the way home, she turned on the radio and listened to music. Mom had looked better than she'd expected. After listening to her parents, though, she'd almost discounted Sorrell as Lynda or Noah's killer. Who would kill Noah? And why?

The home phone was ringing when she walked into her apartment. The same woman's voice she'd heard before stated, "I warned you once. Do what you do best and flip houses. Stay out of other people's business."

Her temper flared. "If you know something about Lynda or Noah's deaths, you should share your information with Detective Gaff. If you choose not to, shut up and quit calling my number."

"Two people died in Cal's house. You could be next." And then the phone went dead.

That was freaking enough! Jazzi called Gaff and explained what had happened.

"I'll be right there," he said.

True to his word, he pulled in front of her apartment half an hour later. He called someone, gave them the information he had, and then listened to the message again. In ten minutes, that someone called his cell. After a brief conversation, he flipped his phone shut and looked at Jazzi. "The calls came from a phone at the Country Club. Members use it occasionally."

She frowned. "Do you know, does Beth belong to it?"

"Yes. So does Isabelle. She and Cal often met business associates there."

He'd already checked into it. That didn't surprise her. A shiver made Jazzi rub her arms to warm them. "Would Isabelle threaten me?"

Gaff turned serious. "I didn't think so, but I'm going to take a closer look at her now. You might want to start being a little careful."

"I haven't done anything. I've mostly stumbled onto things accidentally."

Gaff looked worried. "It doesn't matter. You've helped advance the case, on purpose or not. You're the middle person who's sort of glued information together."

Jazzi took a deep breath. "Should I buy a security system? I'm going to move soon."

Gaff nodded. "I would, and I'd make sure you can move it to your new address when you go there. It never hurts to have extra protection."

She'd never worried about being safe before.

"Do you have someone you can stay with?" Gaff asked.

She did, but if she called Mom and Dad, they'd worry about her. So would everyone else in her family. "I'm going to stay at a hotel tonight."

He nodded. "Not a bad idea. I'll start digging harder."

He was already doing everything he could. She didn't blame Gaff. But she didn't want to stay here alone tonight. She packed a bag, locked her door, and walked out with him.

She found a room downtown and spent the night there. It felt odd, when her house was such a short distance away, but no one would look for her here. In the morning, she'd call about getting her apartment secured and she'd buy a baseball bat to keep under her bed.

Chapter 26

Jazzi told Jerod and Ansel about the phone calls, and Jerod snapped, "That's it. You're sleeping at our house until this is over."

"No need to. I'm having a security system put in today. For a little extra money, they'll move it here when I make this my home."

"I'm sleeping on your couch," Ansel said. "George is a great watchdog."

Yeah, right. "Emily doesn't work tonight, does she?"

"No." She could watch Ansel struggle with his choices.

"You and Emily have enough problems right now. I'm not adding to them. I'm sleeping in my apartment, and the system will go off if anyone tries anything. Reuben's upstairs, and I can call him. I'll be all right."

Jerod stared at her. "You're counting on Reuben? What if Isabelle's the one making the phone calls?"

"He still won't let her send goons to beat me up. Plus, the system's really loud. It makes a lot of noise when someone sets it off. My neighbors are close. No one's going to risk that."

Jerod settled down a little. "That makes me feel better. If an alarm went off in your neighborhood, and I was the thug trying to break into your place, I'd take off."

Ansel relaxed, too. "I'll be happy when you move in here, though."

Jazzi didn't disagree with him openly, but she felt more secure surrounded by people. How long would it take the police to check on her out here? The neighbors were far enough away, would they even wake up if an alarm went off in the middle of the night?

She shook her head. "I don't want to think about it anymore. Let's get to work."

The problem was, she couldn't *stop* thinking about it. Was Isabelle capable of killing someone . . . or hiring someone to do it? She'd never considered that before. Isabelle was rich. She could pay someone to do her dirty work. Only one way to find out. Jazzi called Olivia and asked her about meeting at Cal's house for their Thursday night out. "The kitchen's in, and it looks better than I imagined. I was thinking about inviting Reuben and Isabelle, too, if they can make it."

"If it works for them, let's do it. I can't wait to see the place," Olivia said.

Jazzi called Reuben next, who called Isabelle, and it was a go.

"We'll bring supper," Isabelle insisted. "You're doing us a favor. We're dying to see the house."

With three people saying yes, Jazzi was determined to move her dining room table and chairs into Cal's. Her original idea had been to show Olivia, Reuben, and Isabelle the work they'd done on the house and then go to a restaurant. But they were bringing food. They'd be staying to eat and visit. They could sit around the island to eat, but why not do it right? She'd need the dining table on Sunday anyway. Why not bring it now?

"Can we switch plans and bring my table and chairs here today?" she asked Jerod and Ansel.

They agreed to help her. "If we're going to move the table and chairs, though, why not move it all?" Jerod asked.

"A complete move?" Was she ready for that? She'd packed everything in her kitchen to take to Cal's place. She'd even packed most of her clothes, but she'd meant to take them over a little at a time.

"Why not take your sofa and chairs, too?" Jerod asked. "It's not like you have that much furniture. Your apartment's small, and we have all day. There's no better time. Call the security people and see if they've started yet. If they haven't, just have them come here."

She called and she'd been scheduled for the afternoon. The installers were relieved they had to set things up only once. By five o'clock, Cal's house would be secure.

Jerod glanced out the window at their three pickups. "I bet we can get everything in two trips, but don't spread the word you're going to stay here. Let people think you're going back to your apartment to sleep."

"I already invited Reuben and Isabelle for supper, remember?"

"Right." He didn't look happy about that. "What's done is done, but don't tell anyone else."

So that's what they did. They each drove to her apartment, and by lunchtime, they'd completely emptied it. Not a huge chore. She didn't have much. Reuben would be happy to hear that he could start work on the first floor, but she wouldn't tell him just yet.

Jerod was right. It took two trips, and everything she owned was at Cal's. He ran a hand through his brown hair. "Let's carry everything in, put it in the right rooms, then call it a day. I'll get home early enough to help Franny with a big buffet she's refinishing for a client. It's going to be time consuming."

George followed Ansel back and forth between the pickups and the house until everything was carted to its proper place, and then he stretched out on the floor in the kitchen, completely drained of energy. Jazzi's back ached and she raised her arms to stretch and bend to loosen it up. Ansel grinned, appreciating the show. Jerod gave everything a critical look, then nodded.

"Yup, you're good. You can take it from here. I'm off to my Franny."

After he left, Ansel and Jazzi went to look at her cherry-red leather sofa and chairs arranged near the living room fireplace. She'd bought them when she moved out of Chad's place, so they were only a year old. They had the right look for the room.

"They make a cozy sitting area." Ansel shook his head and turned to the front half of the room. "But you have a lot of empty space."

"Yeah, I noticed."

Her farmhouse dining table and chairs looked great near the kitchen island, but they didn't begin to fill the room either. She could circle four lounge chairs around a coffee table by the front window.

Ansel went to get George. "Good, we still have time to go furniture shopping."

"Today?"

"Why not?" Ansel glanced down at himself. "My jeans don't have holes in them and I'm not covered with sawdust. If you find something, I can help you bring it here."

He had a point, and she did need more furniture. "Why not?"

George huffed when she got to ride shotgun instead of him, but then he curled on the floor and rested his head on her feet. They left the windows down when they reached the first furniture store.

"Is that smart?" Jazzi asked. "Anyone can climb into your truck."

"With George here? He'll stand guard. I can't leave the windows up. It will get too hot in here for him."

Ansel had more faith in George protecting his truck than Jazzi did, but George seemed fine with the idea. He stretched out on the backseat, and Ansel poured bottled water into a bowl for him. They had to visit a few stores before Jazzi and Ansel could agree on a yellow leather sofa and two chairs that would work with what she had.

"How do we get the two sitting areas to blend?" she asked.

"Easy, we find a rug with lots of yellow in it to center the red furniture grouping and a rug with reds for the yellow sofa and chairs."

Jazzi stared. "You're better at picturing all this stuff than I am."

He grinned. "I've been looking at lots of decorating magazines. I really wanted to buy a house before Emily dropped her bombshell."

"What have you got in mind for the front window in the dining room?"

"Four chairs around a round coffee table. That's as far as I got."

The minute they saw four club-style recliners, in a blue-and-yellow flower print, though, they both wanted them.

In between the three trips it took to move everything Jazzi bought, her sleigh bed was delivered and Ansel oversaw exactly where it should be put. Jazzi let him. The furniture in that bedroom was his vision, so she left him to it. As long as the room was rose colored, she was happy. By five, every piece of furniture was in place, and the security system was installed. Jazzi was exhausted. All she'd wanted to do was move her farmhouse table here. Things had gotten out of hand.

Yes, it was her house, but Ansel had been determined to get it right. Happy with the finished product, he grabbed George. He hesitated. "You sure you're going to be okay here tonight? I know you have the security system, but I was thinking. There aren't any houses close to you now."

She'd worried about that, too. "The guy who installed the alarms said someone would be here in ten minutes if one of them went off."

Ansel frowned. "Ten minutes is a long time."

"I had them install a deadbolt on the inside of my bedroom door. I'm locking it tonight. If an alarm goes off, I'll move furniture in front of it and barricade myself in." That sounded pitiful, but she'd rather be safe than sorry.

"You're sure?"

"Get out of here," she told him. "I have company coming and I have to get ready."

He left to meet Emily, and then Jazzi went upstairs to take a quick shower.

It felt odd, not returning to her apartment. Her old bed and chest of drawers were in the caramel-colored bedroom, but she'd already hung her clothes in the rose room. Everything was so new, so different. Would she feel lost in a king-size bed?

Clean and dressed, she hurried down to the kitchen and unpacked the box that held the blue-sprigged plates she'd bought two years ago and still loved. She set the table with those and four drinking glasses. She had wine glasses somewhere, but she had no idea which box to look in.

She'd found the silverware and placed them on the table when the front doorbell rang and she went to welcome Olivia, Reuben, and Isabelle. She'd keep a close eye on Isabelle tonight to study her reactions. She couldn't be *that* good of an actress.

Isabelle stepped into the foyer, held a hand to her heart, and let out a deep sigh. "It's beautiful."

Isabelle looked happy for her. Could she smile at her and celebrate, and then hire someone to hurt her?

"Jeez, sis, I'm jealous." Olivia glanced into the living room, then headed to the island in the kitchen.

Reuben carried in two bags of food that wafted the aroma of Chinese. He put them on the island's stainless-steel counter, then turned to study what Jazzi had done. "Perfection." He pointed to the fake tin ceiling and beams. "A blend of old and functional. I love it."

Jazzi smiled. "Coming from you, that's a high compliment."

"I know." He started to the living room. "I want to see it all, every room. We'll do the grand tour first, and then we'll feed you."

Fair enough. She led them into the long, spacious living room.

Standing next to Isabelle and Olivia, she felt downright tawdry. She'd taken a shower, but she should have dressed up. Olivia had come from the salon and wore tight black leggings with a zebra-print tunic over them. Isabelle wore wide-bottomed black slacks with a red kimono-style top. Her black hair was twisted high on her head. Her eyes were black rimmed and her lips red.

Reuben approved the red and butter-yellow leather sofas and chairs. "A nice blend. Good. There's nothing on the walls yet. No small touches. Those can add a lot of character. Take your time with those. Don't rush."

Olivia walked over to plop onto the yellow sofa. "Comfortable. It was smart using area rugs to blend everything."

"That was Ansel's idea. He went with me to pick out furniture."

Her sister raised an eyebrow. "He did?"

"He had a lot of ideas about this house." Jazzi led them upstairs.

Reuben and Isabelle both loved the rose bedroom.

"I want a sleigh bed like this." Isabelle ran her hand over the thin stitched quilt that was heavy and warm. "I like the ribbon work on this, too."

Jazzi smiled, pleased. "Ansel wanted a sleigh bed. I really like it."

Olivia grinned. "Did he want a king-size bed, too?"

"Come look at this!" Reuben saved Jazzi by calling from the bathroom. "It's just plain stunning." He nodded toward the long antique chest of drawers holding the two sinks.

Isabelle sighed when she saw the claw bathtub. "I'm glad you kept that." Her voice hinted at something, and Jazzi wondered if Isabelle had soaked in that tub on occasion.

When Jazzi showed them the two other rooms, all three of them approved. Olivia especially loved the amethyst room, even though it was empty. "I love the color."

"Ansel picked it out. He chose the caramel paint for the other bedroom, too."

"And you let him?"

Jazzi shrugged. "I liked everything he came up with, and it made him so happy . . . why not?"

Olivia's eyebrows lifted. "I didn't think Ansel paid any attention to colors and design."

"He does on the fixer-uppers, but his vote doesn't count with Emily. He had really strong opinions about this house. He wanted to bid on it, but Emily vetoed him."

"But you didn't." Olivia gave a sly smirk.

"What?" Her sister was being obvious. Jazzi had better be careful what she said from now on.

"You like him."

Jazzi rolled her eyes. "Of course I like him. I work with him every day."

Olivia's smirk widened. "Thane would give Emily her marching orders."

"Your Thane?" Jazzi started leading everyone back downstairs. "He's almost as easygoing as Ansel."

On their way to the kitchen, Reuben stopped to look at the half-bath near the base of the stairs. "Nice." They'd kept it old-fashioned with a pedestal sink, beadboard on the walls, and vintage black-and-white Victorian floor tiles.

Jazzi smiled. "Thanks."

Olivia returned to Ansel and Thane. "Thane's quiet, but he's not exactly easygoing. He can dig in."

"Cal was easygoing. That's what I liked about him." Isabelle opened the bags on the counter and lifted out carton after carton of Chinese food. "We weren't sure what you liked, so we bought a variety."

"Am I easygoing?" Reuben asked.

"Darling, you're adorable."

Reuben looked like he might float for the rest of the night.

Olivia started flipping open lids. Lo mein. Sesame chicken. Mongolian beef and more. Eight egg rolls and crab Rangoon.

Saliva flooded Jazzi's mouth. After a hurried lunch, she was starving. They sat around the farmer's table and Isabelle sighed. "The last time I saw this house, it was in shambles. Disgusting. Cal would be so happy with this."

"Thank you."

Isabelle lifted her chopsticks. Her expression grew serious, ready to move to a different topic. "Have you had any more news about Gaff's investigation?"

Jazzi decided to ease into her news to see how Isabelle reacted to it. She grabbed a fork. She was all thumbs with chopsticks. She could never get the food to her mouth. She told them about Sorrell. "He seemed like a possible suspect."

Isabelle shook her head. "Thomas would never meet with Noah alone. He'd only bother with him if Cal was within seeing distance. He had no interest in the boy other than annoying Cal."

"He has ego issues, doesn't he?" Jazzi asked.

Isabelle gave a low laugh. "Thomas's ego overshadows everything else—even his intelligence. I'd feel sorry for him if he wasn't so unlikeable."

"So, you don't think he could kill someone?" Jazzi asked.

Isabelle pursed her lips, considering. "I didn't say that, but it wouldn't be premeditated. He'd lose his temper and do something rash, then panic. That wouldn't be the case twice in this house, would it? It might have been with Lynda, but luring Noah into the basement while Cal was called away on an emergency and hitting him in the back of the head? That smacks of someone planning it all out."

Jazzi took a second helping of lo mein. "Gaff thinks both cases are connected."

Isabelle nodded. "It seems likely. They were both committed here and they both involve Cal somehow. But they feel different, don't they?"

"Someone's trying to warn me off, so that I don't help Gaff." Jazzi explained about the phone calls. She was curious how Isabelle would respond.

Olivia blurted out, "You're staying with Thane and me for a while."

"I took care of it. I bought a security system," Jazzi told her.

Isabelle's hands went to her hips. "Gaff should have someone watching over your house. If he's going to drag you around with him, he should protect you!"

Jazzi smiled. The caller couldn't be Isabelle, not unless she was a wonderful actress. She looked outraged right now. She tried to reassure them. "I think I'm a pretty low risk, and I'm not just sitting here hoping nothing happens. I'm going to be fine."

"Did you buy a gun?" Reuben glanced out the front window at the dark yard. "There are no streetlights out here. You don't have to aim if you have a shotgun."

Jazzi stared. "I didn't even think about one. I'd probably hurt myself with it."

Before Reuben could argue with her, Olivia waved away his argument. She reached for another egg roll and more sweet-and-sour sauce. "I don't want to talk about murders anymore tonight and not on Sunday either. Jazzi's smart. She's protected herself. I want to celebrate her new house."

Jazzi looked at her, surprised.

Olivia mumbled, "And your security people had better be darned good."

Isabelle nodded reluctantly. "Tonight's supposed to be fun. I don't want to ruin it. Your house is beautiful, Jazzi."

"To Jazzi!" Reuben raised his glass of wine, and they all toasted.

Olivia was right. Tonight was about filling Cal's house with new joy. The rest of the supper was low key and filled with laughter. Reuben was still in decorator mode.

"If you're sure you're completely finished with the Victorian, Isabelle and I can move all of my furniture downstairs this weekend, and we're hiring people to gut the upstairs kitchen of our house. We're going to make the second floor into two huge bedrooms and a luxury bathroom."

Isabelle took another sip of wine. Jazzi had never seen her so relaxed. "We're having someone paint all of the downstairs rooms, and we're making your old bedroom into a study. If either of us wants to work from home, we'll have a place to do it."

Olivia sighed. "You guys are making me want a house. Thane has been yammering about it, but I didn't think we were ready."

"A house is a lot of responsibility," Jazzi said. "If anything goes wrong, you have to fix it, not call your landlord."

Olivia laughed. "Thane's handy, and so is my sister."

"Oh, so that's how it is!" Jazzi knew she'd just been signed up for free labor.

They finished the night talking about old houses versus new. When Reuben and Isabelle said their good nights, Olivia rose, too. "It's later than I thought. I'm taking off, too. Tomorrow's busy at the salon. I'll see you on Sunday, sis."

Jazzi walked to the door and waved them off. She shut it and locked it, then set the alarm. It took her a few minutes to clean the kitchen. She couldn't stop a happy zing when she used the big, deep farm sink after the first time she'd entertained. It even made her happy to put the few pieces of silverware into her dishwasher. Then she wandered to the living room and sat down. Darn, this place was big. She turned on the TV, but felt like a lone viewer in an empty movie theater. When her cell phone rang, she was grateful.

Ansel's voice sounded hesitant, but gruff. "Jazzi? I know it's late, but can I come and spend the night at your house? Emily and I had a big argument, and she kicked me out. I've gone to two motels, but they won't let me keep George in my room."

"Why would you try a motel? I have plenty of space, and I'm rambling around in it, a little bit lost. You can use the caramel room." Besides, she'd been trying to tell herself she wasn't afraid. With Ansel here, she wouldn't be.

"Thanks." He couldn't hide his relief. "I'll stay out of your way and try not to bother you."

"Forget that," she said. "This house is sort of overwhelming and lonely. I'm glad I'll have company, but I get to choose what we watch on TV."

His laugh sounded harsh. "I'll be there in twenty minutes."

"I have leftover Chinese if you're hungry."

"You're a true friend." He hung up and Jazzi leaned deeper into the couch cushions. Emily had kicked him out? That woman needed her head examined.

Chapter 27

Jazzi woke before the alarm went off. She thought she'd have trouble sleeping last night. Cal's house was big. It was far enough out of town, there were no streetlights. Houses sat so far apart, neighbors wouldn't notice if someone broke in during the night. When she looked outside her bedroom window, blackness blanketed the yard and surrounding fields. Not like West Central with neighbors on both sides of her and across the street and a streetlamp located on the corner of the yard near the curb. And it was quiet out here, too quiet, but with Ansel and George in the room next door, she felt safe and secure. When she hit the mattress, that's the last thing she remembered.

She woke refreshed, got dressed in her scruffiest shirt and jeans, and pulled her hair into a ponytail. They were finishing the upstairs hallway today, then painting the basement. She couldn't paint without splattering herself. After today, she'd keep the clothes she had on in the laundry room as paint clothes, because she'd never get them clean again. Next, she made her bed. It was too beautiful to leave mussed. Plus, Ansel was a bit of a neat freak. His bed would probably be made with square corners.

When she opened the bedroom door to head downstairs, Ansel stepped out of the hallway bathroom with a towel wrapped around his waist. *Be still my heart.* His blond hair was damp, and water drops clung to his corded muscles. Her breath caught in her throat. Her heart thudded. Oh, boy, how could Emily deprive herself of this? It would be like going off crack.

Ansel didn't notice her and padded to the caramel bedroom and closed the door. Jazzi grabbed the door frame to brace herself. How many times could she see that and not throw herself on him? What would he do?

Knowing Ansel, he'd hold her at arm's length and tsk-tsk her. The man didn't have a clue how gorgeous he was!

Jazzi swallowed hard. She was a strong woman. She could resist temptation and work side-by-side with Ansel as a friend. Couldn't she? Yes, she had some shreds of restraint, unless Emily made him spend too many nights here. Then all bets were off. She might drug him and crawl into his bed to have her way with him.

She forced her feet to move and zipped down to the kitchen. She'd set the coffeepot to brew last night, so she was pouring two mugs when Ansel carried George into the kitchen. She silently handed one to him.

"Thanks." He took a long draw. "I had trouble going to sleep last night."

She felt guilty. Having him here had helped her, but he'd probably stayed awake thinking about how to work things out with Emily. "I'm sorry. Do you want some toast? I usually make myself two slices." Her toaster had four slots.

"Mind if I make myself an egg sandwich instead?"

"Go for it."

He hesitated. "I shouldn't be the first person to use your stove. You should have that honor."

She snorted. "Is that a sneaky way to get me to fry your eggs?"

His blue eyes went wide. "No, I'm used to cooking for myself."

"Then do it. Break the stove in for me."

He hesitated again. "I usually make an egg for George, too. Is that all right? I'll buy some tonight. Do you want one?"

She waved away his concerns. "I'm going to Grandma's tonight. She usually gives me eggs from her hens, but if not, I go to the store on Saturday. I'll buy more."

Ansel went to the refrigerator and returned to break eggs into a nonstick skillet. "I hope Emily's calmed down by now. I don't want to move. She thinks I should go just because she wants to, but I don't want to impose on you too long."

If she could see him in a towel every morning, Emily could eat dirt. "Stay as long as you want. It'll help me get used to the house."

Just then Jerod stuck his head inside the front door. "Ansel beat me here? I thought I'd be early."

"He's making eggs. Want some?" Jazzi asked.

"You got toast?"

"I can make some."

Jerod came to join them in the kitchen. "Hey, I didn't think about the perks of having you move into the house. I could get used to this."

"It will only last until we start on our next fixer-upper. You'd better enjoy it while you can."

While they ate, Jerod asked, "What did you decide about the upstairs hallway? And what about the basement?"

"I'm painting the hallway the same cream as the downstairs. I plan to stain the basement floors, but I can do that myself after we get the walls painted. I'm painting those cornmeal yellow to cheer up the space."

Jerod nodded. "Ansel and I will leave you to the hallway, and we'll get started on the cement blocks in the basement. Those should go pretty fast."

"We're about done." Jazzi rinsed their plates and put them in the dishwasher.

Jerod shook his head. "We always do landscaping for curb appeal. Just because you bought this place doesn't mean you have to tackle that alone. You helped me at my house, so start thinking about what you want."

She might never disown him as a cousin. She nodded and Jerod raised his eyebrows at Ansel. "Come on, bud. You can tell me why you got here so early while we work." They headed for the basement steps.

Jazzi went upstairs and set up her long-handled roller and got busy. It took her till noon, she had to tape so much trim before she could actually paint. But by the time she dragged everything downstairs and out to the hose to clean, the main floors of the house were done.

She called down to the guys, "I'm making sandwiches if you're hungry."

A formality. Jerod and Ansel were *always* ready to eat. Since she'd brought everything to the new refrigerator, she added lettuce and sliced tomatoes to their deli meat and served it on long toasted slices of French bread.

"We're going to get spoiled," Jerod proclaimed. "My kids would love this for supper."

After lunch, Ansel went outside to call Emily. Jerod gave a low whistle and turned to Jazzi. "Can you believe the little nurse kicked him out?"

"It's a smart move," Jazzi said. "He'll miss her and won't want to lose her. It might tip him into thinking California looks good."

"Or it might make him wake up and realize she's a pain in the rear end."

"They have to decide on something. They're running out of time." Jazzi looked up when Ansel stomped back inside.

Frowning, he said, "She never picked up."

When Emily dug her heels in, she could be one stubborn woman. How far would she go to get her way? Jazzi started down the basement stairs. "Does she work tonight?"

"No." Ansel and Jerod followed her.

"Try her again before supper. She doesn't cook. Maybe she'll miss you by then."

They finished only two walls by five. The basement was huge, and the cement blocks soaked up paint, so that it took several strokes to cover them. Before Jerod left, he said, "We should start thinking about the next place we want to buy and flip. I've been looking at new listings, but none of them have gotten me excited. If you see something, let me know."

"I've been looking, too. Nothing. I'm going to pick up one of the for-sale-by-owner real estate magazines at the store on Saturday."

"Good idea. If you drive by a house with a sign, give it a look." He helped them carry everything outside to clean.

"We'll finish up," Jazzi told him. "No big deal."

Ansel and Jazzi cleaned at the hose after Jerod left. Then Ansel tried calling Emily again. She picked up this time, and Jazzi walked away to give him some privacy. When she glanced back at him, though, his face looked like a thundercloud. She assumed it wasn't going well.

When he came in the kitchen to have a beer with her, he said, "Emily told me not to come home until I'm ready to move with her."

"What are you going to do?"

"Let her pack everything herself and see how much fun it is. I'm not going."

Jazzi stared. "You'd stay here and lose her?"

"If it comes to that."

Jazzi wasn't sure he could hold to that, but in case, she said, "You can stay here as long as you want to."

"Do you mean that?" Ansel drained his beer. "If Emily leaves without me, would you want a roommate? I'd pay rent, pitch in on groceries."

That caught her off guard, but when she thought about it, she liked the idea. "Sure, there's plenty of room. Then, when you meet someone else, you won't have a lease to worry about."

His blue eyes sparkled. "What if you meet someone before I do?"

"I'm not looking right now. Maybe later."

"But that's when it always happens."

She laughed. "I'm not holding my breath."

He took her empty beer bottle and threw it in the recycling can with his. "You know, when I first started working with you, I really wanted to make a move on you, but you were with Chad."

She looked at him, surprised. "You never showed any interest."

"How tacky would that be? You were living with a guy."

"I messed up that choice. We didn't have much in common."

"It takes a while to get to know somebody. I didn't do so great either. Emily was quiet. I thought she was shy. Boy, was I wrong."

Jazzi glanced at the clock. "I promised Grandma I'd come over tonight so she can teach me how to make strudel. Want to come along?"

"Strudel?" He licked his lips. "I'm in. George loves pastry. Are we grabbing supper on the way?"

"There's a barbecue guy who parks his rig in a church parking lot on the way. I told her I'd bring the works."

Ansel grinned. "Even better. When do we leave?"

"In twenty minutes."

"I'll be ready."

They both rushed to wash up and change. Ansel was happy letting her drive while George lay on the floor, his head on Ansel's feet. They pulled into the church parking lot and waited their turn to order. Jazzi got ribs, chicken coleslaw, and baked beans. Ansel added cornbread and smoked potatoes.

Grandma was waiting for them on her front porch. She beamed when she saw Ansel and George. "It's about time you came to visit me. A growing boy like you needs good suppers. You need to bring him more often, Jazzi."

Jazzi. Since she came with a man, would Grandma quit confusing her with Sarah? "He wants to learn to make strudel, too," Jazzi said.

"Good for him! But first, let's eat."

Samantha, her housemate, joined them for supper. Ansel had never met her. She never came to Sunday meals. "I live with Dorothy," she explained. "After my husband passed away, it was too hard for me to take care of our farm. I saw the ad in the paper that Dot needed a roommate, and I applied."

"The best thing that happened to our family," Jazzi added.

Samantha blushed. "I have more eggs for you to take home, Jazzi. The hens having been laying better than usual."

"You have chickens?" Ansel glanced out the kitchen windows to the coop with a fenced-in yard. "My parents raised chickens on our farm."

The two started talking about which breeds were best for what, and Jazzi's mind drifted. Ansel had finished off a slab of ribs, and Grandma liked the smoked chicken, but her appetite shrank every year. Jazzi always left Grandma all of the leftovers. When they finished eating, Samantha and Ansel—along with George—wandered off to look at the chickens and a spot in the coop's roof that worried Samantha.

Jazzi started cleaning up the kitchen so that she and Grandma could cook, and Grandma gave Jazzi a look. "He's a nice man, Lynda. You should stay in River Bluffs and raise his baby."

Jazzi sighed. That was a new one. She'd never been called Lynda before, but when she thought about it, she and Lynda both had wavy, blond hair and Lynda always had a man with her. "I'm not ready for kids yet, Grandma. I'm having too much fun right now."

Grandma frowned. "You've already had plenty of fun. You were too young when you gave away the first baby, but you'd better keep this one. Soon, you won't be able to have any, and Cal's older than you. You don't want him using a cane to chase toddlers around."

Jazzi stared. "Did you try to talk Lynda out of leaving River Bluffs for New York?"

Grandma twisted and untwisted her fingers, agitated. "You never did listen to me. And look what happened. Jerod ended up burying your grown son."

Jerod's reputation was suffering more than hers lately. Grandma must have remembered that Jerod was using the backhoe when he found Noah. But Jazzi hated to see Grandma so upset. She went to her and hugged her. "I'm Jazzi, Grandma, and I came to make strudel with you, remember?"

Grandma blinked. She focused on Jazzi's face. "Oh, honey, I put all of the ingredients on the sink counter for us to use. Once you watch me, you'll be able to make it yourself."

Ansel came in then with Samantha. Grandma smiled. "Jazzi brought her Viking with her. He wants to learn to bake. Can you imagine?"

Once Grandma started mixing ingredients and working with dough, the familiarity kept her in the moment. By the time Jazzi and Ansel left, Grandma waved them off and called, "Come again, Jazzi! And bring your young man with you."

Time must circle and twist in Grandma's mind. Jazzi never knew which period of history she lived in moment to moment.

Jazzi decided to talk to Mom this weekend about taking Grandma to a doctor and seeing if there was anything else they could do to keep her dementia at bay. Gran was one special lady, and Jazzi didn't want to lose her any sooner than she had to.

When they got back to the house, Jazzi set the alarm before they both wandered into the living room. Bookcases flanked both sides of the fireplace, and Jazzi decided to put all of her cookbooks on the top right shelf. She wanted to go through a few of them for ideas. Mom wanted a party on Sunday, and Jazzi had only vague ideas for a few things to make.

"Mind if I watch TV while you look?" Ansel asked.

Typical male. The Discovery Channel showed some expedition into the jungles of South America while Jazzi flipped through recipes. Her family could plow through a lot of food. She decided on stuffed mushrooms, a crispy potato skin bar with a variety of toppings to choose from, cheddar-ham cups, and chicken wings. She'd serve plenty of roasted shrimp cocktail, too, and a veggie tray. For dessert, she'd make strawberry shortcake cupcakes and fruit pizzas.

When she read her menu to Ansel, he got excited. "I'll help you get everything ready. I like it all."

She made out her grocery list and then settled in to watch a little more TV with him. Then they both headed upstairs to their separate beds.

Chapter 28

Buying a week's worth of groceries with Ansel proved interesting. She listened to kids begging their moms to add things to their cart and suddenly sympathized with them.

When he stopped in front of the ice cream freezer, gazing in wonder, she asked, "Who does the shopping for you two, you or Emily?"

"I do, but I'm only allowed to buy the items on her list. I don't even let myself look at what else is on the shelves."

Allowed? For heaven's sake! "Even if you pay for your own treats?"

"Emily says if they're in the house, they tempt her."

Okay, she had a point. "I always buy ice cream, so grab your favorite."

It took an hour and a half to make it through the store. Jazzi thought she might never see sunlight again. The groceries filled the backseat of her pickup. When they got home, Ansel helped her carry everything inside and put them away.

"Can we cook now?" He looked at the ingredients she'd left out that she'd need for the party.

Before she could answer, the front doorbell rang and she went to answer it. A delivery man handed her a huge bouquet of flowers arranged in a wicker picnic basket, then hurried to return to his van. Frowning, she carried them into the kitchen.

"Did you send me flowers?" If he had, he'd gone all-out. This bouquet had more flowers than most funeral arrangements.

"Me? No. Should I have—as a thank-you?"

"No. Don't be stupid." She put them in the center of the dining table and looked at the card.

"Uh-oh, something's ticked you off. Don't throw them at the wall."
Ansel came to read the card, too. "Ah, no wonder you look so mad."

Will you have dinner with me tonight? I'm in town. Best Regards,
Thomas. His phone number was on the back of the card.

She shook her head. "Is he serious?"

Ansel's blue eyes sparkled. "I told you that you might meet someone before I did."

"Thomas Sorrell is a reptile, cold-blooded and icky."

"That's not a nice thing to say about snakes."

She couldn't help but laugh. "He probably had to come to River Bluffs to finish the sale of his business, and his girlfriend won't put him up at her place after he dumped her."

Ansel waved at their surroundings. "I bet he'd love to be invited to spend a night in Cal's house. It would feel like he was rubbing it in, still able to outmaneuver Cal."

"It's never going to happen."

"Are you going to call him back?"

Jazzi reached for her cell phone. She texted *No Thanks,* then concentrated on her check list of things to do for the party. She rinsed and poked twenty large potatoes and tossed them in a hot oven. They'd be ready to scoop out for the potato skin bar tomorrow.

"You can dice and cook the bacon for a topping," she told Ansel.

They turned on the hood for the stove, and it was just as quiet as the salesman said it would be. Her kitchen was going to be a dream to work in.

They were mixing the sugar cookie base for the fruit pizzas when her phone rang. She was scraping down the sides of the bowl, so Ansel answered it for her.

"Yes?"

There was a long pause. "I didn't know Jazzi was seeing someone."

"She isn't . . . yet. We're still friends. Can I take a message? She's busy at the moment."

"Just tell her that she's as lovely as her aunt, and I believe she's probably much nicer. I'd love to get to know her better."

"Will do."

"My invitation's still open for dinner."

"I'll let her know."

"I'll try her again later."

Ansel smirked as he relayed Sorrell's message.

Jazzi rolled her eyes, and then she frowned. "You know, his invitation worries me a little. He has a huge ego, but what if he asked me out for some other reason?"

"Like what?" Ansel was pressing the sugar cookie dough into two pizza pans.

"To keep up on Gaff's cases with Lynda and Noah? To try to pry information from me? Detectives never report everything. They keep a few secrets to themselves."

Ansel started mixing another batch of dough. Jazzi meant to put sliced strawberries and kiwi on two pizzas and blueberries and fresh peach slices on the other two. "I thought you'd crossed Sorrell off your list of possible suspects."

"I had, but this makes me wonder. What if he called Lynda and went to visit her after Cal left town, before she went to New York?"

"What if he did? It would probably be to get the ring back, and she was wearing it when you found the skeleton."

True. Sorrell would never lock that ring in a cedar chest and forget about it. "You're right. He'd have taken it with him if he put Lynda in the trunk."

While Jazzi started on the cream cheese and melted white chocolate filling, he began to pat the new dough into two more pizza rounds. He shrugged. "Why would he kill Noah anyway? All he wanted to do was thumb his nose at Cal. He could do that just by meeting Noah and telling him all sorts of stupid gossip."

She didn't have an answer for that either. Finally, she glanced at the flowers and said, "Beats me. And I guess I don't really care what makes Sorrell tick."

"I'm guessing he'd feel like he was upping Cal if he won Lynda's niece in place of Lynda and got full run of Cal's house. I think it's an ego thing."

"I can see that. The man's all about winning."

"Are you going to keep the flowers?"

Sorrell hadn't scrimped on the bouquet. Daisies, delphiniums, and lilies mingled with pink and yellow roses. "Sure I am. They're gorgeous. But I'm not meeting Sorrell any place, any time." She popped the sugar cookie crusts into the oven. They'd have to cool before she applied the spread. Thank goodness the central air pumped out coolness and comfort.

Her phone rang again and she picked it up. Sorrell. She didn't give him time to talk. "It's a no-go. I don't want to see you."

He laughed. "I thought it was worth a try, but I knew it was a long shot."

"Don't call again."

He hung up without another word. She was pretty sure he'd hoped a cheap investment in flowers—for him—might tip the balance in his favor. The man was an idiot.

Ansel looked at her. "What now?"

"Have you ever made cupcakes?"

His eyes lit up when she rolled up the door on the built-in appliance corner and pulled out a stand-up mixer. "This is going to be so much fun."

And it was. Cooking with Ansel made the rest of the day pass quickly. While he took a shower, she ran to the meat market and came home with two big ribeye steaks and some corn on the cob. When Ansel saw them, his jaw dropped.

"I thought you could grill these while I took my shower," she said.

"Our apartment complex wouldn't let us own a grill."

"Mine's on the back patio. Want to give it a go?"

He bent down to pat George. "You're gonna like this, buddy."

Jazzi laughed and left them. By the time she came back downstairs, Ansel was finishing up. He'd even made a salad.

They ate at the island. Cleanup was easy, and then they rented a movie. When it was time to go to bed, Ansel gave a long, satisfied sigh. "This was a perfect day."

She grinned. "Enjoy it. Tomorrow, my family invades us." And they'd have plenty to say about Ansel moving in with her. Mostly, they'd encourage her to keep him here.

"We're in good shape. We made lots of things ahead."

Her grin grew wider. "The food's the easy part. They're all going to want to see every inch of the house. And they're going to tease me about you. It's going to be organized chaos."

"Lots of laughing people. I can handle that."

And the thing is, she thought he just might enjoy it.

Chapter 29

Jazzi and Ansel met in the kitchen when they got up Sunday morning. They'd done a lot of prep work, but there was still plenty to do before her family came at two. They didn't have to rush, though, and that was nice. They checked off finished dishes at a leisurely pace.

They sipped coffee and nibbled on toast as they worked. Ansel wore running shorts and a sleeveless, white T-shirt. Jazzi kept glancing at his muscles and legs. She grinned when she caught him looking at her legs, too.

"You're a distraction," he told her.

"So are you." She couldn't think too long about that. "Any news from Emily?"

"She texted me that I can either take the furniture in our apartment, or she's selling it."

"Will she really leave without you?"

"She took the job in California. I go with her, or we're done."

A knot clenched in Jazzi's stomach. "If you want to leave . . ."

"I don't want to. This was the last straw. I didn't even get a vote. I never get a vote. She can find some other toady to salute and bow to her."

"I *never* thought of you as a toady."

"Jerod did, and he was right."

Jazzi didn't agree, but she wasn't going to argue about it. "Do you want the furniture? You could store it in the attic or the basement."

"I texted her to sell it. I don't want anything that reminds me of her."

Okay, then. Ansel had reached his limit. A tiny tendril of hope blossomed inside her. Shame on her. But if Emily was out of the picture . . . She glanced at the clock. "I think you look great, but do you want to change before everyone gets here? The food's ready to go."

He grinned. "I think you should wear that sundress with the yellow flowers."

She rolled her eyes. That dress had a scalloped neckline that dipped low enough to show a lot of cleavage. "What? You think you get a vote now?"

"You can't blame a man for trying."

But when she came downstairs a half hour later, she was wearing the dress, and he looked happy.

They'd put all the leaves in the table and arranged the food and dinner plates on the kitchen island. Buckets of ice held beer and wine. When people came, the flow between table and food worked so smoothly, Jazzi thought she'd feed her family, buffet style, from now on.

Everyone came—Mom and Dad, Olivia and Thane, Jerod with his Franny and kids, Dad's brother, Eli, and his wife, and for the first time, Samantha brought Grandma.

"I told her she's part of the family now," Gran said. "She has to put up with you, the same way I do."

People laughed and welcomed her. They ate first and then wanted to see the house.

Jazzi's mom turned in the foyer, taking in both sides of the first floor, and shook her head, a big grin on her face. "It's every bit as charming as I remembered. Lynda called it her storybook home. I love what you've done with it."

Jazzi led them upstairs, and Olivia grabbed Thane's arm. "I want one."

He frowned. "One what?"

"A place of our own."

A big man, he visibly coiled to control his excitement. "Really? You're ready? We can't afford something like this."

"Why not? We'll find our own fixer-upper and make it beautiful."

His steps grew lighter as they went to see the yard.

Jazzi warned them ahead of time. "We haven't done any outside work yet. We want to make the patio bigger and add more landscaping."

Grandma sighed as they passed through the kitchen. "I bought a new dress for Cal and Lynda's engagement party. He served wonderful food, too, and had music."

"Should I have hired a string quartet, Grandma?"

"I don't need background music," Gran protested. "I want a band. We should dance."

Mom laughed. "You're usually tipsy when you do that."

"That's when I dance my best."

More laughter rang out. Everyone seemed happy to be here, even Samantha, and she'd never been here before.

When Grandma stepped into the backyard, though, her good mood vanished. She turned to shake her finger at Jerod. "Shame on you, boy!"

Jerod blinked. She'd obviously caught him off guard. "Why? Franny's my wife, and I'm happy she's pregnant."

People turned to stare. Jaws dropped.

Olivia clapped her hands. "You're pregnant, Fran?"

Little Gunner nodded his head. "My mommy's going to have a baby."

Franny blushed all the way to her hairline, her fiery skin clashing with her carrot-orange hair. "We were going to tell people next week. We didn't want to steal any of Jazzi's glory."

"Doesn't bother me," Jazzi said. "We'll make this a double celebration."

Franny laughed, relieved. "Thanks, we're happy about this."

Jerod turned to Grandma. "See? I done good." He was trying to jolly her up, but Grandma still didn't look pleased.

"Why would you dig a hole in winter?" she asked. "And why hide behind the hedges? I could hardly tell it was you."

Jazzi's eyes went wide. "You were here in the middle of winter?" Grandma must have seen someone digging the hole for Noah's body. No wonder it was so shallow. He'd disappeared seven months ago—in the winter. She hadn't really thought that through. They'd had a mild winter, but the ground would be partially frozen. The hedge was so thick, Cal wouldn't see that the ground had been turned over, and it would look fine by spring. Of course, Cal didn't live that long.

Samantha looked as surprised as Jazzi. "Is this where you went? By yourself? Don't ever do that to me again! You promised me you'd never drive again." Samantha sounded so upset, Gran gave a quick nod.

Samantha tried to explain. "We were supposed to visit Eli that day. I pulled the car out of the garage to warm up, then came in the house to find Dottie, except when I came in the back door, she went out the front door, got in the car, and drove away. I had no idea where she went. I thought I'd die, I was so worried. I called Eli, but she never went to his house. An hour later, she came home, angry."

Grandma glanced at Eli. "You'd be angry, too, if someone invited you to their house and then they weren't there."

Samantha softened her voice to soothe Gran. "You didn't go to Eli's. You came to Cal's house by mistake."

Grandma blinked. She looked at Eli. "Is that why you weren't here?"

"I was waiting for you at our place," he said.

Jerod motioned to the house. "It was all one big mix-up, Gran. We all love seeing you, but it's hot out here, and I want to try one of those cupcakes. I've had only a slice of fruit pizza so far. Let's go back inside where it's cool."

They followed him back to the kitchen and people reached for more desserts. While they ate and talked, Mom announced, "Doogie and I are flying to New York next month to visit Noah's family. We want to meet his wife and baby, and they want to meet us. His parents invited us."

Jazzi stared. Mom had wanted to meet her sister's son. Maybe meeting Noah's families would help her heal. They needed to heal, too.

People left the party at the end of the day, laughing and talking. Cal's house had worked its magic. Deaths had happened here, but joy still filled it and permeated the air. Jazzi didn't exactly understand how, but this house was going to help them put the past behind them.

When she waved everyone off and closed the door, Ansel looked downright pleased with himself.

"It was a success, don't you think?"

Jazzi looked at the empty plates and trays. There were a few leftover cupcakes, but that was all. "I think everyone had a good time, even after Grandma accused Jerod of digging a hole behind the hedge."

"She saw Noah's killer. She's lucky he didn't come after her."

"I'm thinking she saw him, but he was too busy digging to see her."

Ansel picked up plates to carry to the sink to rinse. "She got lucky. If someone called Cal with a fake emergency to get him out of the house to kill Noah, the murder was well thought out. That's pretty cold. He'd have been just as happy to toss Gran on top of Noah in that hole."

Jazzi shivered. It would be so easy to hurt Gran. She started carrying plates from the kitchen island to the sink for Ansel to rinse. "I wonder who Gran saw. She thought it was Jerod, so he must have been tall with brown hair."

Ansel chuckled. "Well, that narrows it down a lot."

She punched his arm. "My big question is why. Why would anyone care if Cal spent a week with Noah? What difference would it make?"

"When you figure that out, you'll be close to your killer," Ansel told her. "But that's Gaff's job. And you need to tell him what you learned, but that's all you can do. The rest is up to him."

Jazzi didn't think her lead would get Gaff any closer to solving Noah's murder, but she called him and told him what Gran had said anyway.

When they'd finished cleanup, it was later than usual. They headed to the living room and sank onto the sofa to watch TV—their usual Sunday ritual when Emily worked. Jazzi's cell phone buzzed and she glanced at the caller ID. "Reuben, my upstairs neighbor."

Ansel had met him, but only in passing.

Reuben rushed into speech. "Hey, Isabelle and I are going to the Gas House again tomorrow night. Want to meet us there?"

"Can I bring Ansel, too? He's staying with me now."

Reuben's voice lilted. "You have a man in your life? How wonderful! I'm dying to meet him. Six o'clock?"

She didn't explain that Ansel was only a roommate. Let him enjoy the fairy tale that she was in a relationship. "We'll be there."

When she hung up, she looked at Ansel. "That's okay, isn't it? Or would you rather stay here while I go?"

"Where you go, I go."

Yeah, right!

Jazzi had looked through the Sunday paper and Ansel was sprawled on the couch with George, watching the end of a baseball game, when the doorbell rang.

Ansel looked at Jazzi and she shrugged. "I'm not expecting anyone this late."

He got up to answer the door, and Jazzi could hear his quick intake of breath. "Emily! What are you doing here?"

Chapter 30

Emily pushed inside the house. Only five-four and thin, she was stronger than she looked. Her dull brown hair was tugged into a knot, and her gray eyes blazed. "I thought I'd find you here. Have you moved in already?"

"I needed a place to stay, and Jazzi has a spare bedroom. You kicked me out, remember?"

"What a convenient excuse to spend more time with Jazzi."

Jazzi looked up from her newspaper, but stayed where she was. This was between Ansel and Emily.

"I'd have spent more time at home if I hadn't always bothered you so much. I made too much noise when you were trying to sleep, remember? You barely wanted to see me on your days off."

"I worked nights. You knew that."

"I was fine with that. Sure, you were gone a lot, and I had to fix my own suppers and do my own thing, but I didn't count on you wanting me gone when you slept, too, or when you were unhappy about something, or when I annoyed you when I didn't unload the dishwasher the right way."

"You knew I'm particular."

"You're past that." He turned to walk to the sitting area in the kitchen. "You're a control freak. I could never do anything right. I'd have still stayed with you, but you're the one who wanted to leave here, and you didn't give a thought to my job, what I want."

"I gave you advance notice."

Jazzi could no longer see them. They were on the other side of the downstairs half-bath, but she could still hear them. His voice had an edge to it when he answered her. "I didn't want a notice. I wanted a vote."

There was a moment of silence. Finally, Emily said, "You should have spoken up, told me how you felt."

"I did. You didn't listen."

Another pause. "You've always let me do whatever I want."

"There are limits, Emily."

"I don't like limits."

"That's why I'm living here and you're moving to California alone." Jazzi heard a foot stomp. "I want you to come with me."

"That's not going to happen."

"Then, darn it, we're through."

"Yes, we are."

Her voice small, she said, "I'm leaving in the morning. I sold everything. I'm renting a furnished apartment."

"Good luck on the West Coast."

A long pause this time. "Can I get a hug good-bye?"

Jazzi heard them move in unison.

"Have a good life, Emily."

There were sniffles. "It wasn't supposed to happen like this."

"I know. I wish you the best."

They walked to the door. It opened and closed. Then Ansel set the alarm and came to lie on the couch again. George snuggled close to him. A car pulled out of the drive, and headlights swept past the window.

"Are you okay?" Jazzi asked.

He nodded. "I was ready. I've been ready. Emily made it easier for me."

"I'm sorry it didn't work out."

"Are you?" He sat up to look at her. "I wasn't sorry when you broke up with Chad. The only thing that bothered me was that I was with Emily. Maybe that's why I put up with so much from her. I felt guilty that I moved in with her on the rebound and I'd rather be with you."

Heat surged through Jazzi's body. "You wanted to be with me?"

"I have fun with you. I was lucky if Emily enjoyed anything we did together. If I took her to a fancy restaurant, she'd have rather had sea bass than walleye. They didn't have her favorite wine. The risotto wasn't creamy enough."

Jazzi smiled. "She's a perfectionist."

"She's impossible. I really tried to make it work, but somewhere along the way, I decided it never would." He glanced at the clock. Almost ten. "I've been wanting to go to bed with you for a long time."

Holy crap! Could bones melt? For being so easygoing, Ansel could be more direct than she realized. "It's been hard to keep my hands off you."

His eyes glinted, and then he pressed his lips together, apologetic. "I know it's a little soon . . ."

"Are you kidding?" She tossed the papers aside and went to him.

He opened his arms and dragged her onto his lap. When his mouth crushed hers, her lips parted. He grinned and pulled away. "You have a king-size bed, don't you?" He pushed himself up, scooped her into his arms, and carried her upstairs.

George whimpered at the base of the steps. "Later," Ansel told him. The dog must know that command. He stretched out to wait.

A long while later, George barked at the bottom of the steps. Ansel glanced at the alarm clock. "It's getting late. Jerod will be here early tomorrow. He's going to guess things have changed between us. What do you want to tell him?"

"That we decided to be friends with benefits."

He laughed. "I'd work overtime for benefits like these. I'll let you sleep now. I'll see you in the morning."

"Oh, no, you don't. I'm a cuddler. Go and get your dog."

He sprinted for the door. "I'll be right back." He carried George's dog bed into the room. Once they were settled, Jazzi drifted to sleep. Cal's house was good for her.

Chapter 31

On Monday, Jerod came wearing his painting clothes. Jazzi and Ansel pulled on ragged jeans and stained tees, too. They were painting the trim on the outside of the house. Each of them carted a ladder to a window and got started. George sprawled in the kitchen to wait for them. He didn't like heat and humidity.

The sun beat down from a cloudless sky. Jazzi could feel it burn through the thin fabric of her T-shirt. She wore cutoffs and the jean material clung to her thighs. She had to laugh at herself. She'd gotten spoiled, working in air conditioning. The guys both stripped out of their shirts. They'd have to scrub lots of spattered paint off them at the end of the day.

When Jerod dipped into the house for a beer, he came back licking his lips. "Something smells good in there. What are you cooking?"

"Our lunch. Thought I'd make Italian beef sandwiches and send the leftovers home with you. Franny still gets queasy when she cooks, doesn't she?" Jazzi normally wouldn't make something so heavy on a hot day, but once the guys walked into the cool house and sat at the kitchen island, they'd be ready to chow down, and they'd make easy suppers for Jerod.

Jerod moved closer to the house to stand in the shade while he drank his beer. "When Fran cooks, she gets sick, when she opens the refrigerator, when a kid eats a peanut butter sandwich in the same room . . ."

"That has to be awful. Can she eat anything?"

"Yogurt, Jell-O, hummus. It will pass in another couple of weeks if it's like her first two times. I've been cooking outside on the grill so she doesn't have to smell anything." He sat his beer can in the grass and climbed the ladder to start on another window. When they finished these, they needed to paint the front and back doors and then the trim on the two-car garage.

The garage itself was stone, like the house, with the same rolled roof, so there wasn't much to do on it.

Jazzi's sunscreen melted away before noon, and she could feel a sunburn starting. "Let's break for lunch."

Jerod burned faster than she did, and his shoulders were tinged with pink. Ansel looked even more golden than usual. They headed into the house and went straight to the refrigerator to fill glasses with ice and cold water.

"This summer's a scorcher." Jerod dampened a paper towel to swipe over his face.

They dawdled over lunch before heading back outside. George came for handouts, then returned to his spot near the sitting area. He liked the idea of living here and didn't feel as obligated to go everywhere with Ansel. Even after taking longer than usual, they finished their work early.

"We're going to wrap up here soon," Jerod said. "All we need to do now is landscaping."

Ansel shook his head. "Jazzi and I can do that. You've already put in a lot of work here."

Jerod cocked his head, a grin on his face. "You don't sound like just a roommate, buddy. Anything you want to tell me?"

Color tinged Ansel's face. "Emily left for California today. We haven't been doing too well for a while now, and Jazzi and I . . ." He fumbled to a stop.

"We decided to be friends with benefits," Jazzi finished for him.

"It's about time! I thought you were never going to get smart, Ansel. I'm happy for you."

Ansel looked relieved. "You don't mind that I'm sleeping with your cousin?"

"Heck, no. Jazzi's a little more fun when she's getting some."

"Hey!" Jazzi's hands went to her hips. "I'm *always* easy to work with."

Jerod shrugged, his eyes glittering with humor. "Inflated ego, and tread softly when she has PMS, but she does good work."

"Won't matter." Jazzi looked at the nearly finished house. "If we don't find another flipper soon, we won't have anything to fix up."

Jerod scraped his hand through his hair. "I've been looking in the Realtor mags, but nothing's really excited me. I've watched the auctions, too. I think we're going to have to drive around and look for private sales."

Ansel pulled his wallet out of his back pocket. He removed a note from it—an address and phone number. "When I was looking for places to show Emily, I saw a big old two-story close to Lake Avenue. It had a wraparound porch. For sale by owner. It's a rental now, probably divided into apartments, but I liked the looks of it." He handed the paper to Jerod.

"Let me guess. Emily didn't like it."

"She wanted something newer."

Jerod nodded. "We'll give it a look-see. If it's cheap enough, it's a contender. It's going to take some sweat equity to make it single-family again."

"I'll call to see if we can get in it." Jazzi thought of Isabelle and Reuben. They were restoring their old Victorian back into a single family, too, and she and Ansel would be meeting them soon at the Gas House. She punched in the number Ansel had written down, and the owner of the house answered.

After explaining that they were interested in it, she asked if they could go through it. When she hung up, she said, "He'll meet us there at nine tomorrow morning."

Jerod grinned. "A good sign he's ready to get rid of it."

"I hope that doesn't mean it's a mess inside." The house before this was so bad, it needed gutted. No big deal, except that they'd found one problem after another when they opened things up.

"You can't always tell until you take down walls." Jerod turned to Ansel. "And your offer to give me a break on landscaping is nice, but when I bought my property, Jazzi helped me with every tiny thing until it was finished, including the entire yard and outbuildings. The only thing she didn't do was build the pond. I plan to do the same for her."

Ansel glanced at the back lot and large yard. "Do you think we have enough land for a pond?"

"Don't see why not. When I was digging near the septic tank, you have enough clay soil to make it work."

Ansel grinned and when Jerod started to his pickup, he walked with him, talking ponds, to say good-bye.

Jazzi went upstairs to take a shower and get ready to meet Isabelle and Reuben. A pond would be nice. After a hot day of work, she and Ansel could jump in to cool off. At night, they had enough privacy, they could go skinny-dipping.

She laid three skirts on the bed, not sure which to wear, before hopping under lukewarm water to scrub off the day's work.

When Ansel came upstairs to shower, he was excited. Jazzi was sure earth moving was in her near future. He lowered George to his dog bed and looked at the skirts she'd laid out on the bed. "This looks serious. Should I rent a tuxedo?"

She rolled her eyes. The man who could only say yes to Emily had quite the wit. "You haven't met Isabelle. She's rich and sophisticated. I feel like a hick whenever I'm around her."

Ansel looked her up and down, still wrapped in her towel after drying off. "You're the hottest hick I've ever met."

"And how many rich, sophisticated women have you beaten off?"

"Does that include cougars? When I worked for Uncle Len, they'd ask for me when they'd call to get work done on their houses. I think that's why his sons didn't like me."

"I'd call for you, too." Smart cougars, but this conversation wasn't helping her. "Your Uncle Len doesn't impress me. Neither do his sons. But you have to help me pick out the right outfit to wear tonight."

Ansel pointed. "That's the shortest skirt. It will show the most leg."

She sighed. "I'm calling my sister. Go take your shower." Olivia knew her stuff. She wouldn't lead her astray. When Olivia picked up the phone, Jazzi said, "Reuben asked Ansel and me to join Isabelle and him for supper. I need to look classy. Should I wear my flower-print skirt; my yellow, short skirt; or my longer broom skirt?"

"You still have a broom skirt? No one's worn those since the Ice Age. We're going shopping together." Olivia let out a breath of frustration. "None of those will work. Just wear black slacks and a nice top, but your wardrobe sucks. You need help. And put on some decent makeup this time—the works. And no sandals."

"Am I that bad?"

"Yes. So bad, I'm taking you in hand. We're setting a date to spend the day shopping."

"I hate shopping."

"It shows. No excuses. You're going to be mine for a day."

It could be worse. If she was with Olivia, she'd still have a good time. Her sister was fun to hang with. "Okay, I can handle that. Thanks, sis."

"And don't let Ansel wear jeans. He could use a fashion update, too."

"Like Thane's"?

Olivia sighed. "Never mind. There are higher virtues, I guess."

"Hey, I want you to know, Ansel and I are living together now."

"I was at the housewarming on Sunday, remember? I saw his bedroom across from yours."

"Now there's only *our* bedroom."

A happy screech almost split her eardrums. "It's about time!"

Since that was Jerod's response, too, Jazzi hurried to say, "We're still on for Thursdays, though. The guys can live without us for one night a week."

"They'll probably kick us out the door. A little apart time is good."

Jazzi laughed and rang off. She put her skirts back in the closet and tugged on her black slacks and a cobalt blue, silky top. She hoped it looked good with her honey-colored hair. When Ansel walked into the room, he was wearing Docker slacks and a white button-down, short-sleeve shirt. He made casual scream sexy.

Jazzi gave him a thumbs-up. "Lookin' good. You know, you don't have to get dressed in the other bedroom." She'd missed seeing him in his towel. "You can move your clothes into my closet now."

He opened its door and stared at the few clothes hanging inside. "Don't most women like to shop? Emily filled the entire closet in our bedroom, and I had to keep my stuff in the spare room."

Jazzi sighed. "I just got the same lecture from my sister."

"Really? Good, because when I was looking for a drawer to put my socks in, I never found any sexy undies and bras. Your stuff looked . . . utilitarian."

Her jaw dropped. "I flip houses. Cotton panties and bras hold up a lot better than lace."

"Sure they do, and you're always beautiful to me, but sexy lingerie is the stuff of fantasies."

"Then reality's going to hit you hard. I don't have any negligees either. I sleep in an oversized white T-shirt."

"I know what I'm buying you for Valentine's Day."

She laughed and slid her feet into a pair of low heels. "That's a long time away, but we'd better get going. I don't want to be late. It's a lot longer drive to the Gas House from here."

Ansel carried George back downstairs and patted his head. "You can't come with us for supper. You'd have to sit in the van too long."

As though he understood, George walked to his spot in the sitting area and lay on his side. He looked tired. He'd been moved too many times today.

Once again, Ansel drove, and Jazzi wondered if men just assumed that was the natural order of things, that men drove and women were passengers. She didn't protest, though. She didn't like driving that much anyway. He was a little slower and on the cautious side, though.

Reuben and Isabelle were walking into the restaurant at the same time they were.

"Hey, neighbor!" Reuben stopped to hug her.

"You remember Ansel, don't you? Ansel, this is Isabelle, Reuben's friend."

Isabelle wore a pale lavender sheath dress that complemented her fair complexion and ebony hair, which was pulled into a tight knot near the top of her head. Black liner rimmed her eyes. How did she do it? The woman looked like not a drop of perspiration ever blemished her skin.

Isabelle smiled at Ansel. "You're the contractor who works with Jerod and Jazzi, aren't you?"

He nodded and circled Jazzi's waist with his arm. "Yes, and I moved in with her a few days ago."

His announcement surprised Jazzi. What had happened to the quiet, docile Ansel who'd never step out of line with Emily? But the answer came to her as soon as she asked the question. She and Ansel had been friends for too long. He could be himself around her. She liked that.

Reuben grabbed his hand to pump it. "That's wonderful! The girl's been on her own too long. It's time someone appreciates her as much as she deserves." He stopped and frowned. "You do, don't you?"

"That's a given." Ansel's glance at her confirmed that.

"Drinks are in order." Isabelle led the way inside.

Isabelle and Reuben ordered martinis, but Jazzi chose wine. Martinis packed too much of a punch. Ansel went with his usual beer. They ordered their meals when they ordered their drinks. Isabelle and Reuben both chose ahi tuna. No wonder they were both slim. Jazzi knew they both loved sushi, too. Could a person get pudgy eating fish and rice? Ansel balanced out their healthy choice by ordering a porterhouse steak. He'd consume every bite, she knew. Jazzi decided on good old fish and chips. If food was breaded and fried, it had to be good.

They talked about their house projects until the food came.

"The new walls are drywalled upstairs," Reuben told them, "and the two bedrooms are good-size. So is the bathroom."

"We're ready to landscape." Jazzi glanced at Ansel. "He wants to put in a pond."

Isabelle shivered. "Sorry, that made me think of excavating, and that made me think of Noah's body, buried behind the hedge."

"Gaff tried to find phone records for the day Cal got called into work for the fake emergency. The call came from a public phone at a library."

Isabelle picked at her wild rice. "Neither Cal nor I connected the call to Noah's disappearing. We both thought he'd simply changed his mind and didn't want to confront Cal with his decision."

"Why would you connect them? Who'd think someone killed Noah in Cal's house while he was gone?"

Isabelle reached for Reuben. "Reuben's been so good for me and made me so happy. I'd never have met him if Cal were alive, but I wish Cal could have spent time with Noah to enjoy family love. His sister and nephews were so cold to him. I just hate it that those boys inherited all of his stocks and bonds. He'd seen his lawyer about changing his will to make Noah his beneficiary, but then Noah never came. And then . . ."

Jazzi stared. "Cal was going to change his will?"

"His lawyer was drawing up the papers."

"Did anyone besides you know about that?"

"He didn't want it to go public until it was official." Isabelle's dark brow rose in a severe arch. "He and his lawyer went over the details at the Country Club. They always met there. Lots of businessmen hash out deals around those tables. I suppose someone could have overheard them."

Jazzi blinked. "Gaff traced the threatening call I got, and it came from the Country Club."

"My club?" Isabelle took a deep breath. "Why would someone call from there?"

"Probably because they didn't want to call from home, and they were a member."

Isabelle leaned back, narrowing her eyes. "That Beth who knew Sorrell trolls for men there." Her eyes widened. "I've seen Tim Draper there a few times lately. He must be working on a deal with someone in town, a member who invites him for lunch to hash out details."

"But it was a woman who called me."

Isabelle's deep red lips straightened into an angry line. "Don't let Tim's chummy routine fool you. He and Katherine are two of a kind. They'd both stab you in the back to make money. If he told Katherine about you, she'd make the call for him."

"Was Tim coming to the club when Noah drove to River Bluffs to see Cal? Could he have heard about their visit?"

Isabelle sighed. "I'm not sure. It's been so long ago, and I never paid that much attention to Tim."

"Do visitors have to sign in?"

She shook her head. "Not always."

"I'll call Gaff about it anyway," Jazzi said.

Reuben pointed a finger in her direction. "And that's why you're a danger to someone. You connect things together that seem inconsequential, and you tell those things to Gaff." He looked at Ansel. "Make sure she sets her alarm every night and keep an eye on her."

"Oh, I will." Ansel wrapped the last few bites of his porterhouse in a napkin for George. "When I moved to River Bluffs, my uncle's sons let me know in no uncertain terms that they wouldn't be happy to share their family money with me. I doubt Tim and Katherine would take the news about Noah well either."

Isabelle looked confused. "But the money wouldn't go to them. It would go to their sons."

Ansel shook his head. "Same difference. If the sons got rich, it couldn't hurt them, could it? Maybe one of the boys owed them money he could pay back. Or maybe Tim and a son want to go into business together."

Jazzi had never thought of Noah as a threat to anyone in River Bluffs, but she'd been wrong. Cal's nephews had done nothing to deserve his money, but they'd undoubtedly counted on it regardless. "Could Wade or Will have found out about Cal's change of heart?"

Isabelle's fair coloring turned even paler. "I hope not. They don't belong to the club. That would be too awful. Cal and Noah's deaths can't be attributed to his nephews. It would be too depressing."

Reuben gently touched her arm. "It would be a long shot that they'd hear any news from the Country Club. They live in Michigan. They don't know that many people in River Bluffs."

Isabelle still looked alarmed. "Tim would tell them if he heard about the will. Or Noah."

Jazzi glanced at Ansel. They both knew this was the most solid possibility they'd heard. But Reuben was right. It was a long shot.

Reuben changed the subject. A good thing. Jazzi wanted to end the night on a happier note. "Remember when I asked you about painting the old Victorian three shades of lavender?"

Jazzi nodded, ready to follow his lead. "Olivia loved the idea."

"A crew comes this weekend. I can't wait to see it. You and Ansel will have to come to see it when it's done."

Jazzi would have never considered light purple on a house, but she had no doubt Reuben would make it look wonderful. "Sounds like you've got plenty going on, inside and outside. Bet workmen wake you up every morning."

"We're making a lot of headway." He gave a sideways glance at Isabelle, hoping to cheer her up. "We gave up on the idea of living in a reconstruction site, so I moved into Isabelle's apartment for the moment. We're hoping everything will be finished in another three weeks."

"Then Ansel and I will have to come and bring supper to celebrate your new place."

"We'd love that."

The waiter came with their checks, and Ansel winced when Jazzi paid for their meals and the tip.

"I always paid when I took Emily out," he complained.

Jazzi gave a sweet smile. "I'm not Emily."

Isabelle reached for her and Reuben's bill, and Ansel bit back any more arguments.

They left the restaurant together, promising to get together again soon. On the drive home, Ansel motioned to her purse. "You should call Gaff. It can't hurt to have him meet with Cal's lawyer and ask about Cal's will and to see if he can track guests who visited the Country Club."

She finished the call before they pulled into their drive. When they stepped into the house, Ansel went directly to George to share his steak. They locked the door and set the alarm, and then they both headed upstairs and changed into their pajamas before hitting the couches to watch TV together. George begged until Ansel lifted him up to stretch beside him.

At ten, Ansel wiggled his eyebrows at her. "You look pretty fetching in a white T-shirt. It makes things more accessible."

"It's now or never," she told him. "We got a lot of sun today. I'm losing steam."

"We can't have that." He pushed to his feet and took her hand to lead her upstairs to bed. "Let's see if we can get your engines purring again."

George whimpered.

"I'll be back to get you later."

George flopped on the floor and sprawled at the bottom of the steps to wait.

Ansel's worries were a moot point. A touch here, a nibble there, and the next hour flew by in a blur of pleasure.

Chapter 32

When Jerod came the next morning, on the ride to the house off Lake Avenue, Jazzi sat shotgun in his pickup, and Ansel and George squeezed into the back seat. She told him what they'd learned about Cal's will.

Jerod whistled. "You know what they say on crime shows—follow the money."

Ansel nodded in agreement. "Lots of kids feel entitled to their parents' money, whether they helped earn it or not. My two older brothers have earned their share of Dad's dairy farm, but they never intended to share anything with my sister or me, and I earned a share, too. Money doesn't always bring out the best in people."

Jazzi had never thought about her mom and dad's money. Mom and Olivia were partners in the salon, and Jazzi didn't expect a share from their business. Hopefully, her parents would live so long, she'd be set before she had to worry about their will. But to be told, like Ansel, that you were cut off from the family fortune before you even graduated from high school had to hurt.

"Didn't that bother you?" she asked.

He scowled. "Yeah, it did. My oldest brother announced it at the supper table when I started my senior year of high school. He told me I'd better find a job when I got my diploma, because if I stayed on the farm, I'd be a hired hand and that didn't pay well. Dad explained that the farm could support two families, but not three. That's why I left to work with Uncle Len, and I ran into the same thing, so I struck out on my own."

She worded her next question carefully. "In the two and a half years that I've known you, you've never gone home to visit them."

"And it's going to stay that way. They chose Bain and Radley over me, even though I had just as many chores to do on the farm. They didn't even consider Adda because she was a girl."

"You said she was spoiled."

He smiled. "She at least had that. They treated her like a princess. I'm glad. She was a pain, but I love her. I was happy she married a good man with a solid future."

"Do you like your brothers?"

"They're my brothers. I love them, but I don't want to see them."

"Do your parents ever offer to come to River Bluffs to see you?"

"Every once in a while. I tell them I'm too busy. I don't have time to visit with them."

Well. Ansel was easygoing, but when he hit his limits, that's as far as anyone could push him. His family hurt him when they sent him away, and he didn't intend to forget that.

Jerod pulled in front of the big old house with the wraparound porch they were going to check out. "We're here, kids. Keep your fingers crossed. Let's hope this house works."

The owner was sitting in the porch swing, waiting for them. He stood when they joined him and unlocked the front door. "Before you even get started, the furnace is over twenty years old. The hot water heater is on its last legs. The roof has a leak. I don't want to deal with it anymore. I'm ready for the next person to tackle the projects."

Ansel tied George's leash to a spike he pounded into the front yard.

"Any foundation issues?" Jerod asked.

"Check for yourself. I'll wait for you here." He returned to the swing.

They started in the basement and worked their way up. The foundation was good. They'd have to replace two or three support poles, but they'd dealt with those before. The plaster was cracked upstairs, but they were going to gut the entire second floor anyway. The rooms were big and airy.

"This works for me if we can get it at the right price," Jerod said. "You two?"

They both nodded.

Ansel and Jazzi let Jerod haggle with the owner while Ansel went to pet George. "We're going to have to replace all the old galvanized pipes," he told her. "If we get the house, that's probably where we should start."

Jerod and Ansel were both good with plumbing, but that was a big project. They might have to hire someone to pass code. They looked up at Jerod as he hurried toward them. "He'll take eighty thousand. I think that's too high. What do you think?"

Ansel shook his head. "We won't make a profit. The median price range around here is eighty-five grand. This is one of the better houses, but a neighborhood sets the price. We might even lose money."

Jerod looked surprised. "You've done your homework."

Ansel grinned. "I might be a blond, but I'm not stupid."

No, no one would accuse him of that.

Jerod smirked. "We'll see if I can budge him. He's pretty shrewd."

"Then he knows the going rate around here," Ansel said. "I wouldn't go over sixty-five thousand. We have a lot of repairs."

The next time Jerod came to them, he wore a smile. "Sixty thousand?"

"Done." Ansel nodded toward the house. "We were wondering, since we have to replace a lot of old plumbing, if we'd have to hire someone to meet code."

"Even if we do, they can finish the job in one day. It's doable."

By the time they left, if their lawyer didn't find any liens or problems, they had a new house to work on. Paying cash and signing a contract for a home "as is" made things move quickly—*if* everything checked out.

"Vegler will let us know by Friday," Jerod said as they pulled away and started home. "If there's a hang-up, he'll find it."

George lowered his head on Ansel's lap and Jazzi admired the Lakeside rose gardens as they passed them. Her mind returned to Ansel's family and the farm and then to Cal's will.

"Has your dad met Cal's nephews?" she asked Jerod. "Did they ever bring their cars into his garage?"

Jerod snorted. "No way. Will's an electrician and Wade's a plumber. They drive white vans just like Ansel. I worked with them on a project a few years ago. A friend needed help for a week, so I went to pitch in. Will showed up every day on time. Wade was almost always late. He's super thin. Likes his beer and drinks his meals."

Jazzi couldn't believe it. "Katherine's sons are tradesmen, just like us?"

"Their dad ran through all the family money. They had to get their hands dirty. The rumor back then was that Wade was deep in debt. He probably danced a jig when he got Cal's money."

"Would he kill Noah to make sure he got it?"

Jerod went silent. "I sure hope not. I liked him a lot more than I liked his older brother."

"Why is that?"

Jerod waited to comment until he'd turned onto the road for Cal's house. "Will's one of those guys who likes to pat himself on the back for being the *good* son. He makes sure that his parents know every time Wade slips up. He even went to the supervisor for the project we worked on and asked if he'd seen Wade because he wanted to ask him about something. That backfired. The supervisor gave him a dirty look and explained that Wade had scheduled the morning off to drive his elderly neighbor to a doctor's appointment."

"A backstabber," Ansel said.

Jazzi nodded. "Sounds like he took after his mother."

"Glad he's no relative of mine." Jerod pulled into the driveway and glanced at the time. "Only ten forty-five. Let's start with the front yard. It's easier than the back. What have you got in mind?"

"There's nothing here. I guess Cal wanted to have people focus on the house, but I'd like some rose bushes and two flower boxes."

"Ansel and I can build the flower boxes if you want to mow and clean up leaves around the foundation that no one bothered with. You and Ansel can go to a nursery tonight to buy all the plants you want."

They finished the front yard before lunch and got a good start on the backyard before five. They'd weeded and trimmed the hedge, picked up and thrown away any trash the renter had left, and shaped every bush.

"Tomorrow, we can plant and landscape," Jerod said. "I'll see you then."

After he left, Ansel loaded George into his white van, and he and Jazzi went to buy flowers and bushes. They stopped at a root beer stand to grab supper so that George could eat with them.

Jazzi sighed. She was getting as fond of Ansel's pug as he was. She never saw that coming. And later that night, when she spooned against Ansel to sleep, she had to admit she didn't see that coming either.

Chapter 33

Oh, Lord. When Jazzi zipped downstairs the next morning, Ansel was already outside, talking to Jerod, who was sitting on a bulldozer, looking pretty happy with himself. Their backhoe sat in the drive.

Ansel turned to her with a huge grin. "Jerod filed for a permit for a pond, just in case you'd ever want one, and we've been approved. The dirt has plenty of clay, so if you're still good with the idea, we're going to start digging."

Of course they were. If Jerod could play on a bulldozer, why wouldn't he? "Is that expensive to rent?" she asked.

Jerod shrugged. "I got a deal for seventy-five dollars a day."

"And how many days did it take to dig your pond?"

"For a half acre one,. Ansel and I will be at it a week."

Not as bad as she'd thought it would be, and Jerod had already been through what to do and how. She shrugged. "Why not? Go for it."

Jerod drove behind the hedge to get started, but Ansel mounted the flower boxes at the house's two arched front windows and dug holes along the foundation for bushes before he went to join him. He wanted to make it easy for Jazzi to plant what they'd bought last night instead of leaving her to do all the work alone. They'd bought a miniature lilac for the corner of the house. She planted that first. She filled the flower boxes and had the rose bushes in place and watered before lunch. They ate quickly to get back to their projects. Ansel and Jerod returned to the pond, and Jazzi rolled huge, plastic flowerpots to the patio to fill them with soil. She arranged them near the outdoor furniture they'd bought.

She was planting geraniums and petunias in the pots when Gaff came to join her. "I knocked and rang the bell, but when no one answered, I figured you must be out here." He glanced around and shook his head. "You guys have done a great job. The place is picture perfect."

"Thanks, we're happy with it." She patted dirt around the last petunia and ignored the herbs she meant to plant beside the garage. "Can I get you something to drink?"

"Do you have any of your iced tea made?"

"I'll be right back." She tossed her gardening gloves on a chaise lounge and stepped into the kitchen. The coolness of the air conditioning took a minute to adjust to after the intense heat of the sun. She poured tea for her and Gaff and carried the glasses outside.

She dropped onto the chair across from him at the patio table. "We haven't seen you for a while."

"The case sort of stalled, and I got busy on other things, so I'm glad you called me about Will and Wade. I talked to Cal's lawyer, and he'd already given Cal the new papers to sign so that Noah would be his beneficiary. Tim was at the Country Club four times to talk with a member who owns a construction company. Tim and Will are thinking about going into business with him."

"No Wade?"

"Wade bowed out. Wasn't interested, from what the guy said."

"So, Cal didn't divide his will between Noah and his nephews? Noah would have inherited all the stocks and bonds?"

Gaff nodded. "I thought you might like to go with me to talk to Will and Wade when they get off work. Their shift ends at four."

"To Battle Creek?"

He shook his head. "They've been working in River Bluffs for a while now on the new lofts they're building downtown. The owner's turning an old warehouse into condos."

"Did they move here?"

He set down his glass after taking a long sip of iced tea. "Good stuff. I don't suppose you have a recipe for my wife?"

"I'll write it out for the next time I see you."

"Thanks. You asked me about the nephews. They share a room in a cheap motel during the week and drive home every weekend."

"How long have they been doing that?"

"Almost a year. They worked on the converted apartments near the Landing, too. Rumor is Cal found out they were in town and didn't bother to see him, and that was the last straw."

Jazzi frowned. "They never took the time to see Cal? Even when they lived here?"

Gaff drained his glass. "Nope. I thought maybe you'd like to ask them about that, since you knew Cal and all."

"I didn't know him."

"Close enough."

She shrugged. He'd made her curious, and she was feeling braver now that she was with Ansel. Why would Katherine's two boys live and work in River Bluffs and still snub Cal? She glanced at the clock. Almost three. "I'll go find Jerod and Ansel and let them know I'm going with you."

Gaff nodded and reached for her unfinished tea. Ansel grinned when she told him she'd be gone a while.

"Good, then when Jerod leaves, I can play on the backhoe."

Now she knew where she rated. He'd rather spend quality time on an earthmover than eat supper with her. She could live with that.

By the time she got back to Gaff, it was time to go. She didn't have a chance to wash her face or fix her hair. But then, the crew at the warehouse wouldn't look much better. On the drive downtown, she thought about Cal's nephews. They shared a cheap motel together. Were they married? Did they have kids?

In no time, Gaff parked in back of the building. Its lot ended at the beginning of Headwaters Park. A perfect location. It would be easy to get to any downtown festivities from here. The city had bulldozed buildings to create the park with its winding trails and tall stages. When the river that wound through it flooded, nothing was damaged.

Gaff didn't give the park a glance. He went directly to a supervisor and showed him his badge. The man directed them to where Wade was working and gave them instructions on where to find Will. "Are they in trouble of some kind?"

Gaff shook his head. "I'm only here to ask questions."

"Better hurry then. They'll be out of here in another twenty minutes."

They found Wade in a second-floor loft that was only framed in. He was installing plumbing for the kitchen that would hug the front wall.

"Mr. Draper?" Gaff showed Wade his badge. "I'm Detective Gaff and this is Jazzi Zanders, her aunt was engaged to marry your Uncle Cal Juniper. We'd like to talk to you and your brother, Will."

Wade had been kneeling in front of a pipe, fitting an elbow piece onto it. He stood, and Jazzi was surprised by how tall and lanky he was. His hair was longish, the same soft brown as Jerod's. He sported a scruffy beard, too.

"What's wrong?" Wade asked. "Cal's dead and we sold his property."

"That's what I need to ask you about. I need to talk to your brother, too. He's working on the first floor."

Wade glanced at his watch. "They're going to lock up the building soon, shut things up for the day. What if we find Will and grab a picnic table in the park to talk?"

Wade led the way to where Will was working, and Gaff went through his explanation again. Will was as tall as Wade, but more filled out. His brown hair was cut short and his goatee trimmed and neat. He frowned at Gaff. "Is there some kind of problem? We went through Cal's lawyer to sell his place."

A loud buzzer rang, and Wade said, "That's quitting time. Let's go."

They crossed the parking lot to Headwaters Park and found a picnic table overlooking the river. Once they'd settled, Gaff turned to Jazzi and said, "Tell the men what you found in the house."

She understood why he'd invited her along. She had two ties to Cal's nephews: her aunt Lynda and finding two dead bodies. "We opened a cedar chest in the attic and found my Aunt Lynda's skeleton."

Wade's eyes went wide in shock, but Will had obviously heard that on the news. He nodded. "We never even went to the attic," he told them. "We didn't even climb the steps to the second floor."

"That's what Jerod and I guessed," Jazzi said. "You left lots of expensive antiques that the renter sold off."

Wade gaped. "He sold them? They weren't his to sell."

"He had no respect for the house or anything in it. When Jerod and I bought it, the place looked like a dump. Trash covered the living room and kitchen, and all the good furniture was gone."

Will's eyes narrowed. "How valuable were the antiques?"

"Worth thousands, each and every one of them." *Think about that, idiots.* Anger still simmered over how careless the nephews had been with Cal's belongings.

"Tell them the rest," Gaff prompted.

Jazzi inhaled a deep breath. "Things weren't draining like they should, so Jerod brought our backhoe to check on field tiles. He found another body buried near the septic tank."

"The renter's?" Will asked. "We thought he skipped out since he was two months behind on payments."

Jazzi shook her head. "No, the son my Aunt Lynda gave up when she went to New York."

Wade and Will exchanged glances.

"Mom told us Cal found Lynda's son," Will said. "She wasn't too happy about it. She didn't like anything about Lynda. She said it only proved she was right about Cal all along. He cared more about Lynda than his own family."

"His family snubbed him and wouldn't have anything to do with him." Jazzi could hear the bite in her voice and tried to tone it down. "He invited you boys to visit him over and over again."

Wade bent his head, as if ashamed. "Mom would have disowned us, too. She had a thing about Cal and Lynda. There was no changing her mind."

Gaff intruded. "Did you know that Cal was going to change his will and leave his stocks and bonds to Noah?"

"What?" Wade stared.

Will's expression turned hard and angry. "So Mom was right. Cal didn't care about us."

"Who could blame him?" Wade shook his head. "If Noah came to River Bluffs to see him, he did more than we ever did."

"But we're family. Noah was what? Someone else's son."

"I talked to Cal's lawyer," Gaff said. "Cal had already signed the papers. But then Noah disappeared."

Wade leaned forward on the picnic table. "What do you mean, disappeared? He must have been at Cal's house, right?"

Gaff explained. "Cal wasn't home when Noah got there. He'd left a note on the door and a key in the lock. When Cal got back, he didn't even realize Noah had been there."

"Wasn't his car in the drive?" Will asked.

"We found Noah's car in Cleveland, Ohio, abandoned."

Wade ran a hand through his hair. "But you found his body on Cal's property?"

Gaff gave another nod. "Somebody buried him in a shallow grave behind the hedge, near the septic tank."

Wade stopped fidgeting and stared. "Wait a minute. You're saying that someone killed him. At Cal's house?"

Gaff spelled it out. "Someone killed Lynda and laid her in a trunk in the attic. And someone killed Noah and buried him in Cal's backyard."

Wade turned to Will. "Was Cal a murderer?"

"No." Jazzi explained about finding Cal's papers in the basement. "He hired a detective to find Lynda. He thought she'd met someone else and took off with him, but he never understood why she didn't write or contact anyone in River Bluffs. He was devastated when he thought Noah had changed his mind and decided not to visit him."

"If not Cal, then who?" Will asked.

Gaff shrugged his shoulders. "We don't know. That's what we're investigating."

Wade's hands shook. He looked rattled and upset.

"Did either of you meet Cal at all before he died?" Gaff asked.

They both shook their heads.

"What about the car in Cleveland?" Wade asked. "Can't you find all kinds of evidence these days? Hair? Fingerprints? Something?"

"We went over it," Gaff said. "Nothing. Whoever drove it probably wore gloves, didn't leave any traces behind."

"But he had to get home somehow." Wade was flying through ideas faster than Jazzi had.

Gaff nodded. "We checked for that, too. No car rentals for River Bluffs. No connection we could find."

Jazzi was curious. "When was the last time either of you saw Cal?"

Will glanced at his brother. "The last I remember was when he came to wish us good-bye when Mom and Dad moved to Battle Creek."

Jazzi couldn't help asking, "And neither of you thought to see him when you came to River Bluffs to work? He'd have probably put you up in his house instead of making you share a cheap motel room. He'd have wined and dined you."

Will tried to explain. "I know we must look terrible to you, but you haven't met our mom. If we'd have gone to see Cal, one of us would have slipped, and she'd have known. Fury and misery would have broken loose. We'd never hear the end of it."

Gaff handed each of them his card. "If either of you thinks of anything—anything at all—that might help us solve this case, give me a call."

They both put the cards in their wallets for safe keeping.

Gaff rose and tossed over his shoulder, "By the way, you probably don't remember where you were on January seventeenth, do you? That's the day Noah disappeared."

"Walk with me to my van," Will said. "I keep a record of everything I do."

As they followed him to his van, the restaurants down the street cranked up their kitchens and the aromas of sizzling meat drifted toward them. Saliva pooled in Jazzi's mouth. She'd eaten a quick lunch, and she was hungry.

Will unlocked his van and reached for a notebook on the passenger seat. He flipped through the pages and stopped on January seventeenth. "I was working on the condos near the Landing."

"Was Wade with you?"

Will frowned. "He drove separately. He had to leave early that day."

Gaff turned to Wade.

Wade spread his hands. "Give me a break. That was seven months ago. I don't have a clue."

Fair enough. Jazzi couldn't remember what she did in January either.

Gaff shrugged. "It was a long shot. Thought I'd ask."

But Wade looked worried. She'd feel stressed, too, if she couldn't come up with an alibi.

Jazzi hesitated. "I heard that you and your dad were going to go into business together, using some of the money you inherited from Cal. Good luck."

Wade shook his head. "Not me. I owed out too much money. I'm finally clear of debt and have money in the bank. I'm happy with that."

Will took a minute to respond, obviously choosing his words with care. "I'm going into business with Dad and another investor, but we all get equal votes on every choice we make. I'll work as an electrician until all the details are settled. Dad gets overly optimistic sometimes. We can help balance him out."

"Thanks again for your time." Gaff started back toward his car and Jazzi trailed behind him. Once they'd pulled into traffic, she said, "You were sort of mean to Wade. How many people can tell you what they did even a few weeks ago?"

"You'd be surprised how much people can remember or try to find out when they're a little rattled. Every little bit of information might help me solve the case."

"I still feel sorry for Wade."

"You're a civilian. You can afford to. I need to dig for facts, even if it makes people uncomfortable."

She'd make a lousy cop. It's a good thing she'd gone into house flipping.

On the drive back to Cal's, Jazzi frowned. "I haven't given much thought to Katherine until we talked to her boys. She's so vindictive and loves money so much, she wouldn't like it if Cal's stocks and bonds went to Lynda's son."

Gaff gave a smug smile. "I was thinking the same thing. Neither would Tim. I want to divide them up, though. Interview them separately. I'd like to meet Cal's sister. Want to come with me?"

"To Battle Creek?"

"Unless I can convince her to come to me."

Jazzi would like to see what kind of woman could cut off her brother and never forgive him because he fell in love with someone she didn't approve of. "Count me in."

Gaff smiled. "I'll call you when I set things up. Then we can try for Tim."

Ten minutes later, he pulled into her drive. Dust billowed behind the hedge, and he asked, "What are you guys doing now?"

"Jerod and Ansel are building a pond."

"To swim in?"

"Once it's ready to go, bring your swimsuit, and we'll supply a towel. You can cool off."

"Can I bring my wife?"

"Why not?"

He grinned. "I love water. I just might take you up on that."

If he did, she'd invite him and his wife for supper. She never wanted to have Gaff grill her. She liked him, but he was too good at his job. She watched him pull away and then went in search of Ansel.

Chapter 34

Gaff called later that night. "What about Friday? Does that work for you? It's a little under a two-hour drive. I thought I'd pick you up at ten, grab take-out somewhere, and then visit Katherine."

"I'll be ready."

"I'll call and make sure Katherine will see us, but if you don't hear back from me, the trip's on."

She didn't hear back, so they must be going. She and Ansel had taken quick showers before throwing hamburgers on the grill. She went braless and pulled on short-shorts. He walked around in his pajama bottoms. After supper, they settled on sofas across from each other. They flipped through channels until nine, and then watched *Property Brothers* together. You'd think after doing remodels all day, they'd be tired of it, but it was fun to see what other people did and how they decorated.

At ten, Ansel pointed to the clock and they headed upstairs.

"I thought you'd be too tired tonight." Jazzi pulled down the comforter on their bed. "You did a lot of heavy work today."

"So did you. Landscaping takes it out of you. Are your muscles sore?"

"It hurts right here." She rubbed the small of her back.

"Maybe I can kiss it better."

If hospitals offered this service, people would flood them.

Tonight, they turned in opposite directions, with only their fannies touching, to sleep. In the morning, they sat next to each other at the kitchen island for breakfast.

"Remember, I go out with my sister every Thursday." Jazzi buttered her toast while it was still hot so the butter would melt. Ansel spread peanut butter on his two pieces of rye.

"Where are you going to eat?" He got up to pour himself some orange juice.

"Henry's Bar & Grill. We haven't been there for a while. We miss it. What are you going to do?"

"I'm picking up Thane when your sister leaves him, and we're going to a sports bar to eat wings and drink beer."

"Fun!" She was glad the guys had decided to have a good time, too.

They were rinsing coffee cups to load in the dishwasher when Jerod gave a quick knock and walked in. He clapped his hands at Ansel. "Time's a wasting. Let's do this!"

"I won't be here tomorrow," she said. "Gaff wants me to go to Battle Creek with him to interview Katherine."

Jerod grimaced. "I'd rather be eating dust here than spend time with her. You can finish everything today anyway, can't you? You picked the perfect time to leave us."

That settled, the men took off and she went outside to plant the herbs along the side of the garage. She swept the patio and watered all of the new plants and she still finished everything before three. There was nothing else for her to do, so she took a shower and decided to bake pies. There was a farm stand a few miles from their house. She drove there and bought six pints of berries, then returned home and got busy.

By the time Jerod and Ansel quit for the day, she had two berry pies cooling on the kitchen island and two cream pies in the refrigerator. Jerod walked through the back door and sniffed appreciatively. His gaze went straight to the pies.

Jazzi smiled. "I got done early. I have one berry pie and one cream pie for you to take home."

"Chocolate cream?"

"With whipped cream on top. That's your favorite, isn't it?"

He smiled. She loaded the pies in carriers and packed them in a cooler to send home with him. He was gone five minutes later.

Ansel peeked in the refrigerator. "I don't suppose I could have a piece before I pick up Thane?"

"Why not?" She took it out and cut him a slice.

"You're not having one?"

"I'm getting the filet sandwich and fries at Henry's. I need to save room."

She stood across from him while he ate. "How's the pond coming?"

"We're going to work on it all day tomorrow. I'll dig on Saturday. Your family's coming on Sunday, but I might bulldoze in the morning before they get here. And then I'm going to try to finish it on Monday while you and Jerod start work on the house on Lake."

"Do you think you can finish it on your own?"

"The digging. I might have to move dirt farther away from it with the backhoe for a few evenings, but we'll get there."

"Don't kill yourself. If it takes another day or two, we'll be all right."

"I want to get it finished, so we can hire a well driller. I'd like to get it filled so we can use it as soon as possible."

She wasn't going to argue with him. Instead she glanced at the clock. "You'd better get cleaned up or no one's going to sit next to you at the bar."

He grinned and bent to kiss her. "You'd still love me."

"Love you, yes. Touch you? No."

He laughed and started upstairs. A half hour later, he drove to get Thane, and Jazzi drove to meet Olivia at Henry's. When Jazzi lived in West Central, she was right on Olivia's way to the bar, but now it was inconvenient for either of them to pick up the other.

When Jazzi parked in the side lot, she was surprised at how many cars were there on a weeknight. Usually, in the summer, people were downtown at outdoor festivals. This must be a dull night without much going on. When she walked inside the old brick building, she was wrapped in its dim lighting and air conditioning. The interior hugged her with its old paneling and aged wooden floors. This is what a bar should feel like. The waitress led her to a booth and five minutes later, Olivia came to join her.

"Hey, sis!" Olivia slid into the booth across from her. She wore an off-the-shoulder red top that clung to her and a white flirty skirt with red and black splotches. Her blond hair was pulled into a loose knot. She looked fun and saucy.

"Darn it." Jazzi glanced down at her Docker's and turquoise top. "I didn't know you were dressing up."

"Dressing up?" Olivia gave her a look. "I wore this to work."

And that's why Olivia and her mom did such a great business. They were savvy and chic. "You look great. How's Mom doing? She's getting over Lynda and her letters, isn't she?"

Olivia nodded. "She's moved on to Noah's family. I know this sounds odd, but your living in Cal's house helped her somehow. Now when she talks about Lynda, she talks about the parties she and Cal threw there."

Jazzi felt the same way. Somehow, Cal's house offered more happiness than unpleasant memories. Donna, their usual waitress, came to bring their drinks and take their orders. They settled in, ready to yak and gossip, when Will and Wade walked through the doors.

Please don't notice us. Jazzi lowered her head, trying to hide her face, but Will tapped Wade on the arm, pointed, and headed toward them. How lucky could she get? Wade slid into the booth next to Jazzi and Will sat next to Olivia.

Olivia scowled, ready to give them a piece of her mind, when Jazzi said, "Olivia, this is Will and Wade Draper, Cal's nephews. This is my sister, Olivia."

Will looked Olivia up and down and smiled. "Nice to meet you."

Her sister didn't mince words. "Just so you know, I'm taken. So is Jazzi. But it's nice to meet you, too."

Will's eyes narrowed when he looked at Jazzi. "Our mom told us that you and your detective are driving to Battle Creek to interview her tomorrow."

"Gaff isn't *my* detective. He's the person who came to take Lynda and Noah's bodies out of Cal's house."

Wade grimaced. "I haven't had any good experiences with cops, but that had to be horrible, the stuff of nightmares."

"We'd have rather found buried gold," she agreed. "It started a whole sequence of digging into stuff we'd gladly left behind. It was hard for our mom. Lynda was her sister."

"And you still like Gaff?" Wade asked.

"Why wouldn't we? Once we calmed down, we all wanted him to find out who put Lynda in Cal's attic. Noah was more of a shock. He's so recent, Gaff might have better luck finding his killer."

Wade grimaced. "Every time I'm around a cop, he's trying to escort me to jail. Mostly so I'll sober up."

Will gave him a dirty look. "It would be nice for Mom if she didn't have to go collect you in the morning."

The conversation stopped when Donna returned to take the brothers' orders. Wade went for a burger with a fried egg on top and a glass of water. When Olivia raised her eyebrows, he said, "If I drink one beer, I'll drink more."

She nodded.

Will ordered a burger, too, then returned to their earlier topic. "Why do you and Gaff have to pester our mom? She lives two hours away from here, hasn't talked to Cal since we moved to Michigan. Why not leave her alone?"

"Gaff says one small lead can lead to a bigger one." Jazzi studied him. "Why wouldn't he talk to your mom? He's interviewed everyone else who knew Cal. She's his sister."

He pointed a finger at her. "Why does he cart you around with him? You're not a cop. You're just a flipper who snoops in other people's business."

Wade stared. Jazzi gave him a long, assessing look. "You must take after your mom. I've heard she's not pleasant either."

"You didn't answer my question. Why does Gaff want you to go with him?"

She didn't like his tone. "I'd guess that was obvious, but I don't care whether I answer you or not. Figure it out yourself."

His face mottled with anger. He must not be used to people not doing as he asked. He pushed to his feet and motioned for Wade to follow him. "You've upset our mom. I don't like your company." He took his drink and walked to the other side of the restaurant. Good, the brick wall in the center that separated the two spaces blocked him from view.

Olivia blinked, then burst out laughing. "He's sure a charmer."

"Everything's about his mother. A little weird, huh?" He'd rattled Jazzi. She didn't like conflict. She could hold her own, but she didn't get a charge out of it like Jerod did. If you irritated him, her cousin pushed buttons just to start trouble. Come to think of it, Olivia let conflict roll off her like water off a duck. It didn't ruffle her either. "He must be really protective of his family."

Olivia thought about that. "He never mentioned his dad or brother. He must be mommy's favorite."

Jazzi shrugged, ready to forget about Will and enjoy her evening. "Our mommy didn't have a favorite."

Olivia pretended to pout. "True, and we both know she should like me more than she does you."

That started a friendly debate that led to their usual gossip and small talk. Their food came and the evening shifted to having a good time on a Thursday night. They were on their second glasses of wine when Jazzi saw Will and Wade walk past the front window to the parking lot. Good. They left before she and Olivia did. Will was such a pill she worried he'd yell something at her in parting.

"How's Thane?" she asked when Donna brought them their checks.

"A happy camper. We're looking for houses."

"Any luck?"

"We found one close to Getz Road we're interested in. It's a short drive from the beauty shop. We were going to ask you guys to go through it with us to see if it's in good shape."

"Are there any trunks in its attic?"

Olivia smiled. "No, and no septic tank. It has city water."

"Then I'm in. Let us know when you want us."

They paid and didn't quit visiting until they reached their cars in the parking lot. Then they drove in separate directions to head home. Jazzi hoped Ansel had had as much fun tonight as she did—not counting Will, that is. She was glad that everything went well after he and Wade trounced to the other side of the bar. She was driving to Battle Creek to see Katherine tomorrow, and she wasn't looking forward to that.

Chapter 35

Gaff pulled into the drive at ten in the morning, and Jazzi went out to his car. Jerod and Ansel were already out back, working on the pond. She'd left deli meat in the fridge for them and a loaf of bread on the counter. George was in the house, lying by the back door, to greet them when they came in for lunch. It was so hot, he didn't mind that Ansel was sweating while he lay in air conditioning. The pug was devoted, but didn't like to overexert.

When Gaff pulled away to start their trip, he said, "I don't know when we'll get back for sure. Is your guy okay with that?"

"We're going out for supper tonight, so it's not a problem, and he has pie in the refrigerator to tide him over."

"Pie?" Gaff glanced at her at the stoplight. "My Ann stopped baking when the kids grew up and left."

"Makes sense. She probably doesn't want to have to toss leftovers."

He shook his head. "There are no leftovers."

"Then she probably doesn't want to watch you gain twenty pounds."

He smiled. "There's something to that."

When they got out of heavy town traffic, Jazzi told him about running into Will and Wade at the restaurant last night.

Gaff frowned. "I dug into both of them. Wade was floundering before he got Cal's money. He'd always squeaked by with steady jobs until the contractor he worked for retired and moved to Florida. The girl he'd lived with for three years ran off with someone else at about the same time. The kid had always liked his Modelo, but he didn't self-medicate until last November, and then he went to crap. Must have some stored-up resentments, because word is he can get belligerent when he's drunk. He's been in a few fights."

"Belligerent enough to kill somebody?" Jazzi asked.

"Or desperate enough to work himself up. Friends say he's the nicest guy around when he's sober."

Jazzi didn't know anyone like that, but she'd heard of them. Would the timing fit? "If I'm right, Noah died in January, didn't he?"

Gaff nodded. "That's right when Wade hit the bottle really hard. He skirted through the holidays in decent shape, but when he sat on his hands with nothing to do—no job, no girlfriend—he lost it. He almost lost his house and van, too."

Jazzi sighed. "It still doesn't make sense, though. I mean, even if Wade wanted Cal's money, Cal was still alive. He was only in his sixties. He might have lived a lot longer. No one could predict he'd die a month after Noah."

"That's where the gamble comes in. Cal's father died at sixty. His uncles died at sixty-one and sixty-three. They all died of heart attacks."

"Genetic." Jazzi had recently read about a runner, who lived a healthy lifestyle, but dropped dead of a massive heart attack when he was in his early fifties, just like his father had. "The killer counted on that."

"The odds are better than buying a lottery ticket."

Was Wade backed so far into a corner, he made a bet Cal's money would save him? She pushed that idea away. "I like Wade. I don't want it to be him."

Gaff tossed her a sympathetic look. "Sometimes it's the bastards who live forever and force nicer people into acts of desperation."

She didn't like that opinion. "Will wasn't wearing a wedding ring. Was any girl stupid enough to marry him?"

Gaff chuckled. "You really don't like him."

"He's a jerk. Is he married, or has every woman he's met run from him?"

"He's single. Hasn't had any significant others. He's the love-'em-and-leave-'em type."

"How many love 'ems?" Jazzi couldn't imagine any woman wanting to spend time with him.

Gaff frowned, trying to remember. "If I'm right, and if people told the truth, he's never stayed with anyone more than five months. He took a couple of girls home to meet his parents, but his mother didn't approve of either of them."

Katherine. From everything her parents told her, Cal was not only nice but down to earth and friendly. How could two people be so different? "Have you asked around about Katherine?"

"I haven't had to work very hard to get people to talk about her. Everyone has something bad to say about her. No one likes her, and I mean no one. Maybe not even her husband."

That surprised Jazzi. "Tim? When he called me, he made a big deal about how she was right when she cut Cal out of their lives."

"He doesn't know you at all, and you don't know him. He's great at putting on a front, and he never disagrees with his wife in public. People I called told me that Tim and Cal got along pretty well when Tim lived in River Bluffs. Cal's friends said that Cal worried about Tim and his business sense. He tried to give him good advice every chance he got. Tim was doing all right when they lived here, but then he got a chance to run a small company in Battle Creek and Katherine encouraged him to go for it. Cal advised him to pass, but I guess Tim's home life was pretty much the pits when Katherine wasn't happy with him. They moved."

"Was that the first business he made go under?" Jazzi didn't know a thing about running a company. She and Jerod kept things pretty simple. She had no desire to judge Tim. It couldn't be easy to make a small business compete with big ones.

"Tim lost money on that deal, had to ask Cal for a loan to keep things afloat." Gaff glanced at the sign that said welcome to Michigan when they passed it, and so did Jazzi. They'd made good time.

"Did Cal loan him the money?"

"Not exactly a loan," Gaff said. "His friends said that Cal never expected to see it again, but yeah, he gave it to Tim."

"And Katherine still cut him off?"

"Oh, it gets better." Gaff cranked up the air conditioning in the car. The sun blasted through the windows, heating things up. "Tim borrowed money to start up the second and third businesses, too."

Jazzi liked Cal even more.

"Cal's friends tried to talk him out of it the third time. Lynda was against it, too, but Cal wouldn't hear of it. His sister and her husband needed help, and he had more than enough money to help them."

"Did that business take?" Jazzi asked.

Gaff shook his head. "Nope, but it looked like it might. Cal had gotten engaged to Lynda, and when Katherine heard that Lynda didn't want Cal to loan Tim any more money, that was it. Katherine called him and issued a blistering speech. She told him he could choose between a hussy or his sister. Cal chose Lynda."

"Why would Katherine do that when Cal always came through for her?" Jazzi stared out her window, trying to understand Katherine. "If the third business went under, too, what would they do?"

"Katherine knew they were safe. Tim's mother died. His father had died a few years before her. Tim was an only child, and he inherited everything. His parents left their money in a trust fund for him, so that he couldn't spend it all in one shot. He and Katherine have been living off the monthly payments ever since, enjoying pretty cushy lives."

Jazzi rolled her eyes. "Must be nice."

"It has been, but there's no money left for the boys, and there wasn't enough to send them to fancy colleges. Katherine's enjoying the country club lifestyle, but she can't pass it on."

"Does she care?" The landscape changed from the lush green of Indiana to the pine trees of Michigan. The terrain looked wilder. The last time she'd driven this route, Jazzi had seen a bald eagle swoop to a pine tree in the grassy meridian between lanes.

Gaff frowned. "From the people I've talked to—so all of it's just hearsay—Katherine strikes me as the kind of person who puts herself above anyone and everyone else, including her husband and children."

Jazzi had formed the same impression. Too much pride. And selfish. "What about Tim?"

Gaff thought through his answer for that, too. "I think that as long as Tim can put on a good façade and enjoy the extras in life, he's okay."

Jazzi had never been rich. Her parents made good money, but not a crapload of it. "It must be hard to grow up with lots of money, like Will and Wade, and know you'll run out of it and hit real life head-on the minute you leave home."

Gaff nodded. "It has to come as a shock."

How much of a shock? Jazzi wondered. Enough to kill an innocent man so that you'd inherit your estranged uncle's money?

Chapter 36

To visit Katherine, they didn't have to drive into Battle Creek. She and Tim lived on the south side of the city on a golf course. Jazzi was a little disappointed. She'd visited Marshall, Michigan, often and even toured the city's historical homes, but she'd never driven farther to Battle Creek. She had no idea what it looked like, and she wouldn't learn today.

Katherine's house reminded her of a fortress, a big square of dark brick with a three-car garage. A thick, heavy door sat in the center with a huge, painted Chinese vase on each side. She was surprised no moat surrounded the foundation. Gaff parked in the drive, and he and Jazzi walked up the sidewalk. A weeping cherry tree sat in the corner near the extended garage. Three rose bushes sat under the living room windows. Each vase held a bonsai tree. Gaff rang the doorbell and they waited a long time. Katherine was obviously not in any hurry to greet them.

Finally, the door opened and an extremely thin woman wearing a beige pantsuit greeted them. Her graying hair was cut in a blunt, chin-length style. Her makeup was flawless, her brows pencil thin. A slit of red lipstick coated her thin lips. She quickly looked Jazzi and Gaff up and down, then motioned them inside, herding them into a room to the right. A living room. Very formal. She took a seat on the stiff-backed sofa and motioned them into matching chairs opposite her.

She didn't offer them food or drink. "You wanted to talk to me? You have an hour. I have an appointment later this afternoon."

Gaff didn't waste any time. "I'm sure your sons told you that when the new owners of your brother's house"—he motioned to Jazzi—"went to clear his attic, they found his fiancée's body in a cedar chest."

Katherine narrowed her eyes at Jazzi. "You're that hussy Lynda's niece, aren't you?"

"Yes, I am, but she wasn't a hussy." Jazzi locked gazes with her. "You're the sister who never spoke to a brother who rescued her from bankruptcy three times, aren't you?"

Katherine's lip curled on one side. "The pretty blond has claws. Am I supposed to be intimidated?"

"I don't care one way or another. I just want to know who killed my aunt and who buried Lynda's son near Cal's septic tank."

"And you think I have the answers?"

"I don't know, but you might have a piece of information that will help us find them."

Katherine turned to Gaff. "I don't really care who killed Lynda."

He looked up from his notepad. "You should since your sons are suspects in this case."

"What?" Her voice was sharp, aggravated. "They weren't even born when Lynda died."

"But they expected to inherit from Cal when Lynda's son, Noah, came to visit him. How far would they go to protect their future money?"

"How impudent!"

Gaff didn't blink. "I'm simply stating facts. Noah Jacobs was visiting River Bluffs. He didn't know anyone there, so not many people would be motivated to kill him. That narrows down my suspect list. So far it looks like your sons had the most to lose if Cal and Noah got close."

"What about his fierce protector, Isabelle? He left all of his businesses to her, didn't he?"

"How did you know that?"

Katherine snorted, an inelegant sound. "The lawyer read Cal's will for all of us. My brother left me five dollars with a note that stated that sum was probably worth more than I ever cared about him. He left the boys his stocks and bonds and property, and he left Isabelle his businesses. All of them. He didn't will one of them to us. We were his family."

Gaff glanced at his notes. "You wouldn't visit or speak to him. Not even your sons, not even when they lived in River Bluffs during the week."

"He brought that on himself. He should have understood that."

"I got the feeling, after speaking to many people, that he resented it."

"Then he was a crybaby. If he'd have apologized, I'd have forgiven him." Gaff glanced at Jazzi.

"Maybe he thought you should apologize to him," Jazzi said.

Katherine stared. "Excuse me? I wasn't the one in the wrong. And you never answered my question. Did you investigate Isabelle's whereabouts when Lynda and her son died?"

You never answered my question. The same words Will had used last night. Like mother, like son. But Jazzi *would* answer Katherine. "Isabelle told me that she was in her office, working, when Noah died. Gaff checked into it. She was. She was in New York when Lynda died."

"Isn't that convenient?"

"Or else Isabelle had nothing to do with their deaths." Jazzi raised an eyebrow. "Where were you when Noah died? He was killed seven months ago on January seventeenth."

Isabelle's gaze turned glacial. She rose and walked to an elegant desk in the corner. Flipping through an engagement calendar, she said, "I had supper with my husband and Will that evening in Marshall, Michigan."

Gaff stood and went to look over her shoulder. "You have nothing listed on that day. Why would you lie to us?"

"Our lives are none of your business. You've ferreted around in them enough."

"Your sons both happened to be working in River Bluffs on the seventeenth." Gaff waited for a response, but she simply returned to sit on the sofa. She glanced at him. "Is there anything else? Our time's growing short."

Jazzi leaned forward. "Why did you provide an alibi for your husband and Will, but none for Wade?"

Katherine sighed. "Our younger son's proved somewhat of a disappointment to us. I couldn't include him because, for all I know, he might have spent that evening in a lockup somewhere, something I'm sure that's quite easy for a detective to check on."

"Do you love your second son?"

Katherine grimaced. "I love him every bit as much as I loved Cal. They both disappointed me, and they both owe me apologies." She looked at her watch. "I must leave now. I'll walk you to the door."

The interview was over. Jazzi and Gaff climbed in his unmarked car and drove away. Neither of them spoke until Gaff turned onto Highway 69, Then he let out a long breath and said, "Wow."

That pretty much summed it up. Katherine Draper was unlike anyone Jazzi had met before. And she'd count her blessings for that for a long time.

On the drive home, Jazzi tried to unjumble her thoughts. Way back, when they'd first found Lynda's body, she'd thought that Maury, Thomas Sorrell, or Cal might have killed her aunt. Then they'd found Noah's body, and she'd tried to connect the two deaths. Gaff hinted that maybe one of Maury's sons could have killed Noah to protect his share of their family deli. For a while, she'd even worried that Isabelle might be the killer to ensure she'd inherit Cal's businesses without any interference from Lynda or Noah, but she gratefully ruled Isabelle out when Gaff confirmed she'd been at the company to meet Cal when he rushed to fix an emergency that had never happened. And then Isabelle had told her that Cal meant to change his will to leave all of his money to Noah, cutting out Will and Wade. And today, she'd met Katherine. That woman was cold enough to kill someone, but had she? Or maybe her husband, Tim, had killed Noah. He'd been counting on Cal's money, too.

Gaff glanced at her. "We've come up with some suspects. That's a good thing. Now we just need to narrow everything down to the killer."

"Do you still think there was only one?"

"It often works that way, but this time, I'm not sure. We'll just follow the leads and see where they take us."

We? Jazzi would be more than happy to leave the rest to him. On Monday, Ansel would finish work on the pond. She and Jerod would go to the new house on Lake Avenue and start knocking down walls and rearranging rooms. That was more her speed.

She felt guilty when she realized she hadn't thought about her Aunt Lynda's murder for a while. She'd been more preoccupied with Noah's death. "It's sad, but I sort of forgot about my aunt once we found Noah's body."

"You were only one when Lynda died. You don't even remember her, and it was so long ago, it's part of the past. Everyone's more focused on Noah. Maury called to ask me if we had any new leads. He's leaving on vacation soon and wanted to make sure I'd call his cell if we found anything new."

"I feel sorry for him. He didn't find out he had a son until after Noah was dead."

They crossed the state line and were back in Indiana. Gaff gave her a quick glance. "That's the thing about murder. There are a lot more victims than the dead person. He's gone and won't feel any more pain, but families and friends live with the aftermath a long time."

Jazzi always thought about that when she read about a new shooting or stabbing in the newspaper. This time, though, she had a new thought. "The killers have to live with what they've done, too. You'd think that would eat at them."

Gaff grimaced. "Sometimes, yes. Sometimes, no. You'd be surprised how much a killer can rationalize away what he did."

"But whoever killed Lynda cared about her. He put a pillow under her head and folded her hands in her lap."

"And didn't take two expensive rings." Gaff shook his head. "That doesn't happen all that often."

"So her death must have mattered to whoever put her there." It felt a lot different than tossing Noah's body in a shallow hole.

They were getting close to a town an hour away from River Bluffs, and traffic picked up. Gaff concentrated on his driving. Jazzi pushed thoughts of murder out of her mind and enjoyed the scenery. By the time Gaff pulled into her drive, she was ready to shift gears and enjoy her Friday night. She and Ansel were going out to eat.

She waved Gaff off, and when she stepped into the house, George ran to the door to greet her. Was Ansel still working? She glanced at her watch. Almost six. Jerod was already gone. She heard movement upstairs. Had Ansel left George down here while he got ready? She bent to pet George, and a few minutes later, Ansel hurried down the steps. His white-blond hair was still damp. "I just took a quick shower. George was sleeping in the kitchen, so I left him there. How was your trip?"

"Fine. If I ever see Katherine Draper again, though, it'll be too soon."

"Want to have a glass of wine to relax before we go out for supper? You can tell me all about her."

They went to the sitting area of the kitchen and caught up on each other's day before hunger motivated them to find food. They decided on the TGIF in the mall on the north side of town. Nothing fancy, but fun. They had to wait to get a table. When they finished eating, they went to a pet shop and bought another dog bed for George. This one was for the kitchen. And then they went to the bookstore and each grabbed a couple of books to read.

Once they returned home, they were ready to call it a day. They crawled between the sheets and an hour later, Ansel went to get George. Jazzi had intended to read for a while to relax, but the words swam before her eyes. She turned off the light on her nightstand and let sleep claim her.

Close to two in the morning, George went to the window and barked. Ansel sat up to check on him.

"What is it, boy?"

George snuffled, pushing his head under the blind to stare outside. Ansel went to look, too. "It's too dark, no light. I don't see anything, but everything's fine or the alarm would go off. Let's go back to bed."

A howl sounded from one of the fields. "A coyote. It's a good thing you're inside." He petted George and got him settled again, and then Ansel slid back under the sheet, and they all fell back asleep.

Chapter 37

Jazzi liked to sleep in a little on Saturdays, but not this morning. Ansel bounced out of bed earlier than usual to start work on the pond. She'd love it when it was finished, but she wasn't so fond of it at the moment. She dragged herself downstairs and tried to overdose on caffeine to find energy.

Ansel raised an eyebrow. "You don't have to get gung ho just because I am. If you want to be lazy today, go for it."

She glanced out the window. Had the coyote come into their yard last night? Was it that brave? The yard looked ragged. She'd mowed it once since they'd started work on the house, but it had been so overgrown, once wasn't enough. She decided to mow it again. Her family was coming for the Sunday meal tomorrow, and she wanted it to look its best. She was making easy food since it was so hot. Ansel loved fish, so she decided on grilled salmon, pasta salad, sautéed summer squash, sliced tomatoes, and peach cobbler with vanilla ice cream. She'd make two pans of cobbler later tonight.

When Ansel went to climb on the bulldozer, she went to the garage for the riding mower. The yard was big enough, it took her most of the morning to finish it. By the time Ansel came in for lunch at noon, though, she'd made tuna salad sandwiches, one of his favorites. She'd put out potato chips and carrot sticks, too. He grinned.

"I'm going to get spoiled living with you."

"Good." Maybe he'd never want to leave.

He ate three sandwiches and washed them down with iced tea. She wondered if he'd be hungry by suppertime, then remembered she'd thawed a flat-iron steak. Ansel could always eat red meat.

They walked outside together, and he followed her to the shed where all of the outside tools were stored. "What's your next project?"

"I'm going to tidy up under the hedge with the weed whacker and then water all of the new plants again." She reached for the last section of hose. She'd strung three together, but it was still hard to reach the herbs growing at the back of the garage. The hose coils were caught in the wheelbarrow's tire, so she pushed it aside. And there, sitting halfway behind a watering can, was an empty can of Modelo.

Jazzi frowned. "I never buy cans. You and Jerod like bottles better."

"Did your renter ever do any yard work?" Ansel asked.

"Are you kidding? He couldn't get up to throw away his garbage." Then a horrible thought struck her. "Gaff said that Wade Draper is a Modelo fan."

Ansel glanced at the shovel resting against the wall a few inches away. "If he came in here and put his beer on the wheelbarrow to reach for the shovel . . ."

Jazzi didn't like where this was going. Ansel was right, though. It would have been easy for the beer can to drop back behind everything where they couldn't see it. If Wade had meant to retrieve it after he dug the hole for Noah's body, he must have forgotten. But that was a guess, a long shot. "Do you think I should call Gaff and see if there are any fingerprints on it?"

Ansel glanced at the padlock on the shed. "It was locked when you bought the house, wasn't it?"

She nodded. "I changed the locks on Cal's house, but I didn't bother with this. There's nothing of value in here."

"Then who else would have a key?" Ansel asked.

"Cal's nephews. They owned the property."

Ansel nodded. "Then I'd call Gaff."

She made the call, but Gaff was in Indianapolis with his wife, enjoying a day off. He sent an officer to bag the can and take it back to the station, so Ansel returned to his bulldozer and she got busy on the hedges. By the time the officer came and went, she was ready to duck into the house and give it a quick dust. She even ran the dust mop over the floors. She was showered and changed and had run to the grocery store by the time Ansel called it quits for the day.

"Want some help with supper?" he asked when he dragged his dusty self into the house.

"Nope, you look like Pig-Pen in the Charlie Brown comics. Go, get cleaned up. I'm throwing a flat-iron on the grill. Nothing fancy."

They both loved that cut of steak. So did George, and she'd bought a bag of salad to go with it. She'd thought about eating outside on the picnic table, but it was too hot. She and Ansel ate at the kitchen island instead, and after they cleaned up, she threw together the cobbler and put it in the oven. That was the end of her ambition for the day.

"Is it my pick?" Ansel asked, sinking onto the couch.

"Only if you pick a movie I like."

He laughed. "We'll only rent one that gets two thumbs-up."

Jazzi made it through the first half, and it was a good movie, but when the buzzer on the oven rang for her to take the cobbler out of the oven, she was done for the day. She bent over Ansel on the couch, gave him a kiss, and took herself to bed. She didn't hear it when he slid under the blankets next to her.

Chapter 38

When Jazzi woke up Sunday morning, Ansel was already gone. It was the first time that had happened since they'd moved in together. She looked at the dog bed, and George had left with Ansel. She got up, pulled on a pair of short-shorts, and padded downstairs. A note greeted her on the kitchen island.

Ate some peanut butter toast and I'm working on the pond. Love ya, Ansel.

Love ya? A rush of heat spread through her body. The kitchen door was open so that George could look out the screen. The pug was sprawled on the floor, eyes closed, keeping guard over them.

She nibbled on toast as she started to heat water to cook the pasta. While it boiled, she made the salad dressing with tahini, Dijon mustard, honey, and diced Kalamata olives, among other things. She'd found it on the Food Network, a Geoffrey Zakarian recipe, perfect for hot weather. She chopped celery, onions, and peppers to start a mound of vegetables to add to the pasta, then sliced tomatoes and fresh mozzarella to layer on a platter. Once both salads were ready, she sautéed the summer squash, then turned off the heat under them once they were tender. All she had left to do was the salmon, and she'd wait until closer to two to grill those.

The food was ready. Time to spruce herself up. She changed into a pair of capris and a sleeveless T-shirt. Her family didn't dress up to come here, so even Mom and Olivia would be in shorts or jeans. She did take extra time with her hair and makeup, though, or Olivia would comment on it.

Nothing else had to be done, so she sank onto the couch cushions to read the morning paper. She'd made it to the living section when a car parked in the drive. It was only a little after noon. Did someone come early? She opened the door to greet her guest and groaned when she saw Katherine and a man who must be her husband walking toward the house.

Her smile slipped and she stepped outside to greet them.

Katherine raised an eyebrow. "May we come in?"

She didn't want them to, but Katherine had let her and Gaff inside, so she motioned them into the sitting area in the kitchen. She took a seat across from them. "How can I help you?"

The aromas from her cooking lingered in the air, tantalizing them.

Tim couldn't stop gawking at the house. His sons got their height from him. He was almost as tall as Jerod with the same light brown hair as Will and Wade. He waved at his surroundings. "This was a premier house when Cal lived here, but you've made it into a showcase."

She didn't like most showcases. She preferred houses that looked cozy and lived-in. "Thank you."

Tim leaned forward, resting his elbows on his knees. "You've visited everyone else in our family, so Katherine and I assumed I'd be next. I'm a busy man, so I decided I'd come to you instead of waiting for you to come to me."

Jazzi shrugged. "I accompany Gaff only when he asks me to, and he hasn't asked."

"Good, then I beat him to it. What would you like to know?"

He made it sound friendly, but Jazzi suspected Tim was trying to bypass Gaff. "You're not saving yourself any time. If Gaff wants to talk to you, he will, whether I have or not."

"Let's find out, shall we? Get a pen and paper and ask away. Try to cover whatever you think might please Gaff."

"I don't have much time before my family comes."

He smiled. "Then you'd better make it quick."

Okay, if that's what he really wanted. She went to a kitchen drawer and returned with a pen and notepad. It was go time. She wanted to get this over with. "You've been visiting the Country Club to talk business, to start a company with Will. Were you the one who saw Cal there with his lawyer and overheard them talking about changing his will?"

"No, that was me." Katherine interjected herself into the conversation for the first time. "I still visit the club occasionally for a few of the organizations I belong to. We'd met in one of the small, private rooms, and I was leaving when I noticed Cal. I slowed to get a better view of him. I hadn't seen him for a long time, and that's when I heard him discussing details to leave everything to Noah."

"And you shared that with your husband and sons?"

"Since it affected all of us, yes."

Jazzi pursed her lips, thinking. "Which one of you did it upset enough that you'd kill Noah?"

Tim laughed. "Every single one of us, but none of us killed Lynda's bastard son. We have standards, whereas Cal obviously didn't."

How could he sound so urbane when he was such a piece of garbage? Cal had saved his fanny three times in a row, and that meant nothing to him? Jazzi gave him a hard stare. "You're not very loyal, are you?"

"I assume you're referring to Cal loaning me money, and yes, I appreciated that. But there's acceptable behavior, and then there's not. Cal should have known better than to associate with Lynda."

"Was that the real problem? I thought it was because she didn't want him to give you money."

Katherine's expression iced over. "You wouldn't understand. You have no class either."

Jazzi grinned. "Is that what you call it? I thought you were just greedy and mean-spirited."

Katherine pushed to her feet. "I'm tired of being insulted by you."

"Then maybe you should start being nicer. You can dish it, but you can't take it."

Katherine drew back her hand, and Jazzi thought she was going to slap her, but just then Ansel walked through the back door. He looked at Katherine and narrowed his eyes. Two inches taller than Tim and with muscles bulging beneath his dirty T-shirt, he looked intimidating.

Jazzi nodded at their visitors. "Ansel, this is Tim and Katherine Draper, Will and Wade's parents."

He went to the sink to wash his hands. "I hope they're leaving. Your family will be here soon."

Jazzi stared. She never suspected he could cut someone so efficiently. She'd never seen him be anything but polite.

"We needed to talk to Jazzi for a few minutes while we were in town," Tim said.

Ansel turned, drying his hands with a paper towel. "You should have called ahead. We're busy."

"I have only a few more things to cover."

"I must not have made myself clear. Your minutes are up. We're expecting guests."

Tim smiled, but it was strained. "Of course, we'll be leaving now."

"I'll show you to the door." Ansel herded them outside and watched them drive away, then turned to Jazzi. "They're gone now."

Jazzi stared. "My god, you *are* a Viking."

He looked surprised, then grinned. "They pushed themselves on you, didn't they? If someone bothers you, they have me to deal with."

She could live with that. "You did such a good job, you get to pick the movie tonight. Anything you want."

"Even horror?"

"If you hold me during the scary parts."

His grin grew wider. "Oh, babe, it's horror for sure if you're going to cling to me."

She went to him and stood on tiptoe to deliver a kiss. "Thanks for chasing them off. I've got to get the salmon seasoned now, though, before I grill it."

He tipped her chin up. "Don't think I haven't noticed you're cooking all my favorites."

"You know what they say: the way to a man's heart is through his stomach."

"You'd have me with cold meat sandwiches." He lowered his head and gave her a long, serious kiss that made her bones melt. "Warn me before you fall asleep tonight. I have plans for you."

How lucky could a girl get? She swatted his butt as he went to climb the stairs to shower. She went to the kitchen and decided they'd eat fish or seafood every third night if it made Ansel happy.

She was carrying in the grilled salmon when Jerod, Franny, and kids arrived. Ansel, six-five of squeaky clean, led them into the kitchen and got Jerod a beer. Franny decided on iced tea, and the kids went to the cooler to choose their sodas. The doorbell rang again, and in under ten minutes, the kitchen was so full, it was hard to hear yourself think.

Ansel and Jerod helped Jazzi lay out food on the kitchen island, and everyone came to dish up, buffet style. Olivia and Thane talked about the house they'd found. They were going to take Jazzi, Jerod, and Ansel to see it Tuesday night. Samantha said she and Gran had driven to Salamonie Reservoir to have a picnic with one of Samantha's old friends and that Gran had enjoyed hiking one of the park trails.

Jazzi glanced at Gran. Her gaze was clear and lucid. If only her mind were in as good of shape as her body.

George plopped himself at Ansel's feet and shamelessly begged. Jazzi was surprised that the pug had a thing for salmon. And pasta. He even liked summer squash. The only thing he didn't want were raw tomatoes.

Mom told them she was looking forward to having Monday off. Dad had to work, so she was going to a day spa with her next-door neighbor. When you got those two women together, they could think of all kinds of ways to have fun. Uncle Eli and his wife were putting in a new fire pit at their house. Everyone had things to talk about. The meal lasted longer than usual and it was back to being filled with gossip and fun. The only people who thought about Lynda and Noah were Jazzi and Ansel, and a large part of that was because Tim and Katherine had intruded on their Sunday.

When everyone left and they'd finished cleanup, Ansel took Jazzi's hand and led her into the living room. They watched sports, as usual, and then he rented a movie that she'd sworn she'd never be brave enough to watch. But cuddled next to Ansel on the couch, with George curled on their feet, the scary parts weren't as scary.

After the movie, Ansel led her upstairs. "The best antidote to fear is lots of heavy breathing and making love."

"Really?" She'd never heard that before.

He grinned. "Come on. I'll show you."

And he did. And he was right. They'd have to watch more scary movies so that he'd chase her fears away often.

Chapter 39

On Monday, Ansel stayed home to work on the pond while Jazzi and Jerod went to the house on Lake to start ripping down walls.

"I can finish up here today," Ansel told them. "Save something for me to do tomorrow."

Jazzi rolled her eyes. This house needed a lot more than cosmetic fix-ups. They'd be at it a while. Jerod drove today. Usually, they met at the job site, but her cousin couldn't wait to see how the pond turned out, so he volunteered to drive her back. She grabbed a cooler full of sandwiches and Jerod grabbed the one she'd filled with cold drinks, and off they went.

They decided to gut the entire upstairs. Armed with sledge hammers, they got busy. Walls crashed down and the toilet and sink got tossed into the dumpster. They were scraping the popcorn ceilings smooth when Jazzi's cell phone buzzed. She looked at the ID and frowned. "Wade Draper," she told Jerod.

He nodded for her to go downstairs to take the call.

Once it was quiet, Jazzi said, "Sorry. We're gutting a house. I needed to find someplace where I could hear you."

Saws and hammers sounded in the background on Wade's end, but he must be in a private spot. His connection was clear. "Detective Gaff called me today. He wants to interview me again. I was wondering if you'd come with him. He makes me nervous. I know you're not my friend, but it's nice to have a regular person there, you know? I'd ask Will, but he'd think I was guilty of whatever Gaff thinks I did, and I'm not. Will you come?"

"When is it?"

"Quitting time, three thirty."

"Ask Gaff to pick me up on Lake Avenue." She gave him the address. "I didn't drive my truck today. He might even have to drive me home."

"If he won't, I will. I know you're doing me a favor."

After he hung up, Jazzi looked at her cell for a minute before returning it to her jeans pocket. It was sad that he called her instead of asking his brother. But after meeting Wade's family, she understood.

She worked with Jerod until Gaff yelled upstairs at them. "Hey, is Jazzi ready to go?"

Jerod came to the top of stairs and yelled down, "Are you taking her home?"

"Yeah, no problem."

"Then I'm quitting here for the day to go see how Ansel's doing. He might be done by now."

She and Jerod locked up and walked out together. He got in his truck, and Jazzi climbed into Gaff's car to head downtown. They waited in the parking lot until Wade finished work and came to see them.

"Picnic table?" Wade asked.

It felt like a broiler outside, but they followed him to the same spot in Headwaters Park. Wade sat down opposite them and fidgeted. "What is it this time?"

Gaff explained about the Modelo beer can Jazzi had found in the shed. "Your fingerprints are on it."

Wade frowned. "In the shed? I never looked inside it."

"You didn't do any yard work to get the house ready for the renter?" Gaff asked.

"I mowed, but the riding mower was in the garage. That's all we did."

"Do you still have a key for the shed?"

Wade nodded. "Will gave his keys to the lawyer when we sold the house. I forgot to bring mine."

Gaff went on. "The beer can was close to the shovel that someone used to bury Noah."

Wade's face drained of color. "I never saw that shovel."

"Your brother had an alibi for January seventeenth, the day Noah was murdered. Do you?"

Wade hung his head. "I left work early that day. I know that looks bad, but you can ask my mentor at AA. I met with him that day for the first time. I was tired of messing up because of my drinking."

Jazzi couldn't hide her surprise. "You didn't tell your brother?"

Wade looked embarrassed. "Will wouldn't believe I can kick the habit. He'd make it worse, nagging me every time he thought I might mess up.

Mom and Dad both think I'm a lost cause, too. I decided I'd do better on my own. None of them have even noticed I haven't had a drink in months."

Jazzi sat, stunned for a moment, then reached for his hand. "That's their loss, but I'm proud of you."

He blinked. "Thank you. Anyway, here's Doug's number. You can call and ask him about that day. I was with him. I was scared. I wasn't sure I could do it, and he talked me through the panic."

Gaff grinned.

What was so funny? Jazzi hadn't found Wade's explanations amusing. "What is it?"

"Someone went out of his way to pin Noah's murder on Wade. He had no idea he had an alibi. He's going to be really disappointed."

It was Wade's turn to stare. "You think someone tried to set me up?"

Gaff nodded. "I don't think it. I know it. I'll check your alibi, but someone's getting nervous, and to save his own skin, he was willing to throw you under the bus."

Wade fidgeted more. He glanced at Jazzi, confused. She thought about the night George went to the window and barked. "I think they planted the beer can on Friday night." She explained why.

Gaff jotted the time in his notepad. He looked at Wade. "Where do you keep your key to the shed?"

Wade pulled his keyring out of his pocket and pointed to it.

"What were you doing at two Friday morning?"

"Sleeping. Will and I were working overtime on Saturday."

"So you stayed in the motel in town?"

Wade caught his gist and shook his head. "You're going in the wrong direction. It's not Will. He's my brother. He pushes me to do better."

Did he? Jazzi wasn't so sure. It sounded to her like Will went out of his way to make himself look good by making Wade look bad.

"Did anyone else have a key to Cal's shed?" Gaff asked.

"Only my parents and the renter."

"Your parents?" That surprised Jazzi.

"Mom was coming into town and Cal used to have two beautiful Chinese vases that he filled with flowers and put on each side of his front door. Mom wanted them, so I made her a copy of the key. Dad wanted to look through stuff, too. Cal only bought high-quality things."

Between the renter and Katherine and Tim, none of those things were left. Jazzi remembered seeing the Chinese pots on Katherine's front stoop. Before she could edit herself, she blurted, "Would your mom throw you under the bus?"

Wade didn't answer right away. Finally, he said, "I hope not."

But he couldn't be sure. No one should have to worry about that with his own mother.

"Your father?" Gaff asked.

Wade didn't hesitate. "Probably. If he was worried you'd look at Will, he'd point at me. Will's the one who's going to help him start a business."

That was even worse. Jazzi wondered how Wade turned out as nice as he had.

Before they left, Gaff said, "You're still a suspect, but only one of them. And if your mentor remembers he met with you on January seventeenth, you're almost out of the running."

"Good, I'm starting to get myself together again. I don't want to mess that up."

Jazzi felt so sorry for him, she went to hug him. "Hang in there, and if you ever just want someone to talk to or you'd like a free home-cooked meal, give me a call."

He narrowed his eyes, studying her. "You mean that, don't you?"

"Yes."

He thought a minute. "I might take you up on your offer."

"Good, you'll like my boyfriend. He's a contractor. You'll have a lot in common."

When she climbed into Gaff's car, and he turned on the air conditioner, she leaned closer to the vents to cool off. It was supposed to rain tomorrow, and the temperatures would drop, but today was a muggy mess. She and Jerod were working inside the house on Lake, so rain wouldn't slow them down. Bring it on!

Gaff pulled into traffic to drive her home. "That kid got a bum deal with his family."

"If he were smart, he'd move to River Bluffs, find an apartment, and get away from them."

"I have another thing I can check on now," Gaff told her. "Since your shed was broken into, I can check to see where people were at two am. They'll lie to me, but I might be able to check stoplight videos if there are any in the area. I can ask around."

"Sounds like a long shot."

He smiled. "It is, but that's what we do. Detectives are always looking for the needle in the haystack."

"I hope you find it."

In a short time, Gaff turned onto her street and pulled into her drive. "Thanks for coming with me today. It helped Wade."

"I'm glad. I like him." With a wave, she went into the house. Ansel was waiting for her. He looked smug.

"The pond's done. I've already moved all the dirt to rim it and give us some privacy. A crew came to get the bulldozer, and it's supposed to rain tomorrow. It can gather in the bottom."

"Want to celebrate?" she asked.

He opened the refrigerator and took out two lobster tails and two filet mignons. "I already thought of that."

"Holy crap." He *was* in a good mood.

"Come here." He wrapped his arms around her and picked her up off the floor, then whirled her in a circle. George barked excitedly. "We're settled in. We're perfect together and our home is perfect, too."

She laughed. "You're not going to want to leave here. Some girl's going to have to work really hard to win you."

"I'm not leaving. I have everything I want: my dream home, a pond, and you. They'll have to carry me out in a pine box."

She wanted to believe him. He meant what he said right now. But he'd just broken up with Emily. She was his rebound girl. The odds of success for rebounds was lower than low. But she'd enjoy this while she could. If she had her way, he'd stay forever.

Chapter 40

A thunderstorm swept into town before Jazzi's alarm went off. Lightning flashed. The sky rumbled, but George slept through it. Jazzi's mom's dogs went frantic when they heard thunder, but not the pug. It took a lot to disturb his inner peace. At first, the rain pummeled everything, flattening flowers, and Jazzi worried about all of her new plants, but eventually it eased to a nice, heavy drizzle before she and Ansel left the house.

Instead of opening their umbrellas, Ansel lifted George, and they ran to the garage. Only damp, they clamored into the van. Windshield wipers kept a steady rhythm on their drive to Lake Avenue. Ansel parked at the curb, and they dashed to the front porch. Jerod had left the door open for them.

"I'm down here!" he called when they entered the house. Ansel held George close to carry him down the basement steps.

Today, they were putting new support posts in the basement. They carefully jacked up the floorboards and got started. They were sliding a new post into place when Gaff called.

Jerod sighed. "Again?"

"He probably checked out Wade's alibi," Jazzi said. "I hope Gaff's crossing him off his list."

She walked a short distance away to take the call. Gaff got right down to business. "Wade's mentor, Doug, kept a record of meeting with him on the twenty-seventh. I'd like to go in person to let Wade know, and I'd like to question Will again. Care to come with me?"

Jazzi muffled a groan. Will didn't bring out the best in her. "Do you think it will help?"

"Yes, you bring up things that move the conversation in the right direction."

She glanced at Ansel and he nodded for her to go. "When do you need me?"

"I can pick you up in fifteen minutes."

That soon? Jerod and Ansel had wrestled the support pole in the right position. They could wait on the next one until she got back. "Sure, I'll be ready."

When she hung up, Jerod said, "Let me guess. He needs you now."

"Sorry." She felt bad, leaving them in the middle of a big job.

Jerod grimaced. "Hey, whatever leads to finding the guy who killed Noah is okay with me."

That made her feel better. That's how she'd look at it, too. She helped them bolt the post into the metal frame that held it in place, then went upstairs and walked onto the porch to wait for Gaff. The rain had gotten a little heavier again, so she grabbed her umbrella to run to the curb when Gaff pulled up.

"It's been so long since we've had a gray day, I'm enjoying it," he said as she got settled.

She was, too. "Ansel can't wait to see if the pond will hold water. He's hoping the skies open and flood us."

Gaff laughed. "He built a pretty big pond. It's going to take a lot of water to fill it."

"That's why he's getting a well dug near it. This rain won't be enough."

It was a short drive into town. Thunder crashed and rolled while they walked into the building where Will and Wade worked. The supervisor saw them and nodded to the second floor. "Wade said to watch for you."

With a short salute, Gaff headed to the stairs. They found Wade in a different loft this time. He was installing a garbage disposal.

"I have good news," Gaff told him. "Your mentor confirmed your alibi."

He backed out from under the sink to turn to them. He really was a good-looking guy. And he seemed nice. His steady girlfriend might have ditched him, but when he was ready, he wouldn't have trouble finding someone else.

He gave a grateful smile. "Thanks for taking the time to tell me. I didn't know if Doug wrote down our appointment or not."

Gaff looked around the large, open space. "I was hoping to talk to Will, too."

"He'll be here soon. We told him you were on your way."

They made small talk for another ten minutes before Will walked into the room. He shook his head in apology. "Sorry, but I had to run to the lighting shop. It only delivered one of the sconces for me to wire in the bedroom. I needed its match."

Gaff's expression shifted. "Does that happen often?"

"Not usually, but once in a while the shop gets the order wrong."

Gaff looked at Wade. "Does that happen to you?"

"Once in a while the plumbing shop leaves out a fixture or an elbow joint."

"Do you have to sign out when you go?"

Wade's brows dipped in a worried frown. "No, we just tell the supervisor. He knows the drill." He paused. "What are you getting at? Are you hinting I killed Noah before I went to see Doug?"

"It couldn't have been you. Cal was home then. He was waiting for Noah to get to his house. Someone called him and told him there was an emergency. When Cal left, that person met Noah, gave him some excuse to check the furnace in the basement, and killed him there."

Wade rubbed his forehead, agitated. "Then why are you asking me about running to get parts? I wouldn't even be gone that long."

"But when one of you is working alone, in a room, like you are now, no one really knows for sure where you are, do they?"

"I guess not." Wade sounded worried.

Gaff turned to Will. "That means no one can actually swear that you were here, working, when Noah was killed on the twenty-seventh. That's how you did it. You came to work, told the supervisor you needed something for your project, and left. No one thought a thing about it."

Will's hands balled into fists. "I suppose that could happen, but it didn't. I *was* here working, and you can't prove differently."

Gaff turned to Jazzi. He *couldn't* prove it, and they all knew it.

"My grandma can." Jazzi was telling a flat-out lie, but Will wouldn't know that. "She went to visit Cal, saw you digging a hole, but didn't realize what you were doing, so she left." That part was true.

Will shook his head. "She must have seen Wade. The privet hedge is high enough, she couldn't see much. We'd look about the same."

Gaff gave him a hard stare. "How did you know the grave was behind the hedge?"

"I must have heard or read about it somewhere."

"We didn't give out that information. Only a few people knew. It wasn't on the news."

Will's face drained of color.

Gaff grabbed his arm and started for the door. "I'm taking you in for questioning."

Wade let out a long breath. He looked shell-shocked. "You can't really think my brother killed Noah."

Jazzi raised an eyebrow. "Yes, I can. And if you think about it, you can too. Who else would Noah threaten but you and Will? If Cal changed his will, you'd get nothing. Hadn't you counted on that money too?"

"Not really. I mean, Cal was only in his sixties. Doctors can treat a lot more than they used to. I remembered him as a nice person. I was hoping he'd stick around."

Gaff gave a brief smile. "I believe you, but the rest of your family was waiting for the day he dropped over."

Wade shook his head, trying to take it in. "My brother killed Noah?"

"And tried to make it look like you did it." Jazzi wanted that part of the conversation to sink in. "He tried really hard to frame you, Wade. Your brother's a jerk. Are you going to be okay?"

He looked around, dazed. "I didn't see this coming. I'm taking the rest of today off. I won't be worth crap."

"What are you going to do?" Jazzi didn't think he should be alone. "Do you have a friend you can stay with?"

"Honestly? All I want right now is a drink. Boy, I wish I hadn't given it up."

If he left here, alone, he'd be sitting on a bar stool soon. He'd worked too hard to stay sober. She didn't want to see that destroyed. "Call Doug. If he's busy, you're spending the day with me."

Doug picked up right away. When Wade told him what had happened, Doug said he'd meet him at the motel Wade was staying in. They'd talk and then maybe go out to eat. Doug was a mentor. He'd know what to say and do. He'd handle this a lot better than she could.

Jazzi called Ansel for a ride back to Lake Avenue, then walked to Wade's van with him. The rain had turned to a drizzle, so she saw him off and waited under her umbrella for Ansel. She didn't want to go back in the building. The dreary day fit her mood.

Ansel studied her when she got in the van. "You okay?"

"I think so. I'm just upset."

He nodded. "Why wouldn't you be? It's a short drive to Lake Street. Jerod and I both want to hear what happened."

It was lunchtime when they settled around the two coolers they'd brought. She shared the morning's events while they ate their sandwiches.

Jerod shook his head when she finished. "You took a chance telling him that Grandma saw him."

She knew that. "Yeah, if he'd ever met her, he wouldn't have worried about it."

"His own fault." Jerod reached for another roast beef on sourdough. "If they weren't such snobs and had gotten to know us a little better, he'd know Grandma couldn't testify."

Ansel stared at his sandwich. "I feel sorry for Wade. We have to invite him over sometime. His own brother tried to send him to prison. I thought my family was bad, but his sucks."

A few hours later, Gaff called again. "Will confessed. When his mom told him that Cal meant to change his will, he flipped out. He'd already talked to his dad about going into business together when Cal died. His mom thought that would be sooner rather than later. He considered Cal's money his, and he wasn't about to lose it."

"Have you talked to Wade?"

"He's taking it pretty hard. He called his parents and told them what happened, but all they could talk about was poor Will, how they were trying to find a good lawyer for him."

"Figures." Jazzi thought Katherine and Tim were about as bright as dim lightbulbs.

"Doug invited him to stay at his place for a while, until he gets himself a little more together."

"That was nice of him."

"Wade could use some friends now."

"Ansel and I are on it." She'd invite him for supper Friday night.

Gaff hesitated. "You've been a big help, Jazzi. Thank you."

She hadn't felt like a help. She'd felt as if she'd fumbled her way to an answer. "I'm glad this is over. I don't envy you your job."

He chuckled. "Most people don't. And thanks again."

Jerod looked at Jazzi's face and he cleared his throat. "You know, I've had a big enough day. Let's knock off early and hit it hard tomorrow."

They packed up their gear and headed in different directions. On the drive home, Ansel said, "Well, that takes care of one out of two." When she frowned at him, he added, "You know who killed Noah now, but someone murdered your aunt Lynda, and it can't be Will. He'd just be learning to walk when she died."

He was right. There was still another murder to go.

Chapter 41

Gaff called on Tuesday. She, Jerod, and Ansel were finishing the support posts before they gutted the first-floor kitchen. Then they knocked out the wall between the kitchen and what had once been the dining room before the owner converted it into apartments.

"I wanted to let you know that I called Noah's parents, and they're happy Noah's killer will be punished. You called your mom, right?"

"I told her, and she passed on the news."

"Good, I still need to let Maury know. I'm going to his deli this afternoon. Care to come with me? It might make it easier for him. He feels comfortable around you."

She'd promised Maury she'd tell him about Noah. "Sure, when will you be here?"

"Maury said two would be a good time. The lunch crowd's gone by then."

"Okay, see you at two."

Over lunch, she told Jerod and Ansel about Gaff's call.

Jerod winced. "Glad it's not me. Old Maury's going to take it pretty badly."

"That's why I'm going." Jazzi wasn't close to Maury, but Jerod's uncles were. And she felt sorry for him. The Lynda-Noah case had been an ordeal for him.

She kept sanding floors after lunch and didn't stop until a little before two to knock the dust off herself. The heat had shot into the high eighties after the rain, but the humidity was more tolerable. She ran to Gaff's car when he stopped in front of the house, and then they headed north to the deli.

Customers still dotted tables, but Maury's sons could handle them. Maury left the counter to lead them to his office. Once he closed the door behind him, he said, "You have news?"

Gaff explained about Cal's nephew Will killing Noah.

Maury slumped back in his desk chair. "It's better knowing. That helps, but not as much as I'd hoped. I still feel so much anger, so much of a sense of loss."

Gaff nodded. "Grief takes time."

Jazzi struggled to come up with something that would lift everyone's moods. She nodded at Maury's deep tan. "You've soaked up a lot of sun lately. Did you take a vacation?"

Maury smiled. "The boys ran the deli. Gina and I just got back from visiting my parents in Tampa."

"Tampa?" Her heart felt like it stuttered. "How long have they lived there?"

He visibly caught himself. "It's been a while now."

"Lynda's postcard came from Tampa."

"Did it? I don't remember."

Yes, he did. Jazzi's thoughts sped back to previous conversations she'd had with Maury. "You told me Lynda was wearing both of her engagement rings when she left River Bluffs. But she never left. How did you know that?"

"I . . ."

She didn't wait for him to finish. "And you told my mom you saw Lynda get on the bus with her suitcases. She didn't get on the bus."

"I must have . . ."

She interrupted again. "You killed Lynda, didn't you?"

"No! Why would I?"

"You sent the postcards from Tampa, the ones typed from Lynda. You probably sent the card from New York."

"I . . ."

Gaff leaned forward. "We can start checking out dates and flights."

Maury put his elbows on the desk and buried his head in his hands. "It was an accident. I didn't kill her."

Gaff reached for his notepad. "Maybe you should explain."

"When Lynda told Cal she had to go to New York, I knew she was going to hurt Cal like she did me. I knew she must be pregnant. Cal had left for Europe, so I went to his house to argue with her. Her suitcases were by the door downstairs. She was upstairs, packing her toiletries and makeup. I told her that I'd follow her to New York and track her down. I'd tell Cal that she was going to give away his child, like she had mine."

"What happened?" Gaff prodded.

He scraped his hand through his tight, gray curls. "She laughed at me. She asked if I'd told Gina that I'd gotten her pregnant. She told me to keep out of her business. Then she started to leave. I went after her and grabbed her arm to have it out with her." He looked down and rubbed his hand over his eyes. When he looked up, his complexion looked ashen. "She jerked away from me. We were at the top of the stairs, and she lost her balance. She fell."

He stopped talking, and Gaff waited for him to gain his composure.

"I raced down to help her, but her neck was at an odd angle. I panicked. I'd come to Cal's house to argue with her, and I knew it looked bad. People would think I pushed her. I couldn't leave her on the floor and pretend I didn't know what happened. Someone might have seen my car in the driveway. Gina had just had her second miscarriage. She needed me. My dad was working fewer and fewer hours so I was running the deli. I couldn't let everyone down. I felt bad, but I carried Lynda upstairs and put her in Cal's attic. I knew Cal would be gone for a year. I could move Lynda later. But I never did. I cleaned the floor where she fell and locked the house and never went back. I've had to live with that all these years."

Jazzi gripped the arms of her chair. "*You've* had to live with it? At least you knew what happened. Do you know how much my mom suffered thinking Lynda just disappeared? That her sister didn't care about her? It ate at Grandma, too, messed her up. Now she's confused most of the time. And Cal. I thought you were his friend. He *never* got completely over it."

Maury looked away, not meeting her eyes. "I'm sorry about that. I really am. I hated to watch Cal suffer, and I felt terrible about your mom, but what could I do?"

"You could have grown some balls and told the truth!"

"I had other people to worry about, other people who'd be hurt if I told anyone what happened."

She turned away from him. She didn't want to look at him. "You sure wanted to know what happened to Noah. You wanted answers, justice. You, of all people, should know how Mom felt."

Gaff stood, interrupting them. He looked at Jazzi. "I'm sorry. I brought you here, but I have to take Maury to the station. I have to ask you to find another ride home again."

"I'll call Ansel." She couldn't wait to get out of the deli, away from Maury.

Maury pushed to his feet. "Will you give me time to talk to my sons, my Gina?"

Gaff nodded. "But I'll be there with you when you do it."

Maury sighed. "The boys can run the deli now. They'll be all right. So will Gina."

Jazzi couldn't complain about that. She hated it when innocent people suffered. She didn't know what would happen to Maury and she didn't much care. He'd used her to get information and gain sympathy while he left her mom and Cal to fight through grief and misery for years.

She stalked out of the deli and walked three blocks away before she called Ansel. The minute he heard her voice, he said, "You can tell me later. Where are you? I'll be there."

He must have gone over the speed limit, because he was there before she expected him. This time, Jerod came with him. He sat in the back and listened while Jazzi told them about Maury. When she finished, Ansel said, "Is your mom at work now?"

Jazzi nodded.

Jerod said, "I'll call Olivia. They're closing the shop today at five so Olivia and Thane can look at houses. When it's time, Ansel and I will go with you to your parents' place. We'll stay with you when you tell them."

"Thank you."

They threw themselves into work when they got back to Lake Avenue. They needed something to keep their thoughts at bay. At five, they took separate vehicles to Jazzi's parents' house. Telling Mom was every bit as miserable as Jazzi thought it would be. In time, there'd be closure. It would be a relief to know what really happened. But for now, Mom reeled at the shock that Maury never hinted about what really happened. She felt betrayed. Again.

When Mom calmed a little, Dad nodded that they could go. He'd be there for her, and she could cry and fuss and let some of it go. Jerod drove home to Franny and his kids. Olivia went home to Thane, and Ansel and Jazzi returned to Cal's house.

Once they entered the house, Ansel crushed her in a protective hug. Even George leaned his head against her leg. She soaked it all in.

Finally, Ansel lifted her chin and bent to give her a gentle kiss. "This has been one miserable day, but from now on, things will only get better. Everything's out in the open. Lynda would have had her baby and returned to River Bluffs to marry Cal. She'd have given lots of family parties here. We can do that for her. For her and Cal."

He'd put a nice spin on it. But he was right. They could finally put the past in the past. It was going to take a while, though.

Chapter 42

The next Sunday meal was subdued. The entire family knew about Maury and Lynda. The shock that it was Maury who'd stuffed her in the cedar chest hadn't worn off. Jerod's dad, Eli, had thought of Maury as a close friend. They all trusted and liked him.

"This will be our mourning meal," Ansel had told her. "We never had the big carry-in after Lynda's funeral. Every passing deserves a moment of silence, a sharing of sadness. This will be it."

What did you cook for that? It was hot and humid outside, but Jazzi had decided on chicken and dumplings and mashed potatoes. She always thought of that as comfort food. And her family needed comforted right now.

She must have chosen the right thing, because there wasn't one scoop of food left when everyone started gathering their things to leave. Grandma came to give her a warm hug. "You're a good girl, Sarah. I love you."

This had been too much stress. Jazzi hugged Grandma back. "I love you, too."

Ansel helped with cleanup when they were finally alone, and then they dropped on their couches in the living room to watch sports. "I think it's time for a scary movie," he told her. "A good scare chases everything else out of your head. I can hold you and keep you safe, and then we'll chase all those fears away."

She rolled her eyes. "That's your advice?"

"It works for me every time."

"When did you test this out?"

"When my parents packed my bags and told me to move out the morning after I graduated."

She stared. "That fast?"

"They didn't want me to get too comfortable working on the farm."

"I'm sorry."

"So am I, but I drove to River Bluffs and rented a room for a week in a motel, and I was scared and mad."

"So then you slept with someone?"

He flushed all the way to his hairline. "It was a one-night stand."

"Did it work?"

"I still live in River Bluffs, don't I?"

She laughed. "No blood and gore. The movie has to earn its scares. No cheap thrills."

He nodded and went upstairs to dig through his stash of DVDs. He came back with *The Shining*.

Doggone. She'd avoided that movie up until now. But it was a good one. And after he'd scared her, he took her to bed. And he was right. When he brought George upstairs, and they cuddled to fall asleep early, she was in a much better mood. The stress of last week and today had drained her energy. She spooned against Ansel and felt herself drift off.

She woke in the middle of the night to snoring. Ansel had never done that before. She was about to tap him and tell him to roll over when she realized it was George, lying in his dog bed. She had to laugh at herself. She got up and patted George instead. When the pug rolled over, the snoring stopped.

She returned to bed and pressed herself against Ansel again.

"I love you, babe." The man knew how to say the right thing.

She nuzzled her cheek against his back. "I love you, too." And she drifted off again, happy.

Chapter 43

Jazzi was sanding the Lake house's wooden floors on the first floor. She was humming. Jerod and Ansel were working on plumbing. George was in the basement with them. When she answered her cell, she must have sounded too happy.

Gaff asked, "Jazzi? Have I got the right number?"

For heaven's sake! "Yeah, it's me. What's up?"

"I just wanted to let you know everything on Lynda and Noah is wrapped up, and I wanted to thank you one last time for all the help you gave me."

"No problem."

"My wife and I are still welcome at your pond, right?"

She laughed. "Did you think I'd changed my mind?"

"It did occur to me that you might be sick of me."

"Never, feel free to come over any time."

"I'll call you first, give you fair warning."

His call put her in an even better mood. By the time Ansel lifted George to leave work for the day, the Lake's floor plan was in good shape. The living room's wide arch led to the dining room, and the dining room was open to the kitchen.

"It looks good," Jerod decided.

Jazzi agreed. "It's going to be great for having people over."

"Or for a large family." Jerod stopped and shook his head. "If Franny and I have any more kids, we're going to need a bigger space with a bigger table. I might have to add on to the house."

On their way out the door, Jazzi asked, "How's Franny feeling? Can she keep food down now?"

"We're past the barf stage. Now she changes cravings twice a week. I'm stopping at the store on my way home to buy two chocolate pies, one for the kids and me, and one for her."

"She can eat a whole pie?"

"In less than twenty minutes."

Jazzi laughed. "How long do cravings last?"

"As long as she wants them to."

She patted his back as he headed to his pickup. "Hang in there, cuz."

"I'm trying. I might have to moonlight to keep feeding her, though."

Ansel had listened to them and chuckled on the drive home. "Maybe I should start saving now for when you're pregnant."

"That's going to be a while. I'm not ready, and you'll have met your new girlfriend by then."

"You're not getting rid of me that easily. I figure I'll have at least two kids with you before I get sick of your stretch marks and move on."

Her jaw dropped. She turned to stare at him, and he threw back his head, laughing.

"I know you don't think we're going to last," he told her, "but I'm counting on it. And Vikings go after what they want. So start getting used to the idea that we're in this for the long haul."

"You're on the rebound. Emily left you for California. You're just licking your ego right now."

He pulled to a curb and turned off the van. He reached across the seat and pulled her to him, crushing her mouth beneath his. When he let her go, she was breathless. "You still don't get it. Emily was my rebound girl because you showed no interest in me. I feel bad about that, but I'm not beating myself up too much. I tried with Emily. She didn't help. She left, so I finally had a shot with you, and you're not wriggling off my hook. I caught you, and you're staying caught."

He meant it. Happiness flooded through her. "I'm not trying to get away."

"Good, then that's settled." He pulled back into traffic and drove home. Without a word, they both started up the stairs. George whimpered, but Ansel said, "Later."

George snuffled and stretched out at the bottom of the steps, his head on his front paws. This time, George had to wait longer than usual, but when Ansel and Jazzi finally came back down, they gave him extra tidbits during supper. And Jazzi felt complete. A silly way of putting it, because she'd felt complete before, but Ansel added more to her life. And she was grateful.

Please turn the page for some delicious recipes from Jazzi's kitchen!

Ansel's Baby Back Ribs

In Indiana, I smoke my ribs in good weather, but my husband doesn't want to grill when the weather's miserable, so I make oven-barbecued ribs. This is the recipe.

For the rub, combine in a baggie:
2 T. Kosher salt
2 t. coarse black pepper
2 t. paprika

I cut a slab of ribs in half, so it's easier to seal with foil.
Line the bottom of a cookie sheet with parchment paper (for easier clean up).
Put a cooking rack on the cookie sheet.
Put enough foil to seal the ribs on top of rack.
Place the ribs on foil. Lightly sprinkle with rub. Then seal the foil.
Pour water with a little apple cider vinegar into the bottom of baking sheet and put it in oven to keep ribs moist.
325 degrees for 3 hours. Refill water halfway through.
After 3 hours, take the ribs out of the oven and open the foil.
If you want to, you could finish the ribs on the grill at this point. In winter, I finish them in the oven.
Slather the ribs with barbecue sauce.
Return them to the oven, foil open, and cook at 400 degrees for 15 minutes, adding more water to the bottom of the pan if you need to. You can add more sauce if you want to.

BBQ Sauce

In large saucepan:
Heat 2 T. olive oil.
Add:
1 small sweet onion, chopped—cook till tender
2 T. minced garlic
¼ c. hoisin sauce
¼ c. honey
½ c. ketchup
2 T. soy sauce

Bruschetta with Bean Puree

Jazzi makes bruschetta in *The Body in the Attic*, but I prefer crostini, so I'm going with that recipe. For crostini, cut however many 1" slices of bread you want from a loaf of French or Italian bread.

Heat olive oil in a large skillet.

When the oil is hot, sauté one side of bread till crispy, then turn to crisp the other side. Sprinkle with garlic salt. And it's ready to serve.

**If you'd rather make bruschetta, slice a French baguette into 1" slices. Put the slices on a baking sheet. Brush olive oil on top of each. (Some people put the bread, olive oil–coated side down, on a sheet.) Bake in 450 degree oven till golden, about 5 minutes. Sprinkle with garlic salt.

Bean Puree to Top Crostini

In a saucepan, combine:
1 can of northern beans, 15 oz., drained
1 t. of minced garlic (I'm lazy. I use the jar variety.)
Sprinkle of salt
1 t. cumin
1/4 c. mild olive oil
Squeeze of 1/2 a fresh lemon
Heat till warm, then smash with potato masher until it's the texture you like.

I add a sprinkle of dried parsley and mix it in.

About the Author

Judi Lynn received a Master's Degree from Indiana University as an elementary school teacher after attending the IPFW campus. She taught 1st, 2nd, and 4th grades for six years before having her two daughters. She loves gardening, cooking and trying new recipes. Readers can visit her website at www.judithpostswritingmusings.com and her blog writingmusings.com.

Printed in the United States
by Baker & Taylor Publisher Services